THE SWORDS OF B'AJJ:

BLOCKADE

James Buehler

ISBN: 9798813892073

DEDICATION

To my son, Benjamin. You have been our gift. Your sense of humor is amazing. Your storytelling is wonderful. Have confidence in yourself, and you will be able to do whatever you want.

BOOKS IN THE SWORDS OF B'AJJ SERIES

TRUTHSEEKER
Paperback - https://www.amazon.com/dp/1466263857
Kindle - https://www.amazon.com/dp/B005UHMI3A
Commemorative Paperback –
https://www.amazon.com/dp/1501057561
Commemorative Kindle -
https://www.amazon.com/dp/B011AY932A

PATHFINDER
Paperback - https://www.amazon.com/dp/1508566526
Kindle - https://www.amazon.com/dp/B011JL6JRQ
Commemorative Paperback -
https://www.amazon.com/dp/1536986240
 Commemorative Kindle -
https://www.amazon.com/dp/B01KGLMGXQ

TIMELINE
Paperback - https://www.amazon.com/dp/1085962601/
Kindle –https://www.amazon.com/dp/B07VZBJG69/

CONTENTS

THE SWORDS OF B'AJJ

ACKNOWLEDGMENTS

Illustrations by

Karinn Welch

Cover by

Victorine Lieske

FICTION ALERT

The following story contains many fun things that couldn't possibly happen. That's called fantasy. It's fiction. There will be some things that you don't think could possibly happen, and you're right. I dreamed them up for your enjoyment. So, don't fret, sit back, relax, and have fun with it!

PROLOGUE

He always hated this place. Why did she have to pick this spot? She could have done better than this. It was dark and dank. The solar-powered panels under the separator between Upper and Lower Stamford did little to chase away the darkness, even in the daytime. During the day there were people, good people, out and about. At least she chose to meet in the daytime, so that helped some.

Lower Stamford was the location of the old city of

Stamford, Connecticut. Long ago, city planners, led by Benjamin Morris, developed a new city above the old one built on a metal platform held up by columns that encompassed entire city blocks. Over time, the wealthier people moved above, leaving the less fortunate below. Eventually, the dregs formed gangs led by cyborg leaders and took over the lower city. However, they only ventured out at night. During the day those gangs allowed those good, hard-working people to go about their business and left them alone. But when the solar-powered panels faded for the day, the gangs came out of their hideouts and took over, beating or murdering anyone that dared stay out. If you were out, then you must be bad. No allowance was given to those that forgot to seek shelter at the end of the day.

She lived here, that's why she chose to have him meet her here. He never knew why she chose to remain down here. It wasn't the place for people like her. She told him to look for the hot dog vendor; that he was a good man, and they'd be safe near him.

With a gloved hand, he pulled his wide-brimmed fedora hat further down over his eyes, hiding most of his face in its shadow. He tightened the belt on his trench coat and continued down the street. He wasn't having much luck finding this hot dog vendor, but she had assured him that he would be in the area.

He rounded a corner. Ah, there he was. He stopped and looked around. She didn't appear to be here yet. Maybe he should order something while he waited.

"Yes, sir," said a weathered old man with a faint

Italian accent. "What can I get you?" He opened the top of his cart, then wiped his hand on a greasy apron and followed with an adjustment to his chef's hat.

"Coney dog; with the works."

The old vendor set to work and in moments, produced a large hot dog piled high with fixings. He handed it to the man, who paid for it with some money he pulled from his coat pocket. "Keep the change."

"Thank you, sir." The vendor's eyes widened when he saw the one-hundred-dollar bill in his hand. "Thank you, very much, sir."

The man walked toward the wall of the nearest building. He leaned against it.

The hot dog vendor continued to sell his goods, yelling, "hot dogs, get yer hot dogs—they're the best in town" occasionally. People ignored him, passing by with nary a look in his direction.

The man took a bite of his coney dog. He raised his eyebrows. That was rather good.

"Where's my hot dog?" An old lady in a gray overcoat appeared next to him. "I was wondering if you'd come."

"Where'd you come from?" He nearly dropped his coney dog.

She smiled. "I'm glad you came."

"You know I always will."

She nodded causing the yellow plastic flower on her gray fedora hat to flop. The yellow band it was stuck into kept it from falling off. She turned away slightly. "We need to find her."

"Right to business, eh. Okay. Yeah, I know. She can't

survive much longer. We need to return her to the chamber."

"How did she get out?" She turned to look him straight into eyes she couldn't see under the hat.

"I don't know. Everything looked fine. There appeared to be no tampering with it."

"The clone?"

"No, couldn't have been. It was brand new."

The old woman glanced over her shoulder. The hot dog vendor was gone. "You better get moving. It's almost the witching hour around here."

He nodded. "I'll take care of her, don't worry." With that, he zoomed off.

CHAPTER I

Bart Taylor ran his fingers through his blond hair. Until a few days ago, it had been wavy, but an encounter with a man wielding a chainsaw changed that. Now, he had more of a buzz cut than he liked. He and his friends had been on a mission for the President of the United States at the time. They encountered a group of humans altered to be physically dominant to normal humans, and one of them gave him an unexpected haircut. After that mission, the President sent them on another mission to stop a military operation against some people that were being unjustly attacked. Now he stood watching part of that military convoy staring him in the face. The soldiers had been on a killing spree as a parting gift to the region, so he and his friend Steve Wolfe had chased them down. Because Bart and Steve owned special indestructible swords that gave them special abilities, these soldiers didn't stand a chance. Bart's sword, called Truthseeker, allowed him to know if someone was telling the truth. Steve's, known as Pathfinder, gave him the ability to track down anybody within a three-day range using the life essence each person gave off as they moved about. On top of this, the swords made them immortal. If they held on to the sword, they couldn't die. Whether they were holding it or stored in its invisible sheath didn't matter. It just had to be in their possession. It provided them with superhuman strength. Each sword also granted them three more abilities that they could choose for themselves.

Bart had chosen telekinesis, two Colt 44 Magnum pistols which rested in invisible holsters on his thighs and reloaded whenever he replaced them in those holsters, and a laser rifle that he kept in an invisible harness strapped to his back. Those weapons also turned invisible when placed in their holsters, effectively becoming non-existent when there. All he needed to do to retrieve them was to reach for them.

Steve's extra abilities consisted of two laser pistols that had invisible holsters just like Bart's Colt 44s, the ability to turn himself invisible, and a red car he named Casey that could fly, talk, shoot lasers and missiles, monitor lots of different things like radar on an instrument panel on his dashboard, adjust to any situation as needed, and was as indestructible as his sword.

They were here with another friend, Bart's girlfriend, Erin McNamara, and a trio of their former enemies that were now also employed by the President. They only knew these people by their first names of Tasha, Reginald, and Isaiah, and the truce between them was tenuous at best.

Erin didn't own a sword even though there were five in the set. The third sword, named Timeline, was owned by another friend of theirs, Matthew Walker, but he had disappeared during the previous mission. They had no idea where he was now or if he was even alive. On top of that, the abilities of their swords kept fading in and out since he went missing. The fourth sword, Blockade, was owned by some lady named Jane that they only knew because they had briefly worked with her by chance. The fifth sword's whereabouts were unknown to everyone except Matt because it was his sword's special ability to know where all the other swords always were. Erin may not have a sword, but she was very capable as a fighter. Her father, Ian McNamara, was a geneticist and had very likely enhanced her abilities as she displayed a few times when she needed to defend herself.

Tasha, Reginald, and Isaiah also had a special ability. These abilities were not related to swords, but to Ian with whom they had been acquainted for years. He had experimented on them as well, bestowing abilities beyond human capabilities upon each of them. To Tasha, he gave the gift of teleportation. The only inconvenient thing about her power was that if she carried someone with her, she always knocked them out for a while. Reginald could fly, or more accurately, glide once airborne, and shoot lasers from his fists. Isaiah was a little more dangerous. He had supersonic speed, and the ability to give anyone a fatal heart attack by touching them with his bare hands.

The military convoy they were pursuing split into three groups, so they divided themselves up. Erin and Casey teamed up with Isaiah to follow the group that had journeyed the farthest away. They would be able to travel the fastest, so it was best to send them after that group. Tasha and Reginald followed another column. Both those groups had headed in a southerly direction, but they were not going in the same direction. Bart and Steve had taken the group that continued to travel north. But this group had decided to turn and fight. Bart was certain that the militants figured they could handle two lone men. Too bad they were wrong. Well, unless their powers fluctuated again, of course. For some unexplained reason, their swords and powers randomly disappeared. He was praying that wouldn't be the case though, but the way things had been going, they had no idea if or when it may happen again.

The vehicles sat arranged into lines with tanks, a few rocket launchers, and troop transports in the front row. The supply trucks sat behind them. Troops poured from the transports.

Steve watched Bart.

Bart continued to stare at the militants. "Ready?" He breathed deep and drew Truthseeker. His laser rifle rose into the air beside him.

"You know it." Steve drew Pathfinder and disappeared. "I'll take the left. You go right. If our powers hold out, they don't stand a chance."

Bart took a step forward when his rifle dropped to the ground and then disappeared. "Not now." He turned toward Steve. He was visible. "Steve, stop!"

"Why? I'm just getting started." Steve was flexing his muscles and doing a little victory dance or a jig of some sort.

"Seriously, do you always do something ridiculous when you turn invisible?"

"I'm visible again, aren't I?" He stopped his little dance in mid-step and glanced sideways at Bart.

Bart nodded.

"Crud." Steve watched the approaching army. "What do we do now? I doubt we can run for it."

"I guess we hope that our powers come back very quickly. They haven't stayed away too long at any point yet."

"There's always a chance they could though. Oh no!"

"What?" Bart glanced at Steve while keeping an eye on the oncoming militia.

"Erin. She was inside Casey. If he disappeared while she was inside, she'll fall to the ground. Who knows how high up he may be, or if he was in the middle of the band of soldiers?"

Bart's heart sank. Why had he sent her off when he knew their powers could disappear at any moment. He hadn't thought it through enough. It hadn't connected in his mind.

Without warning, three helicopters passed silently over their heads. Bart hadn't even heard them coming, and from Steve's expression, Bart knew that Steve hadn't heard them either.

"Are those the same type of helicopters we saw in the Grand Canyon and at that compound that we rescued those hostages from?" Bart raised his hand to shield his eyes from the sun as the ships passed over.

"Yeah, they sure look like it."

The helicopters caught the attention of the mercenaries. Their tanks and missile launchers swiftly switched their aim from Bart and Steve to the helicopters and opened fire. Rocket after rocket, laser after laser, and shell after shell pelted the aircraft. It was all pointless though as the artillery did nothing to damage them. Whether the munitions bounced off or were absorbed, Bart didn't know, but it was clear that the weaponry of the militia was of no consequence.

The helicopters returned fire. They gave the local militia everything they had, and they had a lot. Each aircraft had multiple laser canons, all firing at will. Rocket launchers repeatedly shelled the larger vehicles with a ferocity that Bart couldn't believe.

As the decimation continued, many soldiers in the rear of the caravan began to turn, running in the direction they had been heading. One helicopter pulled away from the others and began to pick them off with such speed that they didn't stand a chance. Others began to run to the left or right of the battlefield only to have the other two helicopters peel off and follow them.

When it was over, nothing was left of the army. Vehicles burned; soldiers lay sprawled across the sand. The helicopters regrouped and sped off in the direction the military had come from.

Bart felt his strength return. He reached for his sword and pulled it from its sheath. "Our powers have returned. Can you track anyone on board those things?"

Steve concentrated. "No, there is no one on board. I see nothing."

Bart stamped his foot. "They manage to stay just out of our reach, do they not?"

***

Tasha teleported by intervals of about a quarter of a mile at a time staying just ahead of Reginald. Her long jet-black hair flapped around her each time she reappeared. They tracked their column to the outskirts of a local town.

"We can't let them enter," Tasha yelled up to Reginald, who had taken to the air through his special gliding ability. His red hair glared in the sun. "I'm going to jump ahead to where they are and engage them. Hurry as fast as the air currents will carry you and meet up with me." She made a popping noise as she disappeared.

When she reappeared, she could see some of the residents of the village running for their lives in the opposite direction. The convoy halted outside the settlement. She had to keep them where they were and stop them from entering the town. Her only ability was teleportation. It was kind of difficult to cause damage to an entire military convoy with teleportation, especially when she could only teleport a few at a time. She had to hold them off until Reginald could add some firepower with his laser bolts.

She scanned the legion. She was looking for some semblance of leadership. With the split military groups, it could be a little more difficult to figure out who may be the leaders of that section and who may be reporting to them.

Near the front of the soldiers, she saw a couple of men motioning to others, appearing to give them orders. The men ran toward the village. As they neared it, shots rang out and the men dropped dead on the ground.

She popped out. Moments later she popped in right in front of the men giving commands. "Boo." She popped out again; this time taking three of the men with her.

She reappeared, along with the now unconscious men, one mile above the army. Before gravity took over, she said, "Bye, gents. Happy landing." She disappeared again, leaving the men behind to fall back to Earth.

She reappeared near the same place she left from. "Who's next?"

"You, I think," said one of the militants, pointing his rifle at her head. Before he could fire, they disappeared.

After leaving the man one mile up, she reappeared toward the end of the army instead of returning to the same place just as Reginald flew in. "I got four of them. They'll be making an impression on their buddies any minute now."

"Tasha, behind you!" yelled Reginald. He aimed a fist at a man bearing directly for her. A laser burst from his fist and blasted the man in the chest. He fell to the ground.

"Thanks. I didn't think they'd seen me yet."

Reginald pointed toward the battalion, "Looks like they all know you're there now."

She turned to where he pointed. All the tanks and artillery in this squadron were facing right at her. Men were frantically running for cover or were aiming any weapon they had in her direction.

"Wow, I didn't know they respected me that much!"

Three helicopters silently passed over her. The militants began their barrage, but not on Tasha.

Reginald landed beside her. "I don't think they respect you at all."

"Well, they should."

They watched as all the different types of ammunition either exploded on or bounced off, or at least appeared to be bouncing off the helicopters as they drew closer. They watched as the aircraft opened fire, mercilessly bombarding the land. In moments, it was over. The helicopters veered off in the direction Erin and Isaiah had gone. Nothing moved. Plumes of smoke rose off the tanks and other vehicles. Bodies littered the ground; no one moved.

Even Tasha couldn't believe her eyes. She reached for Reginald's hand. "Let's go find Isaiah."

***

Casey, Erin, and Isaiah were having an easier time combating the contingent they followed. Casey's lasers effectively cut through the vehicles, disabling all that he encountered. Isaiah, a small waif of a man, sped around so fast touching all he could, that no one could track him. It was a little harder for him to find an open space in their clothing to grab bare skin, but he managed to find an exposed hand or face to touch, causing fatal heart attacks.

Without warning, Casey swerved away from the fight.

"What are you doing?" Erin tried to turn so she could see out the window at the battlefield below. "They weren't even touching you."

"It's not that." Casey continued away from the fray. "I've felt an anomaly in my circuits. I felt this way the last time I disappeared."

"You remember disappearing?"

"Yes, there is a blank spot in my memory core, but I remember before and after. Plus, I am linked with Steve, and it's in his memory as well, so I've filled in the gaps. I felt what you would probably call a queasy stomach the last time this occurred. I need to get you to the ground, or you'll fall a long way."

Without further comment, he raced toward the ground. As they neared, he said, "I'll slow down as much as I can before I go. You will still be moving so just roll with it. Hopefully, if the sand is soft enough there and with the enhanced strength your dad provided you, it will be enough to keep you from harm. I apologize in advance."

He braked seconds before he disappeared. Erin braced herself for the blow. She slammed into the sand and slid and rolled. She lay still for a moment; her long blonde hair lay jumbled in a sandy mess about her. Yep, she felt alive. Casey had found a good spot.

Isaiah zipped toward her. "Are you alright? I saw Casey veer off and wondered what he was doing. Then he disappeared. I saw you fall. Good thing he made it near the ground and slowed down."

Erin rolled over and groaned. Sand fell from her hair. "Yeah, good thing. I'm fine. Casey said he felt this before. Bart's and Steve's powers have been fluctuating since Matt vanished. This might be the first time I'm glad my dad made some enhancements to me, or I wouldn't be able to handle these things."

Isaiah twitched. "Yeah, I guess. We should probably get out of here now though. Without Casey, not even your enhancements could take on part of an army." He reached down and helped her to her feet. "Can you move?"

"Yeah, I think it's only my pride that's hurting at the moment." She looked back at the troops. Her eyes widened. "They're too close. Get out of here, they can't catch you."

"Not without you." He grabbed her hand. "Hang on."

He took off at top speed. Erin somehow managed to keep up.

"How?" she gasped.

"It's one of my lesser-used abilities. I can extend my abilities to people if I want to. I usually don't want to."

They outpaced the advancing company. As the distance between them grew, three helicopters passed directly over them heading straight for the unit.

An artillery barrage commenced, but the helicopters continued undaunted. They returned fire and decimated the regiment. It was over quickly.

Isaiah and Erin stopped. They glanced around. Nothing but ruins were left.

"Good, lord." Erin stared.

"Let's find the others." Isaiah tried to redirect her attention.

CHAPTER II

Matt sat silently waiting for the ceremony. Sha'rell was next to him. He had enjoyed their time together, but he knew it wasn't meant to last. It made him sad. Not only did they literally come from different worlds, but they came from different times too. There should have been no way they had ever met. But, the creator of his sword was in trouble, and through an unknown ability of the third sword, he, and some of the other holders of Timeline had been transported back to that moment to save him. They had accomplished that task, and the others had been returned to their timelines. He had been held back. Sha'rell told him it was because she requested it as part of the right of their family as keepers of the secret to creating these swords. He hadn't minded staying a bit longer, but he didn't belong here long term. She also told him that she would return him after he attended the joining ceremony of her nephew, Xi'heeh with his G'mone counterpart.

Matt scratched his head. This was still strange to him even though he had spent the last month with Sha'rell and her family. He kind of fit in with them. He was black, and their race, known as K'reelians, was purple. No one had said anything to him about being slightly different in color. He was even wearing one of their purple jumpsuits that every K'reelian he ever met seemed to wear. He stroked Sha'rell's beautiful, long lavender hair. It went most of the way down her back.

The K'reelians and the G'mone, who were white and most of whom had long white or exceptionally light blond hair, were the only two races on this planet. The K'reelians were the rightful people of this planet but had been conquered by the G'mone. They formed a truce and became a formidable military force in this section of space. The truce came with a price for their young men. A method had been discovered where a K'reelian boy and a G'mone boy could be joined telepathically to each other and become a potent fighting force that was stronger than if they were separate individuals. That was where the price came in though. If one of the two were killed, the other died as well because the joining brought their minds together in a risky fashion. That seemed like a ridiculous trade-off to Matt, but as he had been told, the combined power of the pair far outweighed the loss of life. Apparently, they won more battles than they lost, and through that, they had gained a reputation for conquests throughout their part of the galaxy.

Instruments that looked a lot like trumpets that

announced the arrival of kings blared into the air. The people sitting in the stands, half of it filled with G'mone and half with K'reelians each to their side, straightened up to attention at the sound. Down on the floor of the instruction grounds, as this area was called, G'mone adults filed in through an arched doorway. They formed a row in front of their side of the stands. Then, K'reelian adults filed in taking the opposite side.

Sha'rell leaned over to Matt, "Those are the parents. T'hi and his wife are over there." She pointed to her brother and sister-in-law.

In between the two rows of people sat a circular depression lined with big stone blocks. A fire raged inside the pit, emitting a blue glow.

The herald trumpets blew again; two short blasts. G'mone boys and K'reelian boys marched in side by side.

"There's Xi'heeh." Sha'rell pointed and grabbed Matt's arm.

Matt thought he looked nervous. He had gotten to know him a little bit over this past month, but he hadn't seemed this nervous before. It was also quite strange to meet him as a boy since he held the fifth sword, known as Gateway, in Matt's time. He was no longer a boy then. It was also weird spending some time with T'hi and Qu'arry, Xi'heeh's dad and grandpa, as well. Each of them held the fifth sword at some point in time. He had recently witnessed Qu'arry receiving Gateway for the first time. To know that T'hi would hold it someday and then Xi'heeh as well seemed out of place.

"Ladies and gentlemen," said a G'mone man walking

in behind all the boys. He was decked out in an elaborate white robe with a collar raised a foot behind his head and a hat that made him look like the Pope. "Let me welcome you all here today to witness this new class of joined youth."

Again, Sha'rell leaned over to Matt. "That's the instructor. He'll guide the boys from here on until they have mastered the complexities of the joining."

The fire in the pit roared higher. The first two boys in each line turned to the fire. They walked toward it and stepped up onto the stone blocks surrounding it. They jumped into the fire.

Matt rose to his feet ready to charge down to save them. Sha'rell held him back.

"It's okay," she said. "This is how they join. The fire isn't what you think you see. It's a special fire that bonds the boys together if they are ready."

Matt trusted Sha'rell and relaxed. He sat back down.

The boys emerged unscathed, but they appeared to be hesitant. Two people from the front of each line of parents moved toward the boys. They led the woozy youngsters to an empty area in the stands and sat them down.

"The first two are joined," confirmed the instructor.

Cheers and exuberant clapping rose from the crowd.

"Sometimes the joining doesn't take," Sha'rell said. "When this happens, the boys are sent off to work the fields. They aren't allowed to join the military. In our village and the surrounding country land, the non-joined and the old, retired military men, work the fields. In the city, those that fail to join are assigned apprenticeships and work in whatever area is chosen for them all their lives. It's not really a disgrace, but it's the closest thing to that."

The ceremony continued. Two by two the boys stepped forward to see if they would be accepted. A majority were, while a few were not. Their parents quickly whisked them out of the stadium to the whispering of the crowd.

It came to Xi'heeh's turn. Sha'rell tensed up. Matt grabbed her hand and squeezed it. She briefly acknowledged him, but her attention was squarely on her nephew.

Xi'heeh and his match walked into the magical fire. They emerged unscathed as had the rest of the boys before them. The instructor pronounced them joined and cheers and applause greeted them. Their parents moved toward them and took them to the seating area in the stands where the other joined youth had gone.

Sha'rell jumped up and whistled. She sat back down and hugged Matt excitedly. "I knew he'd make it. Hasn't been a relative of ours that hasn't yet."

Matt gave her a big smile. Sure, she knew it. That's why she had been nervous for a week. It didn't matter now, Xi'heeh was accepted and by their customs, would be a respected man.

After the ceremony ended, Sha'rell and her family gathered with Xi'heeh, his joined partner, and his family. It was a little tense at first, but after a while, they all settled into a congratulatory conversation.

Sha'rell's father, Qu'arry held up a hand. Everyone fell silent. "Please join us at B'ajj's place for a celebration feast."

They lived in a tiny hamlet. Each dwelling was similar in appearance with thatched roofs highlighted by white stone walls. Wooden framed windows protruded from the sides of those stone walls. Rustic, wooden doors equipped with a heavy iron ring for a doorknob were centered in the side of the hut that faced the street.

It had been B'ajj that Matt and the other holders of Timeline had been brought back to save. By doing so, B'ajj was able to fulfill the prophecy to create the swords. He now held Truthseeker, and Qu'arry held Gateway. No one else yet knew about this other than those that had been present when they saved B'ajj. B'ajj and Qu'arry had once gone through this ceremony as well and were joined to each other.

"So," Matt said, walking hand in hand with Sha'rell back to B'ajj's simple cottage, "try to enlighten me more on this. These boys are joined now, but still have a separate family of their own, is that right? Like B'ajj is married to Bu'an, and your father had you and T'hi with your mother, but B'ajj and Qu'arry are joined. How does that work? I mean, it's almost like you are all family now."

"That's exactly how it works. They are strictly military allies, and while they are in the military, our families are close. When they get out, one way or another, joined men and their families tend to go their separate ways. Sometimes, like my father and B'ajj, they stay near each other, but may not ever speak to the other again."

They walked a little further in silence. Just before they reached B'ajj's place Sha'rell broke the silence. "So," she hesitated, "are you leaving soon?"

"I don't belong here." Matt stopped. He pulled on Sha'rell's hand to bring her to a stop as well. "I must get back to my time. You told me that I could go after Xi'heeh's joining ceremony. You said your family controls when I go back."

"Yes, we do. I was hoping you'd change your mind and stay with me." She looked down.

Matt gently touched her chin and raised her head, looking her in the eyes. "If I could be in two places at once, I would be here with you and where I belong. I have grown to love you."

Sha'rell winced and tears began to form in her eyes.

"There was something special about you from the moment I met you," Matt continued. "If I didn't have other responsibilities, I'd stay in a heartbeat."

"After the party, I shall send you back. Duty is what we value most above other things here. I can understand that." She pulled her hand away and turned toward B'ajj's place.

Matt sighed and followed.

The party where Matt had officially been introduced to Xi'heeh's joined partner, V'ante, continued well into the night. As no one dared venture out into the night when beasts of all sorts roamed the area attacking anything that moved, they all camped out in B'ajj's place.

It was very cozy, to say the least with all the people from both families staying in the small hut. There were probably about thirty total people snuggled all around the living room floor and into the kitchen area a little bit. A few even had to sleep on the floor in B'ajj and Bu'an's room.

The next morning, Bu'an insisted that everyone have something for breakfast before anyone went anywhere. There were no complaints about this, and as soon as everyone had what they wanted, people began to leave. V'ante's family had been the first to leave. They had come from one of the other small villages in the area and had to travel back before the evening when the beasts would return as they did every night. There weren't very many villages on this planet, but the villages were far apart, and they would have to make a stopover in one of the villages along the way. Most of this planet was one humongous city all interconnected across the globe. The country portion of the world was small and contained only a few villages.

T'hi and his wife, H'ona, had taken Xi'heeh and V'ante to the city where the boys would begin their instruction into joined life and the military. They traveled on a transport ship that only went to the megacity.

It would have been easier on both families if they could have used the transportation device in the village tavern. It only took moments for anyone to travel great distances across the planet with these devices, but women weren't allowed in the taverns, so that wasn't an option for them. Qu'arry could have taken them with the new power his sword provided him, but the group decided they weren't ready for the public to know about their powers.

Finally, it was time for Matt to return home. Qu'arry stood up from the chair he was sitting on. "Matt, it is time you return. Where is Sha'rell? She has kept you here long enough."

No one remembered seeing her since breakfast. It didn't take long to realize that she wasn't in the house anymore. Qu'arry, B'ajj, and Matt all went outside to begin looking for her. It didn't take them long to find her, however, as she was just outside the door feeding Bu'an's chickens.

Qu'arry walked up to her. "You cannot stop what needs to happen, sweetheart."

She didn't look up at them. She continued to throw grain along the ground so that the chickens could scavenge for their food. After a few moments, she stopped and spoke, "Father, I want to go with Matt back to his time."

Qu'arry paused. He looked like he had expected that. He smiled at her. "You know that's not possible."

"I don't care. I know your powers that come with the sword. You have been practicing. You can teleport yourself and others great distances. You can take me to Matt's world."

Qu'arry looked at his daughter. He took her by the shoulders and looked deep into her eyes. "Matt is from a different time. I can only teleport within my time. If I take you to his world, you will come out somewhere well in their past. It took the G'mone people a long time to get to his world to populate it. The second armada is probably getting close now themselves, and they left a long time ago."

Tears welled in her eyes.

Qu'arry couldn't bear to look at her any longer. It was painful to watch the hurt in his daughter's eyes.

Matt took her hand. He expected her to wrench it free, probably not wanting anything to do with him, but instead, she threw herself into his arms. "Stay," she sobbed.

Matt held her tight. He couldn't speak.

Sha'rell released him. She looked him in the eyes. Tears streamed down their cheeks. She wiped his face clear of the watery beads. "I love you. I release you. You have my permission to return."

***

Matt appeared at the fortress where he last saw Bart, Steve, and Erin. The stronghold lay in ruins. He couldn't believe his eyes. "What did they do here?" He could sense the swords again. He knew where Bart and Steve were. He needed to get halfway around the world to where they were.

"Well," Matt said to himself, "hopefully Xi'heeh will keep his word and show up soon."

"Of course, I always keep my word."

Matt spun around. An older Xi'heeh stood before him. "You look older."

"I am. I have aged as a K'reelian does. Sha'rell

misses you."

Matt winced. "I've only disappeared from you all a few minutes ago in my time, but it feels like it's been a lifetime. I miss her too."

"Would you like to see her again? She never met anyone else."

Matt tried to speak. "I..." A tear rolled down his cheek.

"The invitation to visit her is always open."

"Take me to Bart and Steve."

Xi'heeh nodded. "Tell me where they are."

CHAPTER III

Bart and Steve had been walking for a few minutes after the helicopter barrage, but they hadn't made much progress.

"This is going to take a long time if we just keep walking," Steve said.

"Is Casey back now that our powers are back?"

"Yeah, but he turned up with Erin and Isaiah. They're trying to help some of the local people adjust. The group they were following had just about reached some civilians."

"Well then, maybe we can help you get to them," Matt said from behind them.

Bart and Steve spun around, each drawing their sword.

"Whoa, man, it's just me." Matt held his hands in front of him. "Well, and Xi'heeh too."

Bart and Steve looked confused.

"Who is Xi'heeh?" Bart asked.

"More important," Steve said, "where have you been all this time? You think you can just disappear and then reappear and we're going to just say, 'Hi, how are you?'"

Matt looked at them. "Well, yeah, of course I do. It's not like you missed me or anything, I'm sure."

"Where have you been?" asked Bart.

"Let's save that for when we get home. It's a long story. I just had to go save B'ajj is all."

Steve looked at Bart, who shrugged.

"Maybe the bigger question is where's Erin." Matt looked around and didn't see much else. Then he noticed some of the wreckage in the background. "Your work?"

"No," Bart said. "That was not us. It is the work of one of those helicopters we saw in the Grand Canyon, then again at that fortress where you disappeared. It laid waste to this troop in seconds. In a way, we were fortunate. We had lost our powers just before it showed up."

"Wait," Matt began, "you lost your powers?"

"Yeah," Steve inserted Pathfinder back into its invisible sheath. "Every once in a while, they would disappear. Usually at a very inconvenient time."

"Interesting," Matt said. "So, it affected you across time then?"

"What did?" Bart sheathed Truthseeker.

"I'll fill you in back at home. As I said, it's a long story. Back to my other question, where's Erin?"

"She is with Isaiah," Bart said. "They were following another column of this militia."

"Who's Isaiah?" Matt furrowed his brow.

"Isaiah used to go by Heartattack," Bart said.

Matt's eyes widened. "What do you mean she's with him? And this doesn't seem to concern you?"

"Oh yeah," Steve said, "you don't know what happened here, do you?"

"Our story is also a lengthy one." Bart turned to start walking in Erin's direction again. "We will have to fill you in as well when we get home."

"You do not need to walk," Xi'heeh said. "I can take us there if you tell me where these Erin and Isaiah people are. My sword has been here and is familiar with this planet. It knows where to go. I only need to tell it where to go."

"Well," Matt said, "I can't tell you where she is because she doesn't have a sword. I only know where those are."

"Casey's with her, can you find her by him?" Steve suggested.

"No, apparently, I can't. Looks like just the swords are part of my ability to find you."

Steve turned away for a moment, "Casey, can you give me coordinates of where you are?" He paused. "Okay, thanks." Turning back to the others he added, "I'd say he's right about there." He pointed to an object in the sky that grew bigger as they watched. "He also has Tasha and Reginald with him too."

"Tasha? Reginald?" Matt still had a confused look on his face.

"Also known as Porter and Cardinal," Bart said.

"You do have a lot to tell me, don't you?"

Casey landed. Erin popped out of the driver's seat and ran to hug Bart.

"So, what, you just run right past me for Bart, eh?" Matt held his arms out. "I see how I rate."

Erin released Bart and turned toward Matt. Her eyes widened, and she covered her open mouth with her right hand. She quickly lowered her hand and pointed a finger at him. "What do you think you're doing just waltzing back here when we've been worried about you?" She paused, catching sight of Xi'heeh. "And... and, you're purple."

Xi'heeh tilted his head in a slight bow. "Yes, I know."

"Sorry," she looked a little sheepish. "We just recently encountered another purple man."

"Yeah," Steve jumped in, "and she pretty much took him down, so I'd be careful if I were you."

Xi'heeh nodded. "I will keep that in mind."

"This is Xi'heeh." Matt held out a hand toward him. "He's the current holder of the fifth sword, Gateway. Someone from his family always holds the fifth sword."

Xi'heeh bowed. "I can assure you that I am on your side. You will not need to 'take me down' anywhere. However, that is interesting that you defeated one of my people."

"Hey, goobers," Tasha interrupted. "This is a swell reunion, but I don't really care. We need to get back to the President to report what happened."

Matt turned to face her. "And just who put you in charge."

She looked at him and rolled her eyes. "The President of the United States. Why do you think we need to return to debrief her?"

Matt looked at Bart, held his palms out, shrugged his shoulders, and had a questioning expression on his face.

"That is part of what we need to tell you when we get a chance," Bart said. "In a way, Tasha is in charge."

"In a way?" Tasha put her hands on her hips. "Whatever. I am in charge. President's orders."

Matt shook his head. "Fine, if Bart says so. Right now, I'll believe only him. Considering our past, you can't really expect me to just go along with what you say."

"We need to move on," Bart said. "We will fill you in on the way back. Although, we will not all fit in Casey."

Xi'heeh stepped forward. "There's no need for us to all fit into Casey. I can get everyone where we need to go."

They all gave him a quizzical look.

"It's okay," Matt said. "It's true. He can take us."

"Just tell me where you want to go. The sword knows where to go. As I become more familiar with places, I will be able to tell it on my own."

"The White House," Tasha answered before anyone else could.

In a blink of an eye, they all disappeared. The next thing they knew, they were on a street in front of a row of neat white houses.

Before any of them realized where they were, Bart said, "I guess we will not fill you in on the way back."

"Wait, where are we?" Tasha gazed around.

"We are in Turnberry, Scotland, the United Kingdom in front of a row of white houses," Casey stated.

Tasha turned to Xi'heeh. "No. The White House in the United States. You know, the president's home."

Xi'heeh didn't seem to understand.

"Sixteen Hundred Pennsylvania Avenue Northwest, Washington, D.C., United States," Casey added. "That will get us where we want to go."

Again, they disappeared. This time they appeared in the right place, landing on a sidewalk outside a fenced-in area.

Security guards quickly surrounded them, pointing laser rifles at them. People who had been walking down the sidewalk moved away quickly.

"It's okay." Tasha moved forward. She took a wallet out of one of her back jeans pockets and opened it up, showing the lead guard something inside. "We're the President's elite force. She's expecting a report from us."

The guard took the wallet. He looked it over and nodded. "Stand down. It's clear. I'll let the President know you're here. Although, she wasn't expecting you back so soon."

"We had a little unexpected help with our job." Tasha took her wallet and stuffed it back into her pocket.

"Let them through." The guard headed inside a small station while the gate began to open.

Bart and Tasha led their respective crews quickly through, and the gates closed behind them. A guard on the opposite side met them and led them toward the main entrance of the White House. He led them straight into the Oval Office where the President was sitting behind her desk. Multiple Secret Service personnel were stationed at various points around the room.

"I didn't expect you back so soon." She stood, smoothed out a couple of creases in her lavender suit dress, straightened a dark lavender amethyst brooch on her lapel, and ran her fingers through her raven black hair.

"We didn't expect any help." Tasha grabbed a nearby chair and sat down.

"Who helped you?"

"We have no idea," Tasha replied.

Bart jumped in. "We were hoping that you could fill us in."

Tasha gave him a sideways look that said she was the one in charge of their group.

"No, I wouldn't be able to tell you." The President gestured for everyone to find a chair.

Bart kept his eye on her while the others found something to sit on. He continued to stand. He hoped that she would say something to trip herself up, but she chose her words carefully. She certainly would not be able to tell him.

Tasha continued their story. "Three groups of helicopters—"

"I think it was one," Bart interrupted.

"Three," Tasha spoke loudly, "groups like the ones that mysteriously appeared before showed up. The troops you sent us to take out split into three separate groups, but the helicopters pretty much decimated them."

"I see," said the President. "We must have someone on our side then."

"What did they offer you?" Matt spoke up.

"Excuse me?" The President's body tensed slightly then relaxed just as quickly.

"T'hi and Javilyn?"

Everyone looked at Matt like he'd just gone crazy.

The President narrowed her eyes and sat back in her chair. "Who?"

"Let me fill you in on one of the abilities of my sword. I know the entire timeline of the sword before I received it. I know where everyone that held any of the swords in the past was, and I know where all the current holders are now. I don't always keep all that information at the tip of my thoughts, but when I need something, it comes to me easily. I know that you met with them often. I don't know what you said to each other, but Javilyn's group was part of your security detail. They secretly did a lot for you. That's one reason you didn't bat an eye when Xi'heeh walked in here with us. None of the Secret Service did either."

Silence filled the air.

"Okay." The President broke the silence. "So, they did. What's that got to do with anything?"

"I don't know that yet, but I'd put some money on them doing more than just helping with security. Maybe they helped build some high-tech helicopters for you?"

The President leaned forward and smiled. "Now that would be something, wouldn't it? That would likely give us a big advantage over the rest of the world.

Indestructible helicopters, that's what we need."

"Wait a minute." Erin stood up. She looked at Matt. "How in the world would they have worked for the United States, and no one knew anything about them?"

"They were a lot more careful than you all have been," said the President. "I'd say you're like bulls in a china shop, but that's such an old saying, that I won't. But anyway, why do you think I want you to work for me as well? Javilyn was a great help to this country and the whole world for that matter. He had a long life. He helped all the presidents. Well, no that's not quite true. There were a few throughout the years that he didn't help, at least, not for long. He also kept it to a minimum about what he would do for all the rest. There were many things that we had to figure out for ourselves and work out on our own. So, now that you know about this, are you still willing to help when needed?" She stared at Bart.

He stared back, not saying anything for a few seconds. Then, he nodded. "As long as you are honest with us and with others you deal with."

She nodded back. "Within reason for the security of this country. There are some things that the public is better off not knowing."

"Of course. That would likely be true. Are we free to go now?"

The President nodded.

"Thank you. I would like you to keep in mind though that we will be looking for these helicopters. I hope they do not turn out to be yours." Bart turned to leave.

Xi'heeh stepped toward Bart. "I can take us where we need to go. Matt can tell me where that would be."

"Just take us home." Matt leaned over and whispered the address into his ear.

"What about Casey?" Steve asked.

"I will adjust for him as well." Xi'heeh disappeared along with Bart, Steve, Matt, and Erin.

That startled the Secret Service agents in the room.

"Well," said the President, "I will say that T'hi never did that in my presence before. That was kind of him."

Reginald stood up and turned toward the door.

"You don't need to leave just yet," the President said. "Is there anything else any of you need to share with me?"

Reginald and Isaiah shook their heads.

Only Tasha spoke. "Other than the helicopters barreling in it all went well. I sure hope those things are on our side, and I don't care how they accomplish their tasks. Frankly, I think they did us all a favor."

"Okay, you are all free to go then."

Reginald strode out the door followed by Isaiah. Tasha turned to follow them.

"Tasha," the President motioned for her to stay. Everyone else except the Secret Service left the room. The President looked at the lead serviceman. "You all may leave as well."

They hesitated, but the President shooed them off with a wave of her hand.

Once they were out and the door was shut, she said, "I want you to keep an eye on Bart and his group. Let me know if they get out of line. I have a feeling that he won't be as easy to handle as Javilyn was. That little pipsqueak was too nice. If Bart gets out of control, you'll need to find a way to get rid of him. It won't be easy, but I know there's a way that if the fourth sword is around, Bart could be taken out. Then his sword would be available to me, and I wouldn't need any of their help. You, Reginald, and Isaiah could control the other swords."

Tasha perked up. To that point, she hadn't paid more than a cursory amount of attention. She hadn't thought there was any way to get the swords away from Bart or the others. "How do we go about that?"

"I don't know. Just keep your eyes open for a chance. It may never come, so don't force something. If they even thought we were considering anything like this, I guarantee it wouldn't be good for us. Got it?" The President's stone-faced stare bore into Tasha.

CHAPTER IV

Tasha paced about the warehouse Isaiah provided for T'den and G'rell where they could set up their alien technology when they attempted to kill Bart and Steve a few days ago. Isaiah had been messing around with the controls trying to figure out how it all worked for the last three hours. It was starting to get late.

"Ah, I think I have it." He pressed a button on the panel and an image appeared in midair. "Are you sure that's what the President said?"

Tasha stopped and turned toward Isaiah. "Yes, she wants us to keep an eye open for an opportunity to take the swords away from Bart and the others. Then we will be invincible and become the most powerful beings on this planet. No one will stop us from taking over the world. Samuel lost his desire for some reason, but we haven't. Oh wow!" Tasha's mouth dropped wide open.

"What is it?" Reginald turned to look at the image

displayed from the alien equipment. "It's her."

Isaiah turned away from the panel to look as well. "It's still working. We can see what Jane and that old woman are doing right now."

"Where are they?" Tasha strained to try to find something familiar with their location.

"I know that place," said Isaiah. "It's Lower Stamford. I wonder what they're doing down there?"

They watched as the old woman and Jane sat on a sidewalk with their backs against an apartment wall. Isaiah was able to adjust the view to see what they were seeing. A group of kids was playing stickball in the middle of the street. It was starting to get dark.

"Those kids better get moving." Reginald moved closer to the screen. "They're playing too hard to notice. It's going to get nasty down there soon."

As if on cue, the girl pitching looked up and tore off toward her apartment building. Some other kids followed the girl's lead and ran for it. They scattered so fast they ran into each other. Two younger kids remained in the middle of the street. They were visibly terrified.

Reginald, Tasha, and Isaiah watched as a woman opened an apartment door nearby. She seemed to be saying something.

"I wish we could hear what's going on." Reginald moved in closer. He was so close that he almost touched the screen.

"I don't remember T'den or G'rell having any sound," Isaiah said. "I doubt they cared about sound. They just needed to know where Bart was."

They watched as the woman in the doorway started to head for the kids. She stopped. A cyborg came into view. He was followed by several of his gang all carrying various types of weapons.

Jane came into view. The cyborg moved toward her, and then suddenly stopped. The other gang members with lasers and guns fired toward Jane, but the beams and bullets hit something invisible and stopped. Then all the gang, except the cyborg, fell to the ground.

"I wish we could hear what was going on." Reginald backed away a bit.

Jane moved toward the cyborg, who struck back.

Isaiah's jaw dropped.

Tasha's eyes widened. She put her hand to her mouth.

Reginald turned away.

"Oh, my goodness." Tasha lowered her hand, but her eyes were still wide open. "That cyborg didn't stand a chance. Wow! Wait." Tasha's eyes narrowed. "What's she doing? She put the sword down because the children were afraid. Bad mistake." She disappeared.

The next thing Isaiah knew, Tasha had reappeared on the screen. "She got the sword."

Reginald turned back just in time to see Jane disappear. Tasha was pumping the sword in the air, waving it around. Then she disappeared.

With a pop, she was back with Reginald and Isaiah. She swished the sword back and forth. "Oh yeah, this is awesome. I'm finally going to be able to take care of Bart. Ever since he first interfered with us trying to get Erin,

I've been waiting for a moment like this." She lunged, stabbing into the air.

"Are you sure you're using that right?" Isaiah's forehead scrunched in a perplexed expression. "I don't think that's how it worked for Samuel. And he was able to conjure up some more weapons."

Tasha swished the sword around again. "Oh yeah, it's radiating power. I just must not know how to use it yet. It's not the same as Samuel's was you know. I probably have to wait a while for new abilities."

"I see you can still teleport," said Reginald. "That's good. When you figure out how to use it, that's one thing you won't have to choose."

"Yeah, I didn't expect to lose that ability. After all, Samuel didn't lose his ability as a tracker and a leader."

"So, where are you going to keep that thing?" Isaiah asked.

Tasha looked around. "Um, I guess I'll need a scabbard or something. I'll get one tomorrow, and then we'll meet up with Bart and the others. We have another job from the President, so we don't want to let on too soon about what we're going to do to Bart. I must be careful of the other two. We can each hurt the others, so I don't want them around when I do something. Maybe when we split up, I'll go with Bart, and you go with the others."

CHAPTER V

The next morning Erin knocked on the boys' door.

Bart answered. "Hey, sweetie, how are you doing?" They kissed. "Pretty good, I would say."

Erin entered. "For the most part. I do feel a little achy today. Must be from all that exertion from fighting those battles the last couple of days." She stumbled a little as she walked into the living room.

"Are you okay?" Steve looked at her, then Bart.

"I'm fine." She stopped. Steve was looking at her funny. She saw him look up at Bart. She turned to look at him. "What?"

"That is how Ian's clones react when they start to decay." Bart stared into her eyes. She could see a mixture of fear and concern.

"Don't look at me like that. It's me. I've been here with you guys for a couple of years now. I'm not a clone. Sure, maybe my dad created a bunch for himself, but he didn't create any for me."

Matt came into the living room from the attached kitchen area. "Actually, we don't know that."

"Guys, it's me."

"She is telling the truth as she knows it." Bart reached out and grabbed her hands. "We believe you. It just seems a little odd."

Before Erin could respond, a beeping sound came through the computer system.

"Enable projection," Steve said.

A three-dimensional image of Tasha's face appeared on the projector situated on the tabletop. "Erin. Gentlemen, and Steve."

Steve glared at the hologram.

"We have another gig from the President. We need to rescue some teens that have been abducted from their school. It's likely a hostage situation."

"Always with the hostages," Steve said. "Why is it always hostages? Why can't we ever just build a bridge or something?"

"Because we don't know how," said Matt.

"You dopes. Meet us on the corner of Webb Street and Crane Avenue." Tasha's face disappeared as the projection faded.

"Well, I guess we are on our next assignment already," Bart said.

"Where's Xi'heeh?" Erin looked around.

"He returned home," Matt said. "He said he'd be back this morning. Should be here any moment. While we're waiting, let's all sit down at the table. I have a little breakfast for us."

"We should get moving." Bart started to head for the door. "If there is someone in danger, we should not wait."

"Erin needs to eat, right Erin?" Matt looked at her.

She nodded. "Yeah, I didn't grab anything in my apartment."

"You never do." Steve grinned at her.

"Well, why should I? Matt's a good cook. He always makes something delicious. I can't cook beans."

"Besides," Matt entered the dining area from the kitchen with a plate of bacon and scrambled eggs, "we need to wait for Xi'heeh to return."

On cue, Xi'heeh appeared in the living room. He wasn't alone. Beside him stood his aunt, Sha'rell.

Everyone looked surprised.

Matt's jaw dropped wider than anyone else's. He bumped into his chair, knocking it over. "What?" That was all he could say.

"Hi, Matt." Sha'rell stood next to Xi'heeh. She was apprehensive.

Matt ran over to her. He gave her a huge hug. When he released her, she planted the biggest kiss on his lips.

After a few moments, the awkwardness of the others became apparent.

"Uh, Matt." Steve set down his fork. "Yo, Matt!"

Matt and Sha'rell broke apart.

"Oh, uh, yeah, uh, everyone, this is Xi'heeh's aunt, Sha'rell."

"Apparently you two know each other," said Bart.

Bewildered, Matt turned to Xi'heeh.

"I knew you would not ask to see her, so I brought her to you."

"But she doesn't look a bit different. It had to be a long time ago."

Sha'rell grabbed Matt's hand. "Not to us. We age differently. If father had sent me when I asked, then I would have arrived on your world thousands of years ago. But, with Xi'heeh now old enough to claim the fifth sword, those thousands of years passed, and I could come to see you. It was only a few of my years for me. It went quickly. I waited."

Matt's hands were shaking. He whispered a muffled "wow" and then hugged her again. "I didn't think I'd ever see you again." He released her from the hug. "Guys, this is the girl I was telling you about yesterday after we returned home. This is my girl."

"Oh great," said Steve, "now I'm a fifth wheel. Fine."

"What is a fifth wheel?" Xi'heeh asked.

"It's when your two best friends have girlfriends, and you don't. You're the tag along, you're the extra, and you're in the way."

"Oh, well, that's ok, you have me." Xi'heeh beamed.

"No, not the same thing."

Bart, Erin, and Matt laughed at the quizzical looks on Xi'heeh's and Sha'rell's faces.

Erin ran over to Sha'rell and took her by the hands. "You can stay with me."

"I want to stay with Matt."

"Well, in our world, sometimes the girls stay in one place and the boys in another until they're ready to be on their own. Right now, I don't think Matt's ready to be on his own."

"Oh, okay."

Erin grabbed a piece of Sha'rell's sleeve. "I do wish that we had some time to get you some better clothes than that awful purple jumpsuit though."

Bart cleared his throat. "Speaking of time, we should be going. We have some kidnappers or something to stop."

"Right," said Steve. "I'll get Casey and we can meet you at Webb and Crane."

"That won't be necessary. I can bring him there as well." Xi'heeh waved his hand. "Take us to where this Webb and Crane is?" They all disappeared.

***

"Where are they?" Tasha paced around a street sign and between a lamppost and a trash can. "It shouldn't have taken them very long to get here."

Before Reginald or Isaiah could reply six people and a hovercar appeared from thin air. Two of the people were purple. This sudden appearance of the group caused a bit of commotion. The street wasn't busy, but there were a few people outside of the businesses that lined it. An older couple sitting on a bench quickly stood up and ran as fast as they could away from the group. Another group of people across the street and down the block did a double-take on them but didn't seem bothered by the sudden appearance as they hadn't been paying close attention.

"Do you think you can do something without making

a big scene?" Tasha shook her head but didn't wait for a response. "Fine, I have one announcement before I tell you where we're going." She patted the hilt of her new sword. "Do you like it? I got it from that Jane lady."

"Really?" Matt glanced a little closer at the sword. "Interesting."

"Yep, and she disappeared. She's gone now."

"What about the old lady?" Bart asked.

"I don't know. I don't care about her. I just want you all to know that I'm like you now. I came down here to this section of town to buy a sheath for it. I found a really cool one. Wait, who's the broad?"

"Um, broad?" It was Matt's turn to shake his head. "I didn't think anyone used that term in the 2050s anymore. This is Sha'rell. She's Xi'heeh's aunt."

"Fine, can she do anything? Or does she just take up space and probably get herself killed or one of us killed?"

"I can take care of myself and speak for myself if I need to." Sha'rell's lavender eyes lit like a fire. "Or to stay out of the way if need be."

"Whatever." Tasha started to turn away to address the others when she turned back. "Although, that's some very cool long lavender hair you have there. I like it."

"Thanks, I think."

"All right," Tasha clapped her hands together. "Let's get this thing rolling. We're headed to a country in Africa. There was another group of children, both boys and girls, that were kidnapped and taken away from their school. We thought this type of thing had stopped about twenty years ago, but apparently, someone thinks it's time to revive it. We're supposed to go in, get the children, and get out. Although, we're not exactly sure where they are. So, it's not going to be quite that easy."

"Okay, so, Bart," Matt began, "is she telling the truth?"

"Yes, she is. These kids are in danger."

"Thanks for the vote of confidence. Of course, I'm telling the truth. It's our next assignment. We can't let anyone know that the United States government is behind this rescue. It'd start a huge war. The people responsible probably have the backing of a foreign government themselves, so you can't do your normal 'look at me, I'm a hero' thing here."

"Oh, come on, we never do that," said Steve. "Maybe we get carried away a bit, but it's usually someone else starting things. And besides, what's more private than discussing this on the corner of a semi-quiet business district with two purple people?"

Tasha rolled her eyes, slightly shook her head, and sighed. "Fine, we'll continue this somewhere out of the way." She looked around. "How about there? So, purple guy, can you take us to the roof of that tall building just down the street? It looks quiet up there."

"My name is Xi'heeh, and yes, I can get us there. Is everybody ready?"

"I'll just fly myself over there if you don't mind," said Casey, turning to maneuver down the street. "I don't want to be up on the roof, so I'll just come on over and park along the street. You can bring me along when you decide how to proceed."

Everyone disappeared and reappeared on the rooftop. It was a basic flat top building with a tar and gravel mixture spread across the top. The roofing curved ever so slightly allowing rain to flow to the edges and out some gutters to the street below. A few turbine vents dotted the roof in different areas. A heating and cooling system rested close to where they landed, and nearby there was a structure with a door in it that provided a way for those inside the building to get out onto the rooftop if the need arose and considering the two men and two women resting in reclining lounge chairs next to the door, it must have been unlocked.

"Really? Who sunbathes at eight in the morning?" Tasha walked over to them. They were asleep. She kicked one of the chairs, sending the female occupant flying.

The other sunbathers woke to the screams of the woman. Dazed, they sleepily looked around. A couple of them spilled their drinks.

One jumped up. "What's the meaning of this?" He caught sight of Tasha and the others.

Tasha drew her sword.

"Hey, man, this is our apartment building." The sunbather backed off; hands held out in front of him as if trying to keep her away. "We have the time blocked off up here. You can't come up here during our time."

Tasha glared at him. "I care, why?"

"Hold on, Tasha." Xi'heeh stepped next to her.

The man's eyes grew huge as he'd never seen a purple man before.

Xi'heeh continued. "Just give us a few minutes of

privacy and we'll be gone."

The other apartment dwellers joined the man. "I don't think so."

"Fine then." Xi'heeh waved his hand. The sunbathers disappeared.

"Where did you send them?" Bart asked.

Before Xi'heeh could answer, screams from the street below arose.

"Okay, that answers that question. Tasha, quickly fill us in."

Tasha sheathed her sword. "As I was saying before we moved, we don't know where these children have been taken."

"How long has it been since they were taken?" Steve asked.

"It's been about a day and a half now."

"Were they all taken from the same location?"

"Yes."

"Then I could track down where they went using Pathfinder."

Tasha stared into his eyes. "Let's go. We'll plan more when we get there. I was hoping to divide up now, but that sounds like a better idea than splitting up now. Xi'heeh, can you take us there?" She pulled out a card and showed it to him.

"I'm sorry, I don't know what that means. The swords translate our words to each other, but not our written languages."

Tasha rolled her eyes then leaned over and whispered in his ear.

Steve poked Matt on the arm. "Wow, she won't even tell us where we're going. Apparently, she doesn't trust us."

She glared at Steve. "The less you know, the better, trust me. It shouldn't matter to you where we go."

The door to the roof area burst open. Four police officers spilled out onto the rooftop. Their weapons were drawn and pointed at the group.

"Hold it right there," said the officer closest to them. Before any of them could say or do anything else, Tasha and her group disappeared.

CHAPTER VI

Tasha and the rest materialized on an open field near a large building, arriving in the late afternoon local time. Military personnel roamed about. A couple of the closest soldiers jumped back at the appearance of the group. They recovered quickly and aimed their laser rifles at them.

Tasha walked forward. "Put those away. We're here to help."

The soldiers didn't obey.

One spoke. "Commander. Over here. We have unexpected visitors."

"My name is Tatenda," said a soldier, walking toward the group. He signaled the soldiers to put down their weapons. "Who are you?"

"My name is Tasha." She stuck her hand out to shake.

Tatenda ignored her hand. "What do you want

around here, Tasha and her long sword?"

Tasha's hand found the hilt of her sword. "We're here to help."

"We didn't ask for help. You look American."

"We look like whatever. We're mercenaries. The best there are. We're here to get your children back."

"You look American," Tatenda repeated.

Tasha ignored him and pointed to Steve. "He's the best tracker around. He'll find your kids very quickly."

"We know where they went. They went this way."

"You're wrong." Steve pointed in the opposite direction. "They went that way."

"What are you talking about?"

"I'm the best, you heard her."

"We have clear tracks that they have gone this direction." Tatenda pointed toward a grove of trees. "That would make the most sense too. They would be able to use those trees for camouflage."

"Yeah, you'd think that would make the most sense, and yes, a small group of them got in a vehicle and headed that way, but they didn't have any of the children with them. The main group went that way. They want you to think they took the most logical path, but I know they went that way."

Tatenda stared in disbelief.

"Look, I can show you. I suppose I wouldn't believe me if I were you, and you're right, that way is more obvious. Too obvious though. Look here." Steve knelt on the ground. He pulled Tatenda to his knees beside him. "Here are the tracks that you see. They're trying extremely hard to make tracks here, so they spun out more than a normal vehicle would. They wanted to make it look like they were in a rush when, in reality, they had time. You can see the tracks from the other three vehicles that went this direction." He pointed to the west.

Tatenda leaned closer to the ground. He scanned the tracks. He felt the dirt where they traveled as if that would tell him its story and hidden secrets. He sat up and dusted off his hands. "How did you see that so quickly?"

"I'm good at what I do." Steve stood, not revealing the real reason was that he tracked the life essence of the children after they had been captured.

Tatenda stood and signaled to his troops. "This way. Everyone, climb into your designated vehicle and follow me." He turned to Steve. "You will ride with me. The rest of your group can fill in as you are able."

Steve nodded as he climbed into the back of the tan, open-air jeep that pulled up beside Tatenda. "I have a vehicle that five of them can use."

Casey maneuvered over allowing Bart and Erin to get into the front seats while Matt, Sha'rell, and Xi'heeh slid into the back seat.

Tasha looked around. There didn't seem to be any room in any of the vehicles for them. "What about us?"

Tatenda looked down from the back of the jeep where he sat by Steve. "I have room for one of you in the front seat beside my driver. You may have that. Your friends will have to find another way there."

Tasha nodded, looked at Reginald and Isaiah, and then went around the jeep to sit in the passenger side.

"Why is it always you and me that have to find a different way to get somewhere?" Reginald asked, turning to Isaiah.

Tatenda laughed. "Just joking. You can ride with my Lieutenant in her jeep. She's right there."

Reginald and Isaiah turned in the direction that Tatenda pointed and saw a young woman gesturing them to her vehicle. They strode over and climbed in the back of her jeep.

Once everyone was settled, they moved out. It was a small caravan consisting of the two lead jeeps followed by Casey and three larger covered troop transport trucks.

Steve turned to Tatenda. "Do you have enough personnel to handle these kidnappers?"

"I have what I have. This is all I was given. We haven't had this type of thing in twenty years, so we have settled into new ways and don't have the resources to handle things like we used to. Most of the soldiers you see here are very untrained in this type of thing. We are progressing as a world society now, but there are still a few holdovers that keep the world from moving forward as one. I just hope my men can handle this. If only I knew how many there were."

"There were ten kidnappers. That doesn't mean there aren't more at the location they're being held at."

Tatenda stared at Steve. "How can you know that? There were so many footprints by the school building back where we started. With all the children mixing in, who knows how many kidnappers exited the vehicles and touched the ground."

"There were ten."

Tatenda shook his head.

"Look, I don't like to let people in on my secrets because it'll just make them either scared or think that they can manipulate me somehow. But you have a right to know. I have special abilities, and one of them allows me to see where people have been for up to three days."

Tatenda's eyes widened then narrowed.

Steve pointed at him. "Yeah, just like that. See, you're either in disbelief right now or a little on the frightened or wary side of things, wondering how you're going to get yourself out of this. Back at the school building, I could see two small vehicles each with one person that went the way you thought. The rest went this way. I can follow them and lead you right to them. My friends and I can take the bad guys out for you as well. You don't need to worry about your soldiers. Maybe have them set up a perimeter behind us but let us handle the bad guys. We can take them out for you."

Tatenda looked unsure.

Steve put a hand on Tatenda's arm. "We'll have this under control."

"Fine. We will do as you say. It may be better than having my untrained soldiers try." Tatenda turned to watch the road.

Steve did too, silently watching as the road wound around the countryside. After about ten minutes a fork in the road appeared.

"Hold up." Steve stood up, hanging on to the roll bar in front of him. "Aw man, they split up."

Tatenda stood as well and turned to signal the vehicles behind him. They all slowed to a stop as Steve jumped out. He moved toward the split in the road.

Tatenda, Bart, Erin, and Tasha joined him.

"They split up here," Steve informed them. "It looks like they stopped and separated the boys from the girls. The boys went left, the girls right."

"Sounds like they have different purposes for them." Erin shielded her eyes from the sun as the wind whipped her blonde hair around her hand.

"We're going to have to split up." Tasha turned to head over to where Reginald and Isaiah were. "Just a second and I'll be back."

Steve didn't acknowledge Tasha moving away. "I don't know where they end up in either direction. They've traveled beyond what I can see from here."

"So," Bart started, "one of our groups is going to have to run blind and hope we stumble upon them."

"I've got an idea." Erin turned and ran back to Casey. She returned with Xi'heeh. "How about Steve and Xi'heeh make little jumps as far as Steve can see to follow the girls and as soon as they find them, they can return here to the rest of us. Then, Xi'heeh can take some of us back there and Steve can take the rest to where the boys are."

"That sounds like a good plan," Bart agreed. "It will require a little bit of time, but it will keep one group from going the wrong way if we split here without knowing where the kidnappers might leave the road."

Tasha wandered back over with Reginald and Isaiah.

"Okay, here's what we're going to do. We'll split into two groups. One will go left, and the other right. So, we'll send—"

"Good plan," Bart said. "I know just what you are thinking. We will send Steve and Xi'heeh down the right path toward where the girls went. Since Steve can only see their trail so far, they will make short jumps until they find them. Then they will return to the group here and then we split up into your two groups with Xi'heeh returning to the girls with one of the groups."

Tasha narrowed her eyes at Bart. "Follow me." She moved away from the others.

Bart sighed. "See you in a moment." He walked over to where Tasha went.

She lowered her voice so no one could hear her. "Every time I try to come up with a plan, you interfere somehow. I'm in charge, not you."

"What? Was that not what you were going to say? It is a brilliant idea if that was what you were planning to say. Think about it. Steve can see where the girls went. Xi'heeh can take him as far as he can see, and maybe a little beyond. Assuming they have not left the country, it should not take them long to track where they are. And, to think that was the idea you were going to mention is sheer brilliance."

Tasha was speechless. She sputtered for a moment, then said, "Sure, yeah, that's what I was going to say."

She walked back to the group. "Okay, like I was saying. Xi'heeh will take Steve on those little jumps and come back when they find the girls. Then we'll split up and go get both groups of kids."

Steve nodded. "Great plan, Tasha. Xi'heeh, I can see to that tree." He pointed down the road, and in an instant, they were gone.

They reappeared close to the tree that Steve had pointed to. Steve gathered his bearings. He could see a long way down this country road, but there came a point he couldn't see any trails further up some hills in the distance.

"Let's try over by that building at the foot of those hills. I can see trails leading there, but I'm not sure beyond that."

They disappeared and reappeared where Steve suggested, right in the middle of the kidnapper's hideout. The girls were lined up outside in what resembled a small courtyard.

"Whoops!" Steve yelled. "Quick, before they know what's going on, teleport these girls back to the others, then come back with Bart and Matt."

Xi'heeh nodded and in the proverbial blink of an eye, he had assessed where all the girls were, and they all disappeared.

"Hey, guys, how's it going?" Steve rotated in a circle where he had been standing and looked at all the men closing in around him. They all had top-of-the-line laser rifles and wore raggedy and disheveled clothing that blended in well with the background of the area they were in.

"What did you just do?" One of the grubbier-looking guys pointed his laser rifle at Steve.

"Let's see. My friend and I just suddenly appeared out of nowhere. We then took all those girls back to where we came from by suddenly disappearing. Oh wait, we didn't go, he went. I stayed behind to teach you all a lesson you won't soon remember."

"You do know that we're not going to be happy with you, right?"

"Eh, I'll take my chances."

"You're pretty brave, shiny boy."

"Wow, 'shiny boy'? Really? That hurts, man, that hurts." Steve removed his sword and melded his hand with the handle so that it couldn't be accidentally knocked free.

"So, you're planning on teaching a lesson with that while I'm holding a laser rifle?" The man's mouth formed a slight smile, and he shook his head back and forth while staring Steve down. He moved toward Steve.

More unkempt men carrying similar laser rifles appeared from the building.

"Are you sure there's enough of you?" Steve took note of how many there were. It was a lot.

"You just don't get it, do you?"

"Oh, I get plenty. Ever think it might be you that doesn't understand what you're about to get yourself into?"

"That's it. Attack!" The man fired his laser. The beams seemed to just disappear as they reached Steve.

Others joined in, firing on Steve. No beams ever came close to hitting him.

Steve moved toward the first man. Closer and closer

until he was a few feet away. Then, he turned himself invisible.

"Where'd he gah—?" The man collapsed to the ground.

The others looked around. Their eyes widened as they looked and waited.

Steve reappeared in front of the next closest one. "Boo!"

The man dropped his gun and stumbled back. He turned to run, but Matt was right behind him preparing to wrap him in some rope he was pulling from his pocket.

Steve furrowed his brow. "Dude, I will never get used to you doing that."

Matt grinned. "You don't know how handy this has been already."

Bart and Xi'heeh had also returned. Bart took out his sword and Xi'heeh held an alien-looking rifle. He started shooting at the kidnappers, easily cutting them down with the energy bursts that didn't seem to quite be laser blasts. Before the others could stop him, Xi'heeh had cleared the area of any remaining abductors.

"Whoa, Xi'heeh, we usually try to capture people." Bart held up a hand to try to calm him down. "We try not to be like them."

"I apologize. I do not understand your ways yet. I shall try to do better next time."

"We wanted someone to tell Tatenda why they did this."

"Matt has captured one," Xi'heeh noted. "We will get him to speak."

Bart looked around. "Well, we had better get back to the others. Xi'heeh, please bring the lone captor with us."

They appeared back at the spot where their group waited.

"We will not have to split up now," Bart said. "The girls are safe, and the bad guys have been neutralized. This individual is the only one remaining."

Matt picked up the prisoner by the rope. He carried him to Tatenda and placed him face to face with Tatenda.

Tatenda looked at him for a moment. Without warning, he slapped the rebel across the cheek, knocking him to the ground. "Get this filth out of here, Lieutenant."

She raced over and jerked the struggling man to his feet.

"Should we try to get him to tell us where the others are first, or who he is working for?" Bart stepped next to the Lieutenant and the kidnapper. "I can help you know if he is telling the truth or not."

"I will tell you nothing." The kidnapper spat.

"I am glad you missed." Bart looked at the loogie that hung in the air between him and the Lieutenant.

The kidnapper's eyes widened as did the Lieutenant's. Tatenda looked mildly surprised.

Bart walked closer to the kidnapper. The ball of spit continued its course. "I made that stop and start again. I can do other things too. You can tell me who put you up to this, or I can let Xi'heeh finish you off."

"I'm not telling you anything."

Bart motioned to Xi'heeh, who came over. He

reached out in front of him and pulled his blaster out of midair.

"You saw what this did to your brethren, correct? It has three settings, pain, death, and disintegration. I'll start with pain." He lifted the gun, aiming at the kidnapper's shoulder.

The kidnapper's eyes widened. "You wouldn't."

Xi'heeh pressed the trigger.

The kidnapper screamed in agony.

"Do not ever guess what I would do. I am K'reelian. We do not have your rules."

After a long bit of wincing the kidnapper spoke. "I don't know for sure who hired us, but I know he has an office in New York City. It's in a building called the Flatiron."

Bart nodded. "He is telling the truth. That is all he knows. I am not sure how much help that is as we do not know where in the building this person is."

The Lieutenant grabbed the kidnapper by his good arm and started to haul him to her jeep.

"Just a moment." Matt placed his hand on the mercenary's shoulder.

The man winced for a moment then he breathed easier.

"There, that should feel better," said Matt.

"So," Tatenda turned to Bart, "you have taken care of the rest of those fighters you say?"

Bart nodded. "Xi'heeh shot them all before we could almost blink."

"Good. They would have received the same

treatment from us." Tatenda turned to the driver of the last truck. "Go with your men and make sure all is as they say and that there are no more still hiding. When you are done, radio me and await further orders. If we handle the next group as quickly, you may be able to return to base."

The driver nodded and jumped into the truck. He started it up and roared off down the road.

"It is only a few miles down the road," Bart said. "They should find it quickly enough."

CHAPTER VII

Tatenda jumped in the back of his jeep as it began to roll. "Let's move out and find the boys."

The remaining vehicles began to follow in line. Isaiah had taken the last spot in the Lieutenant's jeep, so Reginald jumped into the air, taking flight.

Tatenda looked up. The sight of Reginald gliding through the air appeared to startle him.

"Most of us here have something special about them," Steve told him.

Tatenda tilted his head in curiosity.

"I told you a little bit about my tracking ability before, but the whole story is too long to tell. As I said, just have your people set up a perimeter behind us and let us take care of the rest."

Not far down the road, Reginald yelled for everyone to stop. He landed in front of Tatenda's jeep, forcing the convoy to halt.

"What's up?" Tatenda jumped out of the jeep.

"I don't see anything yet." Steve followed out of the jeep.

"I can." Reginald pointed down the road toward a small bend covered by trees. "They've set up a camp right around there. I can see it from up higher. I'm figuring you can't see that they've stopped yet because of the bend and trees."

"Let me pull it up on my holo-map." Tatenda brought out a small device as Bart and Tasha joined them.

"What is up?" Bart asked.

"I can see from above that they've stopped just behind the bend there in the road."

Erin, Matt, Sha'rell, Xi'heeh, and Isaiah joined them.

"Here's what the holo-map projects of the area ahead." Tatenda set the device on the hood of his jeep.

"Okay, here's what we're going to do." Tasha knelt to draw in the dirt on the road. "Unless, of course, Bart has other ideas." She glanced at him.

Bart shrugged.

She continued. "The road takes a bend up there, so the left side of the road will be on the south and the right side to the north. Bart and I will go to the south side which will put us left of the grove. We'll come up to the side from there."

"You're not going alone with Bart." Erin folded her arms, staring straight into Tasha's eyes.

"Fine, you come with us then. Matt and Xi'heeh, I

want you to transport behind them on the right side of that road, right there." She pointed at the location and then looked at Sha'rell. "I suppose you want to go with Matt?"

"No, thank you. I will stay back with the vehicles. I may be K'reelian, but I'm not really a fighter."

"Great. Isaiah, I want you, Reginald, and Steve to start down the road here like you're walking along minding your own business. As you near the bend, slow down and take stock of what's there. I'd like Isaiah to use his super-speed to run through the camp as fast as he can to the other side. If you can, take anyone out along the way or steal their weapons."

Steve raised his hand.

Tasha looked up. "Yes? Do you have a question, and don't tell me you have to use the restroom or something? I know you think you're a funny man."

"Nothing like that, although now that you mention it, I do need to, thanks. I was going to suggest that maybe I walk through their encampment invisible while you all get in place so I can assess what we're up against instead of having Isaiah run through. Once I have an idea of what everything looks like, I could radio everyone, well if we had radios that is."

"Here." Tatenda reached into a box on the side of his jeep. "These should do it for you. They are communication devices that we're testing. You just need one in your pocket, and everyone can hear everyone else." He grabbed a handful and tossed them around to everyone.

Tasha pocketed her device. "I like the idea of Steve going invisible into the area first. So, Isaiah, you wait for Steve to tell you it's clear before going through. Tatenda, you and your troops gather here and watch for any escapees that come in this direction. Isaiah will have the other side of the road."

"I have a request." Xi'heeh turned to Tatenda. "May I see your map apparatus?"

"Sure." Tatenda picked it up off the hood and handed it to Xi'heeh.

Xi'heeh surveyed the map. The image began to rotate, moving faster and faster until the entire world had spun around ten rotations.

"What are you doing?" Tatenda reached for the device.

Xi'heeh turned around, blocking him from grabbing it. "I am familiarizing myself with your planet. This way I will no longer need to ask for directions. My sword already knows this planet, but I do not. This will help me remember where everything is so I can work more efficiently with my sword."

When he was finished, he handed the holo-map back to Tatenda.

"Any more questions?" Tasha asked. "Is everyone on the same page?"

Everyone nodded.

"Great. Let's go."

"Are we going to high five or something?" Steve held his hand up in the air. "Ah, come on, don't leave me hanging." Steve lowered his hand. "Fine."

Matt and Xi'heeh disappeared.

"This is Matt. Can everyone hear me?"

"Loud and clear," Bart answered first.

"Great, we found a fairly good place to wait for the rest of you to get into place. Let us know when you are. Also, keep in mind that others near you can hear you, so keep it quiet and to a minimum."

"Roger that," Tasha said. "Let's go, Bart, Erin."

Bart removed his laser rifle from his invisible back harness. "Here, Erin, you will need this." He tossed it to her as Tatenda and his troops readied themselves to guard the escape route in this direction.

Tatenda shook his head. "Is there anything that you guys don't have?"

"We're pretty much a small army battalion ourselves." Erin grabbed the gun but immediately fell to the ground.

Bart fell to his knees. "Erin, what happened? That gun is not too heavy for you. It should not have knocked you down."

"I'm fine," she lied. "Just give me a moment."

"You cannot tell me you are fine when you are not. I think you should stay back and let Sha'rell help you."

"No! I'm coming with you. It's passing, whatever it was." She stood up and brushed off the dirt. She headed for their side of the road. "Let's go."

Bart and Tasha followed. They darted across open spaces and crouched behind shrubs or trees, whichever they could find until they reached a spot where they could still see the site.

"I'm going incognito," Steve said. "I'll be inside the grounds in a minute. Reg and Isaiah are coming around at a slower pace, but I think they may have been spotted."

"Never call me Reg again."

"How about Inald then?"

"No."

"We can see the area from where we are," Tasha said over the comm device. "This thing is working well, but as Matt said, let's go quiet now until we're ready to move. I see five pairs of guards walking around. Steve, let us know when you've got more information. Try to find the youth."

Tasha, Bart, and Erin sat behind some shrubbery in silence, waiting for Steve to report.

Steve's voice came over the comm. "Ah, there you are. Just what I was looking for."

"What did you say?" An unfamiliar voice floated through the comm.

"I didn't say anything," said a different voice.

"Then we must be hearing a ghost," said the first unknown voice, "cause the door to the outhouse just opened and closed."

"Why would a ghost need an outhouse?" asked the second.

"Whoa! Man, who died in here?" Steve's voice came through the comm.

"See, it was a ghost," replied the first.

"Steve, we are picking up the conversation around you." Bart tried to whisper.

The sounds of lasers bursting came over the comm

device. Bart crawled forward enough to be able to see a couple of militants shooting at a small building. The other four sets of guards were moving toward the little shed. The door flew off.

Steve's voice came from nowhere. "Can't a guy have some privacy?"

Then bodies started flying around or collapsing on the ground. It only took a moment before they all lay strewn about. It didn't appear that any backups were coming out of the bigger building, but there had to be someone there. That had to be where the boys were being held.

"We need to move." Bart stood up. He turned to Erin.

She was halfway to her feet when she collapsed.

"Erin!" Bart reached over to her. "Something is wrong with her."

"I was afraid of that," said Isaiah.

"What?" Bart asked. "How would you know?"

"I am Ian McNamara's assistant. I helped with everything that he ever did. And he didn't do his daughter any good."

"Is she a clone?"

"No, but not much better off. We need to help these boys, and then I'll help her. I'm going to see if I can speed through that building and try to find the rest of the bad guys. I'll let you know where the boys are."

Bart turned to Tasha. He heard the familiar pop of her teleportation process as he saw her disappear. Then he heard a closer pop.

"I can't miss from this close." Tasha drove her sword into his back. "I knew eventually I'd find a way to make this work. The fourth sword will be your death."

"What is all the chatter?" Matt asked over the communication device. "We're supposed to be silent."

Bart fell to the ground beside Erin.

"Ha, I finally killed Bart. I did it. It was me!" Tasha taunted over the radio. "And now I'm going to kill Erin too."

"What?!" yelled Isaiah into his radio. "You can't do that. She's Ian's daughter."

"I don't care about Ian anymore. Look what he did to us; what he turned us into. He made us freaks, and never gave us anything in return. I want more than this, and with this sword, I'll get what I want."

"Guys." Erin stirred, looking at Bart. "Bart isn't moving. I think he's dea..." She passed out.

"Erin, Erin, are you alright?" Matt yelled. "Bart? What's wrong with Erin?" There was no answer from either. "Xi'heeh, get to their side of the road. I have this side."

Xi'heeh appeared beside Erin and Bart. Both lay on the ground. Neither moved.

Tasha attacked. Xi'heeh's K'reelian instincts kicked in. He blocked her sword attack. He slashed his sword in her direction. She disappeared. He heard a pop behind him. With speed she couldn't have expected, he drew his dagger and without looking, flung it right at her. She didn't have time to react. The dagger blade buried into her abdomen up to the hilt. Her eyes grew big. Her mouth opened slightly. She made a popping sound as if trying to transport herself away but instead fell to the ground.

Xi'heeh turned to Bart. He wasn't moving. Erin lay close beside him. She wasn't moving either.

"I need help in here." Isaiah's voice came over the commlink. "There are three bad guys in here. They have what they tell me is a proximity bomb on each of the boys. The boys will explode if they are moved away from any of the three men. We can't move them."

"Xi'heeh, can you teleport the boys and leave those devices behind?" Matt asked.

"I do not believe so. I have never tried to move someone and leave behind something they may be holding. This is not the time to find out if I can. Even if I were able to, the bombs would likely explode before I could get them away. They would probably be dead wherever I took them."

"Agreed." Matt's voice was matter of fact. "We need Jane and the old woman. Can you go get them?"

"What about Bart? He is still not moving."

"Bart, get up, or Xi'heeh won't go."

Bart rolled over. "Thanks for the hand."

"You are not hurt?" Xi'heeh had a blank stare on his face.

"No, I was not. I was playing. She does not have the fourth sword."

"Where can I find these people?" Xi'heeh retrieved his dagger from Tasha's body.

"Lower Stamford, corner of Main and Bank Streets,"

Matt replied.

Xi'heeh disappeared.

CHAPTER VIII

Xi'heeh appeared at the intersection of Main and Bank in Lower Stamford. He had never seen the lower level of Stamford before. He shook his head as he looked up at the panels that covered the lower part of the city. It was mid-morning here, but the artificial lighting didn't do much to make things bright. He certainly wasn't impressed. He looked back toward the ground and saw a statue of, well, he didn't know what it was a statue of. It looked like a naked woman with something around her, but he didn't know what. It was just a jumble of metal to him.

"Are you looking for someone?"

Xi'heeh turned to see an old woman sitting on a bench in front of a small cement park with fake plants.

The woman must have guessed the look on his face. "It used to have real grass and bushes and flowers, but that stuff doesn't grow here anymore."

"Too bad," he replied.

"Yes, isn't it. So, I'll ask again, are you looking for someone?"

"I might be. It might be you."

"Well, I figured you might be looking for me, because we don't get many purple guys that abruptly appear out of nowhere around here. If one were to come around though, he'd probably be looking for me. Or for my friend Jane."

He looked around for someone else.

"Oh, she's not here right now," the old woman continued. "She's across the street in that store over there. She should be out any minute."

"I was told to look for someone named Jane and an old lady at this spot. It must be you. You are the only one here."

The old woman stood up and walked closer to Xi'heeh. "What do you need us for?"

"My friends and I are rescuing some kidnapped children in a place called Africa. We saved the girls, but the kidnappers attached bombs to the boys, and we can't move them."

The old woman turned away, gazing into the little park. "And what makes you think we could help?"

"My friend, Matt, says you have a sword similar to mine." He unsheathed his sword as the old woman turned back toward him, then quickly replaced it. "We need your special ability to put shields around anything. We need you to put it between the boys and the bomb devices."

She thought for a moment, then she walked closer to him. "It's Jane's ability, not mine."

"We need her then. In either case, I really don't care which of you it is. These boys will likely die in any attempt the rest of us can make."

"So," the old woman rubbed her chin, "if Jane doesn't go, these boys die? That's not a good situation you found yourself in, is it?"

Xi'heeh shook his head.

"What makes you think we can get there in time?"

"The special ability of my sword is teleportation. It can take me and anyone I need anywhere in the universe in an instant. It takes me anywhere that I know where to go. It even retains any maps I can absorb. I will have us back there in seconds."

The old woman again turned away. "What if I don't want to go?"

"I will ask Jane when she comes back, and surely she is a hero and will help out."

The old woman laughed. She turned back to face Xi'heeh. "Neither Jane nor I are heroes. We keep things clean down here because no one else will. We do that because we live here, and we do our best to maintain order. Folks around here appreciate it, but we can only do so much. There's too much for the two of us to clean up completely, so we just keep an even keel."

Xi'heeh didn't know what to say. He wasn't sure what he could do to help her make up her mind. "I don't have time to philosophize with you. These boys are in immediate danger. Another new friend of mine, Erin, is in danger as well."

"What?" The old woman's eyes were wide. She moved closer to Xi'heeh. "What do you mean she's in danger?"

"She has passed out and we are not sure why. My friend, Isaiah, says she needs his help."

The old woman ran to the bench. She started to pick up a bag but put it down. "I don't have time for that." She returned to Xi'heeh. "I told that dad burned old fool that we needed to get her back into that chamber. He never listened to me. Let's go, now!"

Xi'heeh hesitated. "But where is Jane? We need her too."

"She'll be along with us, don't you worry. She's coming out of the building, just tag her along."

Xi'heeh looked but didn't see her. "I need to let you know the scenario. We can't just pop in and hope you get the protective shields up in time."

"We don't have time." The old woman was getting very agitated, but the look on Xi'heeh's face said they weren't going anywhere yet. "Fine, fill me in. I'll let Jane know when we get there."

Xi'heeh nodded. "I will set us down outside of the building where the boys are. We will sneak in, and you can put a force field between the boys and the explosive devices."

"Sounds like a plan. Now, let's go. Jane's on the way out."

Xi'heeh walked over to the bench and picked up the old woman's bag. "I can store it for you and return it later when we're done." He reached out, picked up the bag, and put it in front of him where it disappeared. "Let's go."

***

They reappeared outside of the building the boys were being held in. Steve and Reginald stared each other down. Matt peeked into a door in the front of the building.

"You guys killed her." Reginald seemed to be maintaining a level of composure, but the veins in his neck were popping.

"She tried to kill Bart, again." Steve was equally doing his best to maintain self-control. "She always tried to kill Bart. She was just waiting for a chance like this."

"Gentlemen." Xi'heeh cleared his throat. "I have returned with the old woman only."

"We'll make do." Matt turned away from the door and jumped off the stairs toward them. "Isaiah's still inside, and Bart hasn't moved Erin. I checked her out, but there's nothing my healing powers can do for her. I'm not sure why, but it's possible Ian really messed up her DNA or something. So, Mrs.—"

"Just call me the old woman," interrupted the old woman loudly. "And... Jane is here. You snagged her just as we left."

"I did not sense her with us."

"Maybe that's because you set me behind this tree over here," said Jane, emerging into the open.

"Where did you come from?" Xi'heeh couldn't hide his surprise.

"Right there behind the tree where you saw me," Jane replied in her haughty manner.

"I did not bring you."

"Yes, you did. I'm here, aren't I?"

"It appears so." Xi'heeh narrowed his eyes and put his hand in position to grab his sword.

"Does it matter how she got here?" Matt asked, placing a calming hand on his shoulder. "She's here now, and she needs to get inside immediately and put a force field between the boys and those devices."

Jane sighed. She moved toward the door with Matt right behind. The old woman moved behind them as they entered the building. Stairs greeted them. There was a door to the right of the stairs that led into the first-floor area.

"You're in the upstairs, right Isaiah?" Matt waited for a response. None came. He pulled out Timeline and Jane likewise unsheathed Blockade.

"Yes," Isaiah finally said. "Sorry, we were staring each other down for a moment. There are four bad guys with me. It's hard to keep an eye on all of them. They're each in one corner of the room. It is one single, oversized room full of beds for the boys. The boys are standing beside their beds."

"Got it." Matt started up the stairs.

"Let us go first." Jane brushed passed him.

The old woman gave him a knowing look and passed by. "She's just not a people person."

Matt smiled. He followed them up.

Jane stopped at the door. It was just like the door

below and was the only thing in a small vestibule. There were two tiny rectangle windows in the door frame. Jane slowly peeked inside from the right side as the old woman came over to the left side. She slowly moved an eye into the frame as had Jane.

"Okay, it's done." Jane backed away from the door as did the old woman.

"Did you hear that, Isaiah?" Matt asked.

"Yes, we all did thanks to these not-so-private communication devices."

"Do it then." Matt burst through the door, swinging for the guy to the right of the door.

Jane followed through, heading for the guy to the left of the door.

They both turned back to look at each other because there was no one in either corner. They turned to the other side of the room. The four bad guys stood by a bound Isaiah with their weapons pointed at his head.

"Yeah, I know." Isaiah tried to shrug but couldn't very well while tied up. "What're you going to do when they're listening in on you. They do have the explosives on the boys though, well, and me too now. They had all the cards and made me say everything. I couldn't let them blow the kids up."

One of the guerillas spoke. "One move and they all get blown to bits." He lowered his weapon, then took a small device with a red button on it from his camouflage jacket.

"Nice." Matt stood his ground. "First you try to cliché me to death, and then you pull out something with a red button on it. I'd advise you not to press the red button."

"Are you going to stop us? Try, and these kids die. And this old dude too." He pointed to Isaiah.

Matt took a step forward.

"No, really, man, don't make me."

Matt stopped he looked at the frightened faces of the kids. He turned his head toward Jane, who nodded. He turned back. "Don't be afraid, young men. I guarantee your safety." He looked at as many of them as he could in their eyes and nodded.

The boys still looked scared. His assurances hadn't helped them it appeared.

Matt looked at the man with the detonator. "You do realize that you're in the room too, right? Press that, and you'll go boom along with the rest of us."

"We know the risks of war."

Matt raised his eyebrows in an acknowledging fashion. He couldn't argue with that. "Fine." He took another step.

The man raised the detonator to about shoulder level and placed his finger on the red button.

Matt took another step.

The man pressed the button. A big explosion rocked the building. Windows blew out. The roof flew into the air in multiple pieces, some of which returned to fall back into the building. Those pieces landed on top of an invisible shield and didn't reach the ground. The walls on the upper level had huge chunks blown out, making the remaining sides look like Swiss cheese. The floor remained intact.

"I told him not to press the red button." Matt turned to Jane. "You covered the floor too, eh?"

"I didn't want anyone falling through to the first floor after saving everyone. There's a reason this sword is called Blockade."

Matt turned his attention to the boys. "Are you alright?"

The boys looked around. They had no idea how they were still alive. They were free of the vests though.

The militia was nowhere to be seen. Isaiah stood alone and the ropes binding him were shredded. He flicked the remaining bits to the floor. "Thank you, Jane. I appreciate you saving me as well."

Jane nodded then turned to walk out the door.

"Let's get back to Erin," said the old woman as she too turned to head out the door.

"Follow me, boys." Matt led the way out.

CHAPTER IX

Matt, Xi'heeh, Jane, and the old woman ran to where Bart held the unconscious Erin. Isaiah used his super speed to beat them all to the scene and knelt next to Erin. Steve stood over all three with a look of concern on his face. Reginald sat holding the lifeless body of Tasha. The kidnapped boys followed not knowing what else they were supposed to do and having no idea what happened back in the building.

"You!" Reginald stared at Bart. "You are the cause of this." He pushed Tasha's body into a sitting position, shaking her in Bart's direction.

Bart looked up. "I am not the one that attempted to put a sword in my back. We were trying to work with you. She bided her time to attempt to take my life. She did not have to do this. I did not ask for it."

Reginald set Tasha down, then scrambled to his feet. He rushed toward Bart.

Bart didn't look up at him. "Are you sure you want to do that?"

Isaiah jumped to his feet. He held out his gloved hands and blocked Reginald's path. "Calm down. He's correct. We didn't know that she was planning this. At least I didn't, did you?"

Reginald slowly shook his head. His head dropped.

"Look," Isaiah started, "why don't you take these boys back to Tatenda? They can take care of them from here. Bring Sha'rell back, and we'll all go home."

Reginald didn't move. He didn't raise his head.

"I will take the boys," said Xi'heeh, "and I will get my aunt. I do not trust him with her." He and the boys disappeared.

"We're wasting time." The old woman knelt, caressing Erin's forehead. "We need to get her back into stasis."

Bart looked at her. "What are you talking about?"

"There's no time to waste. She's dying as we speak."

Matt knelt beside them and placed his hands on Erin's head. "Let me try my healing power again."

He concentrated for a moment. His face showed concern. "I don't have anything on her. My healing power isn't doing anything for her."

"That's because her fool of a father tampered with her genes." The old woman looked at Isaiah as he knelt back beside them.

He didn't return her gaze. "I couldn't stop him. I tried to tell him not to do it. I knew he would do more harm than good."

"You need to stop." The old woman grabbed his bare wrist and forced him to look at her.

He wrenched his arm away.

Xi'heeh and Sha'rell reappeared with Casey.

Bart looked back and forth between the old woman and Isaiah. "What is going on? What are you two talking about?"

The old woman sighed and scowled. "I think you know somewhat about what Ian did to her. He tried to make her immortal."

"It was to protect his daughter," Isaiah said. "He didn't ever want anything to hurt her."

"And he did the opposite," the old woman continued. "She started to deteriorate instead. He quickly built a stasis chamber for her. Once inside she stabilized and stopped aging. While she stayed there, she was alive. Outside, she would start to crumble inside again."

Bart looked bewildered. "But she's been out two or three years now. How did she get out? And how long can she live outside?"

"We don't know the answer to either question, but she may have lived longer than we expected." Isaiah stood up. "We thought the chamber was foolproof. But that day you met her; she had just escaped. We were trying to get her back."

"She said you were criminals."

"In a way we were. To her, we were. World domination was something we discussed in our lab. She must have heard us and pieced things together."

"But she had a mother that she went back to?" Bart's

face was filled with confusion.

"No, she didn't. Did she ever leave you?"

"We were on our way to take her home when you found us. Then Gan and Koolth came along, taking us to their planet."

"Right, and did she ever make it to a home after that?"

Bart thought for a moment then shook his head. "No, we found that apartment complex as soon as we got back."

Isaiah nodded. "And it was already too late to convince you that we were only trying to get her back into the chamber. You wouldn't have believed us anyway."

Bart nodded. "Yeah, without my sword, we would not have."

"Well, you better believe us now, or Erin will die."

Bart lifted Erin and stood up. "Everything you have said is true. I do not understand because everything Erin has told me is true as well."

"To her, it was true." The old woman stood and continued to caress Erin's forehead. "Your sword's power is only as good as the information you receive."

Erin moaned.

"She's not doing well," said the old woman. "We need to get her to the chamber, now."

Xi'heeh stepped into the conversation. "Where can I take us?"

Isaiah pulled a business card from his back pocket and handed it to Xi'heeh. "Can you take us there?"

"I am not able to read your language. You will need to tell me where I am going."

Isaiah pulled the card away. "I don't want the others to hear where our lab is."

"Oh, for Pete's sake, just tell him!" The old woman glared at Isaiah. "Are your secrets more important than Erin?"

Isaiah thought for a moment. "No." He leaned over and whispered into Xi'heeh's ear and then they all disappeared.

***

They all reappeared outside a warehouse building tucked into a grove of dead and decaying trees. They stood in a street next to a loading area for trucks. Four bay doors lined the outside walls next to the loading area. White paint peeled from the brick façade. Five windows set side by side looked out over the wheelchair ramp into the building. The railing surrounding the ramp was bent and in disrepair.

"This building was once a manufacturing plant." Isaiah swept his hand toward it. "Her chamber is inside."

"I'm not going in." Reginald picked up Tasha's lifeless form. "I'm going to bury her on my own. I don't know if I can be with you again, Isaiah. It appears that you value Bart and his friends over your own. For now, I'll take my leave of you." He turned and walked down the road, out of sight.

Isaiah watched him fade down the street. "I wish you well my friend." He turned to the building. "Let's get her in there."

Still carrying Erin, Bart sped up the ramp while Isaiah zipped around the front and opened the door. Everyone followed inside as Isaiah led the way into the building, leaving Casey outside. They passed what appeared to be a small office area.

"We had one legitimate business in here. With the post office across the street, we couldn't afford to have people figure out what was going on in the back."

Isaiah pressed a panel in the wall. It slid aside revealing a big room filled with all sorts of equipment. There were all sorts of different things, computers; gadgets, big and small; tools, all kinds imaginable; wires and clamps, you name it, and it was probably in here. Tables filled with all sorts of scientific equipment. In the middle of a room sat an ominously empty, hexagon-shaped glass chamber. Its door was open. Inside sat a cushioned chair that reclined at a comfortable angle.

"Get her in there." Isaiah went to the control panel beside the booth. He quickly pushed some buttons and pulled some levers.

Bart ran over to the compartment and placed her gently in the chair. As he stepped back, the door closed on its own. At the far end of the room, he could see three similar booths, but he couldn't tell if something, or someone, was in them or not. They appeared to be clouded over.

Steam poured into the chamber. Erin seemed to relax.

Isaiah sighed. Everyone else stood by without speaking.

After a while, Bart broke the silence. "How old is she?"

The old woman looked over at him. "That's complicated. Technically, she has existed for about seventy-five years, however, she only aged to around eighteen while she was in the stasis field because it prevented her from maturing. Her father made this for her, but he never figured out how to cure her. She never aged while in stasis. With the time she's now spent outside the chamber, she's only aged to twenty-one."

Everyone was silent. It was an awkward silence. What does one say to anyone after learning something such as this? There is no precedence for this.

"That is no way for her to live." Bart placed a hand on the glass.

"You're correct." The old woman walked over and stood beside Bart. "I think I know of a way to help her now though."

Bart looked at her. "What do you mean?"

The old woman hesitated.

Jane walked over. She nodded.

Matt followed her over. "You need to tell everyone."

Bart assumed his most recent state; that being in a state of confusion.

"I agree. I think it's time." The old woman heaved a sigh. "Matt has known ever since he received the third sword. He knows everything about all of us current sword holders and those that held the sword in the past. He knows who I am. He knows what Jane is. I thank him for allowing my privacy. It is no longer time to hide. I am

Felicia McNamara. I am Ian's wife. I am Erin's mother. I am the current holder of the fourth sword. Jane is one of my extra abilities. You could call her a doppelganger of what I used to look like. She always appears with a sword of her own, and not the real one. Tasha didn't know that, but that's why she couldn't kill you. She acquired one of Jane's swords and not the real one. I have it."

It took Bart a while to speak, but he finally said, "I knew Tasha did not have the sword because I could still tell if she told the truth or not. I cannot with you, but I do not think you need to be able to have a sword with the abilities mine has to know you are telling the truth. So, you said you had an idea that might help Erin."

"Yes, she needs to take my sword."

"I can't let you do that," Isaiah said.

"It's not your choice. It's mine."

"Yes, I suppose it is your choice, but Erin is not stable enough to go through that. She needs a little time in the chamber to recuperate. Besides, I think she needs to know what's at stake and who you are before that choice is made."

Felicia glared at Isaiah. "You're just stalling."

Isaiah stared blankly at Erin through the glass container. "You know that we would have to open the chamber again to speak to her. She is in a coma-like state there. She needs to recover before she can talk to you. Give her that time, and I'll guarantee you that opportunity to tell her who you are."

Isaiah turned to face Felicia, and they stared at each other. No one needed to utter any clichés about the tension in the room. It was evident.

"I know no one wants to think about our next move, but I think we need to," Steve broke the awkwardness.

"We have two things, well three really, that we need to accomplish right now." Bart turned away from the chamber to focus on the rest of the group. "First, someone needs to stay with Erin. I would like to, but I am afraid that I need to be at one of the other two things."

"I'll stay." Felicia tore her gaze away from Isaiah and toward Erin. She grabbed a nearby wooden chair which seemed better suited for a dining room table and sat down.

"I can stay," Matt volunteered. "I'm the only one that knew who you were, so I'm a logical choice."

"I'm more of a logical choice," Isaiah chimed in.

"I don't need anyone to stay with me."

"I think it is best if someone else stays also," Bart agreed with the others. "Someone of your capability. Matt is the better choice to stay behind. Sha'rell, you can stay with them."

Isaiah didn't look happy, but he didn't press the argument further.

Sha'rell, however, looked delighted. She quickly found two chairs identical to the one Felicia had and brought them over to the booth and set them down. She sat down and motioned for Matt to join her.

Bart looked directly at Isaiah. "We will need you to be at one of the other places. Someone should go to the President and report on our mission, leaving out the details on Erin. Another group should go to New York City and see what we can find out at the Flatiron Building the mercenary mentioned."

"Fine, if those are my choices, I'll take the Flatiron Building." Isaiah walked away and picked up a couple of flasks and started to move them around on one of the tables full of equipment.

"Steve," Bart turned toward him, with a look of bewilderment crossing his face. "What are you doing?"

Steve was holding a small glass bird with a bulbous bottom filled with some red liquid. "What does this do?"

"Oh man, I've seen one of those before." Matt jumped off his chair and went over to Steve. "Here, you need some water in this cup." Matt slowly filled up the empty glass that was beside the bird using his special ability to generate water from his hand. Then he took the bird device from Steve and dipped its head down into the glass for a few seconds. He set the bird down and the red liquid in the bulb area began to rise inside the tube it had for a body. After a few moments, the bird dipped down into the glass, and then the red liquid fell back into the bulb. It repeated the process.

"Man, that's cool," Steve said, watching the bird dip up and down.

"Boys, can we get back to the business at hand?" Bart tapped Steve on the shoulder.

Steve looked up. Realizing everyone was watching him, he straightened up. "Sorry, carry on."

Bart rolled his eyes. "Steve, you go with Isaiah to the Flatiron Building."

Steve saluted. "Aye, aye, Captain."

Bart rolled his eyes again. "Xi'heeh and I will visit the President. We will drop you two off first and then head to Washington D.C."

Steve nodded. "I'll signal Casey to head toward New York City and wait for us outside the building so that you don't have to come back for us."

"Hang on a moment." Isaiah headed over to another table with a hologram communication device. He clicked it on. An image appeared on the holo-screen.

"Yes, may I help you?" said the image.

"Is the President busy?" Isaiah asked. "We finished our mission and need to go over the results with her."

"She has a free moment right now, but you're too far away to get here."

"Don't worry about that. I have a friend that will get us there in a few moments."

The face in the image looked doubtful. "Whatever. I shall let her know you're on the way then." The image blanked out.

"There, you're all set for a meeting with her. What? Why are you looking at me like that?"

Bart looked suspicious. "You have a direct line to the President?"

"What do you expect? We've worked for her longer than you have. You have one too."

Bart thought about that for a moment then shrugged. "Yeah, you are correct. I guess we do. We just never thought of using it like that. So, Xi'heeh, take us all to the Flatiron Building and we will drop Steve and

Isaiah off there and we will continue to the White House."

They disappeared.

CHAPTER X

Bart, Steve, Xi'heeh, and Isaiah reappeared in front of the Flatiron Building in New York City. The building was tall and shaped like a cream-colored wedge with a covered walkway around the main level.

"It does not look like anyone noticed us popping in," said Bart.

"I can control how we seem to appear. I can make it seem as if we were already here even though we were not. It is kind of like a perception filter, making those around think they saw us before we landed. It works better in a crowded place like this than when we appeared in front of Tatenda's small group. Plus, sometimes I forget I have that."

"Nice. Well, Steve, you and Isaiah poke around the building and see if you can find anything about that person the mercenary told us about."

Bart and Xi'heeh disappeared. Those around went

about their business as if nothing out of the ordinary had just occurred.

"All right," Isaiah moved toward the main entrance on the Fifth Avenue side of the building, "see if you can keep up with me." He zipped away at super-speed and entered the door before Steve could even move.

"What was that about?" Steve ran for the door, but by the time he entered the building, Isaiah was completely gone. There was no sign of him anywhere. "Now where could he have gone. I don't think he's on this level, so I'll have to check them all one at a time."

He proceeded to climb the stairs to the second floor. On the way up when he was sure no one was watching, he turned invisible. "I don't want people seeing me snoop through their offices," he muttered to himself.

He opened the door closest to the staircase on the second floor and walked unseen inside.

A woman lifted her head. She watched as the door closed but saw no one else in the room. "Hello. Is anyone there?"

"What is it?" asked a woman at another desk adjacent to her.

"I-I'm not sure. I heard the door open, but when I looked up, no one was there."

"Probably someone realized they were in the wrong room and just closed the door." The other person went back to drawing a design on a 3D imageboard she was working on.

"Yeah, sure." But she didn't appear to believe her co-worker. She stood up and grabbed a thick book and slowly walked toward the door. Another door in the room opened, but it didn't close. She inched toward the door. When she reached the door, she swung the book as hard as she could. She didn't expect to hit anything solid, so when she did, she let out a little shriek.

The other woman looked up. "Now what?"

Steve stood in front of them both. He shut the door. "It's a good thing that didn't hurt."

Both ladies began to scream very loud.

In a moment, the door Steve had just closed and another one on the opposite side of the room swung open.

"What's going on out here?" yelled a man coming through the door Steve had been at.

Both women pointed to an empty area in front of the man. They couldn't speak.

The front door of the office opened and quickly closed again. Before any of the employees in the office knew what was going on, Steve bounded up the staircase and reappeared after rounding the first half of the flight to the third floor. "That was close. I'd better think of a different way to find out where... Oh for crying out loud. What was I thinking? Do I or do I not have a sword with the ability to track anyone and everyone wherever they went? I can't believe I forgot that."

A couple of people heading down the stairs passed by as Steve spoke to himself. They edged over as close to the stairwell wall as they could and watched him nervously as they inched along.

"What, haven't you ever seen someone talk to

themselves before?" said Steve, as the people quickly maneuvered down the rest of the stairs. "Now, let me filter in Isaiah only. Ah, there goes that little speed demon. I'm glad I didn't have to go back down to find him."

***

Isaiah raced up to the eighteenth floor. He knew exactly where he was going and who he was going to run into. As soon as he overheard the soldier mention the Flatiron Building, he knew what was happening. He had to make it there before Steve could join him. It would only be a matter of a few minutes before Steve caught up to him. He hoped maybe they could get away before that happened. Hopefully, he could convince this person to go down the elevator and get off on a different floor and then head out the doors on the Broadway side of the building in an attempt to throw Steve off the trail so they could talk privately.

He didn't bother to knock. He barged in and found Ian staring up at him. "To what do I owe this intrusion?"

"You need to get out right now." Isaiah didn't stop at the door. He went up to Ian's desk.

"I have no idea what you're saying or trying to do." Ian stood and backed up.

"You might. I was in Africa earlier today and helped break up a kidnapping attempt on a bunch of school-aged kids. One of the soldiers mentioned a benefactor in this building. I know what you're up to."

Ian leaned forward. He had gotten over the shock of the intrusion. "I don't know what you're talking about.

I'm a legitimate businessman."

"Don't give me that. I know you're into a big business opportunity in Africa and that you're trying to build an army. Follow me if you don't want to get caught." Isaiah raised a gloved hand and motioned for Ian to follow him.

Ian thought for a moment. "We can't go out the same way you came in. Follow me, all the rooms on each floor are connected by doors between them. We can go through another room and eventually out to the elevators."

Isaiah followed Ian through a side door into another office space. "Pardon us." Ian plowed through not stopping for anyone, with Isaiah tagging along right behind.

They came out on the other side of the floor next to the elevators. Isaiah grabbed Ian by the shirt and pulled him back just inside the door they had exited. "I see Steve. He's the one tracking us. Let's wait for a second while he goes into your office."

Isaiah peeked out the door and didn't see Steve. He waved to Ian. "Let's go. I hope the elevator gets here fast."

They were in luck as a couple of other people were waiting for an elevator. It opened as they walked over.

Once inside, one of the others pressed the button for the first floor. "What floor?"

"Two, please," said Isaiah.

The door opened on the second floor. They exited and headed for the stairs for the last flight. They left the building through the Broadway side and saw a red aircar parked in a spot reserved for taxis. The door to the car opened as they neared. They climbed in and the door shut.

"LaGuardia Airport, please my good car." Isaiah sat back pleased that he was about to ditch Steve.

***

Steve opened the door to the office that Isaiah had entered earlier. No one was there. He wasn't surprised. Another life essence appeared. It was linked to Isaiah, so it automatically displayed alongside his essence. They both headed out another door into the office adjacent.

"Oh brother, not again." Steve disappeared. This time he wasn't going to reappear for any reason. He opened and closed the doors quickly. No one seemed to notice this time. He observed that they stopped for a moment in the last room before exiting near the elevators. He could see that they caught an elevator.

"I hope they went straight down. I'll have to take the stairs and look on each floor to make sure they didn't get off somewhere else. Good thing I don't have to worry about being out of shape."

He descended each floor and stopped to look at the elevator area to make sure they didn't double back or anything. Who knows, maybe that would be the best way to lose him by never actually leaving the building. He continued down and finally at the second-floor level picked up their trail heading down the stairs to the first floor and out the door.

He saw a red car in the taxi lane and walked over to

it. "Hi, Casey, how are you doing today? I'm glad you were able to make it here in time."

"I arrived before any of you. I have been here since Bart had you send me here."

"Are our friends inside?"

"Of course, I thought about letting you know, but I thought you were having fun."

The driver's door opened. Steve climbed in. "Hi, Isaiah. Oh, and look who's here. Ian, is it the real you, or another clone?"

"Who is this guy, and how does he know my name? And why does he think I'm a clone?"

"This is Steve. I hoped we wouldn't see you so soon."

"What? Didn't you remember that I can track anyone anywhere?"

Isaiah removed his left glove and reached to touch Steve's bare neck.

"Ah, ah, ah, that's not nice. Did you forget that I'm invulnerable too?"

Isaiah replaced his glove and sat back down.

"All right, Casey, let's head back to Isaiah's lab. You remember that location, right?"

"Yes, I do have a computer for a brain you remember, and we were just there only a short while go. Do you think I would forget?"

Steve feigned ignorance. "Right, just making sure."

"We'll be there in a little while." Casey lifted into the air.

***

Bart and Xi'heeh appeared in the president's office.

To their surprise, Reginald sat in a chair in front of the president's desk.

"Reginald here was just telling me about everything that happened." The President didn't look happy. She motioned for them to sit.

"Did he tell you that Tasha tried to kill me?" Bart didn't accept the invitation to sit.

The President turned to Reginald. The look on her face said that he had not given that little detail. "I thought I asked you all to work together for the benefit of our country."

Reginald squirmed. He stood up and drew himself up to the same position and stature as Bart. Clearly, he wanted to be the alpha dog here.

"Can I expect you to work together?" The President leaned on her desk. "I have another lead on those helicopters, but I will only tell the information to whomever I can trust to follow instructions."

Bart grabbed the back of the chair he had been offered earlier, pulled it away from the desk slightly, and sat down. He crossed his legs and folded his hands in his lap. "I have no issues working with anyone. I had no issues with Tasha until she showed her true colors, and I will have no issues with anyone else."

Reginald's body remained tense. After a moment, he eased up. "I can't. That purple mongrel over there killed the only woman I ever loved. I will never forgive him. I will somehow work my revenge on him and all the others. I don't know how yet because they all have these special abilities beyond mine."

He turned to leave. The Secret Service men in the room blocked his exit. He gave them an exasperated glare.

"Just a moment." The President rose and walked over to him. "I want to thank you for your service." She extended her hand, and they shook. "If you ever change your mind, please give me a call." She nodded at the Secret Servicemen, and they moved aside.

Reginald clenched his fist and left.

After the doors closed, the President turned back to Bart and Xi'heeh. "You'd better be good agents for me because they were my favorite ones. I can't believe Tasha tried to do that. She should have known better." She crossed the room and returned to her chair.

Bart raised an eyebrow. "She believed that she gained abilities equal to ours. It turned out not to be the case. I do not think she would have otherwise done this. Ever since we met, she has been bent on my demise."

"Yes, well, I guess that's been taken care of now, hasn't it?" The President leaned forward. She stared at them for a moment.

Bart glanced at Xi'heeh. He tilted his head ever so slightly in Bart's direction but didn't make eye contact. He was keeping a keen eye on the President.

"Okay," Bart began, "what do you have in mind?" "Are you familiar with the cave system in the Afghanistan and Pakistan areas?"

Bart nodded.

"This is where we think they are coming from," the President continued. "We've had reports of sightings of the helicopters around there. We think the reports are legitimate even though we've also had some reports of weird paranormal stuff happening around there. We even had some crazy reports about red-headed giants in the area too, but we're very certain those are just conspiracy theories. There is no evidence of either paranormal phenomenon or giants in the area."

"Then why mention them?" Bart asked.

"Because you will hear things, and we don't want you to get sucked into a wild goose chase. We just need to investigate the helicopter sightings in the area. I do want you to be aware that there is absolutely no evidence of the Afghan or Pakistani governments being involved with these incidents. They are working with us on this, and they also do not believe that any other known groups in the area are involved either. This seems to be an entirely new group that is utilizing the cave networks in that region. Do not bring anyone else into this, we do not need outside factions involved. Understand?"

Bart and Xi'heeh nodded their heads.

"OK, good, report to me what you find out. We do believe this will be dangerous, so you are the ones that will be handling all the details. There will be no military assistance from the United States or any foreign governments."

Bart and Xi'heeh nodded again, but they looked unsure what to do next.

"You may go." The President stood.

"Right, Xi'heeh, take us back to the lab." They stood, then disappeared.

CHAPTER XI

Matt paced around several tables in the area beside Erin's container. "I don't like staying behind and waiting. I need to be doing something other than waiting."

Sha'rell stood. She grabbed Matt as he made a pass by her. She gave him a great big kiss.

"Well, that's not what I had in mind, but hey, it's better than doing nothing."

Xi'heeh appeared with Bart in the exact spot they had left from, causing Matt and Sha'rell to jump out of the way. "We have returned."

"Yeah, I can see that. Good thing we weren't on the same spot where you landed."

"Oh, you were in no danger. I can see the place I'm going just before we land so I can adjust as needed. Others with me don't notice a thing."

"So, uh, then you... uh... could see what was happening?" Matt's face flushed darker ebony.

"Do not worry. You are my brother now as it is anyway. You are accepted in our family."

"Uh? What?"

Sha'rell rubbed his left shoulder. "You and I are one according to our ways."

Matt sank into the chair he was standing beside. "Oh, I didn't know that."

Sha'rell knelt next to him. She peered into his eyes. "Is that all right?"

Matt returned her gaze. "Yeah, I just didn't know how things worked for you. Wasn't sure I was ready, but you are so awesome that it's great."

Sha'rell smiled. She leaned in and gave him a big hug.

"What just happened?" Bart looked at Matt and Sha'rell.

"I think I'm married to an alien or something like that."

Sha'rell's forehead scrunched mildly. "If you mean that we are bonded together, then yes, you are correct. It is the way of my people. I can be with no other."

"Well, congratulations then." Bart walked over and gave Matt a hearty handshake. He then hugged Sha'rell. "When did all this happen?"

"While Matt was on my planet."

"Uh, I think I missed the ceremony." It was Matt's turn to furrow his brow.

"There is no ceremony. You just choose to be together. On my world, by showing affection to another, you are pledging to each other." Sha'rell looked back into

Matt's eyes. "Did you not mean to show me affection? Since you don't know my ways, it could be possible that we had a misunderstanding."

Matt grabbed Sha'rell's hands. "I meant to show you affection. I didn't know your traditions, but I don't care about that. I choose to be with you."

Sha'rell's face lit up. She gave him another big hug.

"All right, all right, that's enough." Steve strode in carrying a struggling Ian. "What's up?"

They all turned toward Steve. Isaiah was right behind Steve and Ian.

"Oh, nothing much is going on," Bart said. "Matt is married now, that is all."

Steve stopped in his tracks and dropped Ian, who landed with a thud on the floor.

"Steve," Bart began, "if your mouth opens any further, you're going to be licking the dirt off the floor."

"But... but... but..."

"Your motor's not sounding too good there, buddy," Matt said, patting Steve on the shoulder.

"So, I see Xi'heeh and myself made it back before you did." Bart looked down at Ian sitting on the floor. "You brought an old friend too."

Steve closed his mouth. He continued to stare at Matt. "Yeah," he said without much conviction. After a moment, he blinked and turned his attention to Bart. "Yeah, sorry, that's some news there. Isaiah found this Ian clone in the Flatiron Building."

"Clone?" Ian stood up, brushing dust off his shirt and pants. "I'm not a clone. I made the clones. I'm the real Ian."

By the look on everyone's face, no one believed him.

Ian sensed their doubt. "No, really, I am."

"That's what they all say," Steve said. "Is he telling the truth?"

"Yes." Bart moved toward Ian. "He definitely thinks he is."

"Because I am."

Bart stopped in front of Ian. "Will you be disappointed if we still do not think that you are? After all, Ian would supposedly be old by now."

Felicia finally stood up. Ian's eyes bulged. She walked toward him.

"How are you still alive?" Ian's eyes returned to normal size. "I thought the process didn't work on you. I... I can't believe it. I've missed you."

She stopped after taking a few steps. It was her turn to look shocked. "You can't be real; you just can't be the real Ian. I thought... someone else was the real Ian. But you know more than a clone should know. Maybe I was wrong about who is real."

Ian started to rush toward her.

She held her palm out. "No, don't. I don't want this, not now, not ever. It's way too late."

He stopped and nodded.

"Interesting," Bart said. "I would not expect the Ian clones we have met to follow a command."

"Not all of the Ian clones were bad," Isaiah entered the conversation. "There are a few that were good. This is one."

Bart looked at him. "So, you think this is a clone?"

"I would guess that he must be, but that's only my guess. After all, as you said, he would have to be older, wouldn't he?"

"I am not a clone. Again, I will say that right now. I'm not. I haven't aged because I perfected my process."

Isaiah didn't disagree again but bowed his head slightly as if giving in to the idea. "We shall see. You can prove that by your actions."

"I agree," said Bart. "We will go on the premise that you are a clone for now, but that can be revisited as time moves on."

"Fair enough," agreed Ian. "So, why have you all brought me here?"

Bart leaned against the nearest table. "We were looking for someone who is forming a mercenary army in Africa; someone from the Flatiron Building. One of the soldiers we met mentioned someone there was bankrolling them. It must be you."

Ian didn't respond. He tightened his lips and clenched his jaws. "I know nothing about this."

"Ah, there we go, a real lie for sure this time."

"Whatever, you're just trying to trick me into giving you some information. You're trying to drag it out of me. You can't tell if I'm lying or not."

"Actually," Bart inched a bit closer into Ian's personal space, "I can tell when someone is lying. I have a special sword that allows me to know exactly when someone is lying. I would suggest your next words be true when you speak."

Ian didn't say anything else. He backed away from Bart and turned away.

"Looks like we'll not get anything from him for a while now," said Isaiah. "How was your talk with the President?"

Ian whipped back around. "President? Did you meet with the President? What did she say?"

"Uh." Bart was taken aback. "I am not sure that we should talk in front of you if you are that interested."

"I'm interested because she's not what she seems to be. I have had run-ins with her before. She's not all dainty and good."

Bart continued to look skeptical, but he too shared the opinion that she was not all she appeared to be.

"Look," Ian moved toward Bart. "I would be wary of me too if I were you. You've run into all sorts of my clones, so why would I be different? I will tell you though that I'm trying to stop whatever it is she's up to. That's why I need to build an army. No country I met with would join me against her."

Bart tried to change his expression, but it just turned into a worse case of skepticism. "You are aware that we are working for her, right?"

Ian turned away and paced around a small piece of the floor. "I must convince them. What can I do?"

Steve walked behind Bart and put a hand on his right shoulder. "This guy's bonkers."

"He is smart," Bart said. "He is too smart." Bart thought for a moment. "Okay, Ian, please tell us what you know, and then we shall see if you need to know any more."

Ian stopped pacing. He looked up at Bart and nodded. "She is amassing a force in the Afghan mountains. No one knows this. She's been sneaky about it. I discovered her plot while I was working for her. She always finds the smart and powerful to do her dirty work." He stopped for a moment as if deciding whether to continue or not, then he blurted out, "She has help from aliens." He looked at everyone in turn. "I can see you don't believe me."

Bart scratched his head and ran his fingers through his jagged haircut. He looked at Xi'heeh and Sha'rell. First not noticing Felicia and now two aliens in his presence, this Ian must be so scatterbrained that he overlooked big details. "We have had experience with aliens before, but I find it hard to believe that she would be doing this."

Ian's face drooped.

"However," Bart continued, "you believe this all to be true."

Ian perked up. "Then you believe me?"

"Not totally. I can only trust my ability to know the truth so far. It can be manipulated by the fact that what you say, you believe to be true. It is also interesting that you mention the mountains of Afghanistan. That is where she is sending us on our next mission. She said someone is using the mountains to stage a military buildup. She says there are some immensely powerful helicopters in the area."

Ian's eyes widened. "I've seen those helicopters.

They are very precise in their operations. Have you seen them too? I didn't think anyone else had."

"Yes, we have encountered them," Bart said. "But they have always seemed to be mostly on our side. What do you know about them?"

"Nothing more than you, most likely. They are incredibly quiet and stealthy. They are part of what I'm trying to stop though. I was trying to build an army. I needed bodies. I only had a few mercenaries so far. I hoped for more, but no one would sign up. I had to find another way."

"So, you abducted kids?" Matt's eyes flashed.

"It wasn't my best idea, but I hoped to get people to listen to me. I wasn't going to use the kids. I wanted countries to send their militaries in to help."

"Do you know that your mercenaries were training these kids and that they had each of the young boys suited up with bomb vests?" Bart's eyes drilled into Ian's.

Ian's mouth dropped open. "Th-they wouldn't."

"These are mercenaries we're talking about, you know, right?" Matt shook his head. "You don't really think your plans through very well, do you?" He turned away from Ian.

Bart sighed. "The President sent us to stop your operations in Africa. You have fewer mercenaries now, just so you know."

"See, she knows that I'm on to her. She will try to thwart me wherever she can."

"Why send us to the Afghan mountains then?" Steve asked. "Sounds like that could ruin her plans if she's involved in building that up. We would probably even accomplish your task of finding out what's going on there."

"I don't know." Ian's thoughts were churning. You could see it in his eyes. "She must think you won't succeed. This is a fortress that they are building there. She must know it. I agree though, that seems to be against what she should want. She must be trying to throw you off her trail."

Xi'heeh stepped forward. "There is indeed something strange about this leader person of yours. I cannot place it, but that brooch of hers seems familiar to me. I'm sure I've seen it somewhere before, but I cannot place where that was."

"I think we are all in a consensus that she is not to be trusted." Bart rubbed his chin. "She lied when she said that she could not believe Tasha would attempt to kill me."

Xi'heeh continued, "She is clearly sending us somewhere that may not be what it is meant to be. I think we should go there but continue with the possibility that this is a trap of some kind. She may have hopes that whatever is in the caves can destroy us. We should proceed with the caution that this man has given us."

"I agree," said Bart. "Only those of us with swords should go. We cannot risk anyone that does not have invulnerability."

"I can't go with you." Felicia sat back down in her chair. "I must stay with my daughter. I will not leave her side ever again. I made a terrible error in doing so before. She is all I have left."

"Can Jane come with us?" Bart asked. "We really need the abilities of your sword."

"I'm afraid she only works when I'm around. I was always the one setting the blockades. It was always me. That's why I followed her into the building to save those boys. I had to set the shields."

Bart nodded. "You are the only one that I will trust with Erin's life. We will figure out something without you."

Felicia smiled. "Thank you. You have been good for my daughter. I hope you two can make some semblance of a life together."

Bart studied Steve, Matt, and Xi'heeh in turn. "Are you gentlemen ready?"

"Ready, willing, and able for anything," said Steve.

"Then, we should get moving." Bart motioned for Xi'heeh to do his thing.

Before he could do anything, a crashing sound came from around Erin's chamber. The tinkling sound of glass dissipated. Everyone turned toward the noise. Steam poured out of the container. Erin stood in the broken doorframe. She looked around; confusion etched on her face.

"Where am I?" She stumbled out of the chamber. She would have fallen had she not caught herself on the nearest table. "Who am I?" She regained her footing. "No, I know who I am." She looked at the others. "Who are you is the question?"

Bart and Felicia rushed to her side. They each took a separate hand, holding her gently. They glanced at each other.

"She hasn't been in there nearly long enough." Felicia tried to get Erin to sit back down, but she was not going to allow it.

"She was strong enough to break the glass this time." Bart also tried unsuccessfully to ease her into the chair. "Can we get her into one of those other chambers at the end of this room?"

"Those don't work," said Isaiah. "They were prototypes of the one she's in. Each of those failed, as you can see by the clouded glass. That's smoke that seared itself to the glass."

Erin's eyes were glazed over. Her head nodded forward, but she managed to weakly tip it back to an upright position. She looked closely at Bart, then at Felicia. "Don't I know you?" Her voice was quiet and incoherent. She pointed to Bart. "I love you." She turned to Felicia. "Aren't you that old woman we keep running into?" She stumbled again, but Bart and Felicia held on tight.

"Yes, dear, I am. It's a long story though."

"I got time." Erin almost passed out.

"No, you don't." Felicia drew her sword. "Take it. You need it more than I do."

Erin stared at the yellow glow. "Oh, that's pretty. Wait, you don't have that. Someone else does. I think her name's John." She laughed. "That's a funny name for a woman."

"No, Erin, listen to me." Felicia took Erin's other hand from Bart. "I was the sword holder the entire time. It is time for you to have it."

"Oh, thank you, it's pretty. It glows."

"She is too far out of it." Felicia held Erin closer. "I pass it down from mother to daughter."

Bart put a hand on Erin's back. "Are you sure that this will help her in her condition?"

"It's the only thing that can help right now. If this doesn't do it, I don't think anything will. The chamber is broken, and she spent only a couple of hours or less in there. The strength that Ian put into her must be the only thing keeping her from dying right this instant."

Erin perked up slightly. "Wait, wait, wait, you said mother to daughter?"

"Yes, dear." Felicia began to hum a tune.

Erin listened. She tilted her head. She wrinkled her forehead. She relaxed. "I know that tune. My mother sang it to me every day of my life. Do you know my mother?"

"I am your mother."

Erin looked more confused than ever. "But you're old. My mother is young."

"I'm a lot older than even you may think. Please, take it. Save yourself. It's the only way."

Erin reached out, but she missed the sword. Her hand flopped by her side. "If I take it, my mother will die."

"Well, she isn't so far gone that she doesn't remember some things." Bart stood still, clearly not knowing how to help. "Erin, listen, if you don't take it, you will die."

"I've lived long enough, my dear. It's time for you to be out of your cage. You have Bart. He's going to need you. Be his rock. You have a life that needs to be lived. Please, as my last responsibility toward you, as my daughter, take it."

Erin reached out again. Tears began to form in the corners of her eyes. "I can't lose you again. I didn't even have you long enough."

Before Erin's hand could drop again, Felicia grabbed it and placed the hilt in it. "I've kept a watchful eye over you for many, many years now. You've always had me near." She released her grip leaving the sword in Erin's grasp. Nothing happened. No power overtook Erin. Felicia didn't disappear.

Erin's eyes popped wide open. She began to tremble, then shake with all the force of an earthquake. She fell to her knees, sword still in hand. She covered her face and screamed so loud everyone covered their ears. Then she fell silent. She tipped over onto her side, then sprawled on the floor. Her long blonde hair spread in all directions.

Felicia looked on in horror. "She didn't make it." She was barely audible. As she bent over to recover the sword, she began to fade.

Erin gasped and popped up. "Mom! No!" She tried to hug her mom as she vanished, grasping only air.

Bart dropped to his knees beside her. She grabbed him, squeezing so tight he wasn't sure that he'd be able to breathe. She cried into his shoulder as he caressed her hair.

Matt and Steve wandered over and squatted beside them. Steve put a hand on Bart's shoulder and Matt placed one on Erin's.

"I remember it all now," Erin sobbed. "The testing, the change, the failure, the booth. I can't believe my dad did that to us."

Bart held her and rubbed her back. "It is okay. You are well."

"I didn't think it was going to work." Erin released Bart from their hug.

"It almost didn't," Matt said. "I couldn't feel what you felt, but I know what almost happened. Your DNA was rewritten, and it didn't reset very nicely. But you are whole again, back as you were meant to be."

Erin looked at the sword in her hand. "I suppose I have a place for this at my side now."

"You do," Matt said.

She placed it in the hidden scabbard at her side. "I wish this could have gone differently." She stood up. "Oh, it's you?" For the first time, she saw Ian and Isaiah. Anger replaced sorrow. "How could you let this happen to her?"

Ian looked shocked. "What do you mean? I gave her a long life. Not many people can say that. Long and healthy."

Ignoring him, Erin glared passed him. "Forget it. It's not worth it." She turned away. "So, what happened while I was in stasis?"

After they brought her up to speed, she said, "Well, then. What are we waiting for? We need to get to the mountains."

Bart held her by the shoulders. "Are you sure you are ready to go out there? You have had a traumatic experience both physically and mentally."

She looked at him. "Did you feel ready to go after you received your sword?"

"Yes and no. I had no idea how my new powers worked; everything was new. I took it in small steps."

"I've seen you guys' work. I have an idea of what I need to do. I have had abilities beyond that of a normal person already. Not that I used them much until I met you, but now, I'm charged up even more. I can handle this. The sword has given me strength. It has helped me recover quickly."

Steve spoke up, "It took me a little by surprise when I got mine because it occurred quickly. I didn't have time to think, much like you. What do you know about your main ability?"

"I know that it just happens. I think. It's done." She concentrated. "There, that Ian is in a box now."

Ian furrowed his brow. "What do you mean?" He tried to move but couldn't move far. "Let me out, now!"

"I can make the same little shields around others. Steve, shoot Isaiah."

"What?"

"It's fine, he's in a shield."

Steve drew one of his laser pistols. "Sorry, I hope this works." He fired. The beam bounced off without harming

Isaiah.

"Did you really have to do that?" Isaiah's face had gone from eyes bugging out to narrow slants.

"No, but it made me feel better," Erin said.

Steve looked at her. "Uh, like I'm the one you made shoot him."

"You didn't have to do it, so I didn't make you."

Steve rolled his eyes.

"Bart, start walking down the aisle here." Erin concentrated again.

As he moved forward, he felt an invisible force at his feet.

"Step up," Erin commanded. "And continue to step up like you're climbing stairs."

He followed her command and rose halfway up to the ceiling."

"Now," Erin said, "start to descend the stairs.

He stepped downward, descending back to the floor as he continued.

Then suddenly, junk crashed to the floor and broke as it fell from a table.

"I can even push stuff with these. That's fun."

"I would say you are ready to go then." Bart looked impressed.

"I have two abilities I want to choose before we go," she began. "I've thought about these things if I ever got one of the swords. First, we tend to make a big mess when we get into fights. I want to ability to repair anything that gets damaged. I want to leave a scene like it was before things got smashed." She stopped. "Oooh, I felt that." She waved her hand. Small bits of shattered glass and other fragments of broken items bubbled around on the floor like boiling water. Pieces started to move together and reform. They flew into the same position they held before Erin cleared the table, sitting as if they never moved.

"Nice." Steve clapped. "Do you think you can come over to our place and clean up once in a while?"

If looks could kill, Steve, with or without his sword, wouldn't have survived the glance that Erin gave him.

"Uh, I'll take that as a no." He quietly backed away.

"My second ability will be to keep all the sword holders and our friends and loved ones safe from being recognized in public. This will apply to anyone that we designate verbally. Each of the sword holders will have the ability to put anyone under this protection. Each of us will always know each other, and those under this protection will know who we are. Other people will only remember that someone exists that can do the things we can do with our abilities, not who we are. If they hear our name, they will immediately forget it once we are out of their presence. If they try to write it down or record it in any fashion, they will immediately forget what they were doing. They won't be able to follow us. If they try, they will get confused about where we went. Once we are out of sight, we are out of mind. They will not remember our names or what we look like. We can walk down streets, sit in restaurants, and generally be in public like normal people. Unless we tell them who we are or our swords are visible, no one will know we are anything but a legend.

They'll just see normal people walking down the street or doing their own thing. This will apply to video and images as well. Any images, video, or recordable media of us using any of our abilities will cast us as unrecognizable blurs. It'll be like the camera malfunctioned while filming. In case I missed something, I reserve the right to modify this ability as I see fit, including anything retroactive as well."

"Nice move." Bart clapped a couple of times. "You have given thought to this."

"So, are we like vampires now?" Steve looked serious. "No, really, we're like vampires on film."

Matt shook his head. "Don't be going there, man. We don't do vampires here."

Steve laughed. "Aw, come on, I just like to have fun."

"I put Sha'rell under this protective shield." Matt grabbed her hand.

"I put Casey under it." Steve looked at the others. "What? He'll need it. You don't think that people remember him?"

"He's one of your abilities," Erin said. "He's already covered."

Steve wrinkled his forehead. "Oh yeah, I suppose so."

Bart turned to Ian and Isaiah. "I think you two need to remember who we are, or we'll be starting this story over every time we try to work with you. So, against my better judgment, you are granted this protection as well. I suppose we will have to let the President in on it?"

"Let's wait on that one." It was Isaiah that spoke.

"We seem to have some misgivings about her right now."

"Wouldn't she need to remember she sent us on an assignment though?" Steve asked. "And probably the Secret Service agents that are in her office. We wouldn't want them to try to arrest or shoot us every time we entered her office."

Isaiah thought for a moment. "You're probably right. But what if she talks to others about us and they don't know what she's talking about, or they think she's gone crazy believing non-existent legends are real?"

"She will remember us as ordinary people and that she has us working for her," Erin said. "She just won't remember our names or powers nor be able to follow us or have us followed. She'll likely think we're special agents."

Bart nodded. "All right then, for now, the President is not under this blanket. Are the sword holders ready to go to the mountains of Afghanistan?" He looked at all the others. They nodded. "Shall we go?"

"Wait." Isaiah held out a hand. "I think I should go too. You may need my help."

"Who is going to watch this Ian then?" Bart held out his hand toward him.

"Who says I need watching?" Ian put his hands on his hips. "I don't have anywhere to go."

"You were trying to leave pretty fast when I came to get you," Steve reminded him.

"That's because this guy," Ian pointed at Isaiah, "wouldn't leave me alone."

"Interesting," Bart said. "You don't know who he is,

but he knows you. Do you know Samuel?"

Ian shook his head. "Never heard of anyone by that name."

"I have an idea." Erin walked over to her broken chamber. She waved her hand, and the glass flew back together as strong as ever. "Sha'rell isn't coming. We'll put Ian in here, and she can keep an eye on him. He won't be able to break out of there."

Bart nodded. "Excellent idea."

"No!" yelled Ian. "I'm getting out of here." He turned to run but smacked into an invisible wall.

"I haven't removed the walls yet," Erin smirked. "But I have now."

Before Ian could move, another force moved him toward the chamber. The door to the chamber swung open. Ian floated into it and was gently placed in the chair. The door swung shut with a click from the latch.

"There, that ought to hold you," Bart said.

Ian jumped up and pounded on the door, but no sound could be heard. He tried pushing with no luck. He slammed his shoulder into the door with no luck. He returned to pounding on the glass door, but nothing changed.

Sha'rell grabbed a chair. "Hurry back, okay?"

The rest of them disappeared.

CHAPTER XII

The sun was setting. There was still enough light out, but the daylight wouldn't last much longer. Bart looked around. He could see enough to know that they landed in the most barren spot that anyone could imagine. The surrounding area was rugged, reddish dunes. Or maybe it was just the shadows of the evening making them look reddish. The land rolled into gentle curves, not too hilly, and not too flat. In the distance there looked like there might be some brownish land that was a grassy area, but at dusk, one couldn't quite tell. Beyond that, some smaller mountains loomed.

Bart shielded his eyes from the setting sun. "This looks about as desolate as we could possibly get. Are you sure you did not take us to Mars instead of Afghanistan?"

Xi'heeh didn't answer. He stared at the small red dunes.

Bart tapped him on the shoulder. "Hey, Xi'heeh, are

you alright?"

At first, Xi'heeh didn't seem to notice Bart trying to capture his attention. He had a far-away look on his face. Without changing his expression, he said, "I did not realize I would return here. It reminds me of where I was when the sword came to me. I was battling the Kutarians on their home planet. It looks exactly like this. It's bringing back the moment I should have died."

Bart glanced over to Erin, Steve, and Matt. He quickly caught Isaiah's eye. They all had that same what can you say to that look. "Uh, I do not think any of us know what to say to that."

Xi'heeh blinked. "Sorry, I was thinking of V'ante, my joined partner." He became silent again.

Matt quickly explained to the others about the joining process between K'reelian and G'mone males and how they used that for a military advantage.

Erin grabbed Xi'heeh's hand. "Can you tell us about him? I would love to know more about him."

Xi'heeh pulled his hand away and breathed a sigh. "We never have the chance to talk about our deceased partners. I am the only one ever to survive. The other always dies too. V'ante died, I should have too. We were on the Kutarian homeworld. It was the final assault before our victory over them. Since G'mone and K'reelian have teamed up, we have never been defeated in war. We were clearing the remaining Kutarian soldiers from their final town." He sighed. "Soldiers, how ironic. They do not have soldiers, but what else can we call them to make ourselves feel better? Sorry, it is complicated. Anyhow, we entered a house. On the floor, huddled in a circle, was this family. They looked just like any other family that had desires of their own. They did not ask for us to be there. We just came in and took over, leaving most of their civilization in shreds." He stopped.

"It's okay," Erin said softly. "You don't have to tell us anymore."

"I do need to. It will be important someday. The G'mone are the drivers of all these wars. We need to do something about them. Anyway, V'ante and I were standing in their main room, watching these giants that should be able to give us a real fight cowering in fear. The sword appeared in front of me. It just hovered there. I knew what it meant, but the others did not. I realized that my father was gone, and my time had come. I reached out and took the sword. I felt the power of it. I knew it had completed its conversion to my ownership. Somehow, the father of this family we were threatening gained some backbone and seized the opportunity. He knew that if he killed one of us, the other would also die. That is no secret. While V'ante was distracted, he shot him right through the forehead. I felt what V'ante felt. I jumped in shock because I knew that I would also die. But I did not die. I stood there. The sword had counteracted the joining and saved me. The family stared in horror at me. The father opened fire on me, but as you know, the projectiles from the weapon disappeared as they drew near me. He shot until the gun did not have any ammunition left, while I stared at V'ante. You get to know someone very well when you go through the joining together."

"I'm so sorry." Erin tried to pat Xi'heeh on the arm.

"Please, do not do that, you are Bart's."

Erin stepped back. She had that look like she was about to let Xi'heeh have it. "I am no one's."

"I thought you liked Bart."

"I do." She looked down for a moment. "I think." She shook her head and looked back up at Xi'heeh. "But he doesn't own me."

Matt stepped between them. "Easy, Erin, they have different customs than we do. Trust me. You missed out on that discussion. Sha'rell and I will fill you in later."

Erin's fire calmed down.

"I am sorry," Xi'heeh said. "We do have different ideologies, and I mistook your ways. I apologize."

Erin shrugged. "We have a lot to learn from each other."

"I turned away from that family," Xi'heeh continued his story. "They watched as I turned to leave. I was no longer the soldier our governments had made me. I stopped and turned back around. I knew they would not be safe if I left them here. Someone else would check on them. Someone else would slaughter them. I still had my sword in hand, and I knew how to use it. I had seen my father and grandfather use it so many times. I raised it. I could see the fear in their eyes. They expected me to slice them all to pieces. Instead, we all disappeared. I brought them here to this place. I do not know how my sword knew to bring me here with them, but it did. I dropped them off several miles from here at a place called Karez

Kalay. They would be safe there. They are shapeshifters and take the form of whatever the indigenous people of the area are. They even learn their language quickly. They would have a new home. I returned to their planet. Outside, I saw our commanding officers. I told them the place was all clear. They asked where V'ante was. I told them he was inside. They went to look for him. I heard them yell as I disappeared. I made many more trips that night and brought many more people from that world to this one. When I transported as many as I figured I safely could, I went home and became scarce. They never looked for me. After a few years, my mother told me it was time to look for you guys. Aunt Sha'rell begged me to bring her with me. I knew what she wanted, but I figured it would end badly. However, Matthew, you have surprised me. I am proud to know you and your friends. I am now joined to you all like family."

No one said a word for a few minutes. Then Bart broke the silence. "Well, it is getting dark. I forgot about the time difference on the other side of the world. I suppose we should get moving into the mountains to find where those helicopters are hiding. I'm not sure we set down close enough the first time."

"Should we even try going there in the dark?" Isaiah asked.

"We can't afford to waste any time," Steve said. "Are any of you even tired? It's early in the afternoon for us. Besides, where else can we go?"

"Let's stop at Karez Kalay first." Xi'heeh turned in the direction of the place. "I need to see them, and maybe they can help us somehow. They have been in the area long enough. They may know something."

Before anyone could utter a word, they disappeared.

***

It was the shabbiest place that Bart may have ever seen. There were three or four small buildings made from a sand and stone mixture from the area. The roof also had to have been made from the same sandy mixture. There were openings in each building, but instead of doors covering them, they had blankets nailed to the top of a wooden frame. Dust and sand covered the area. There were no designated roads to and from the area, but there were some paths that vehicles had traveled on. Some sprigs of brown grass dotted the area, but they were few and far between. There were some brown shrubs next to the buildings. There appeared to be nothing living in the area, and the shrubs didn't count as living.

"Are you sure that you have the right place?" Bart covered his eyes and mouth as a breeze kicked up some sand.

Xi'heeh nodded. "Yes, this is the place. I do not see anyone around though."

"Oh, there's people here all right." Steve glanced around. "I see multiple trails in and out of the area over the past three days."

A hand appeared at the closest building and pushed the blanket aside. "It doesn't look like anyone's here because we're not outside at the moment." A man emerged in the doorway. His high collared white waistcoat stretched down to his knees and covered white trousers. Some brown embroidered stitching lined the two sides of the collar. He wore a gold and brown colored vest adorned with elaborate embroidery draped over the shirt. A golden stitch-style hat covered his hair and matched a pair of flat stitch-style shoes on his feet. A thin, black-haired beard lined the jaws of the man.

Xi'heeh smiled. "It is you. I have wondered how you have managed."

The man stepped outside. "We are alive. I feared that you would kill my family and me, but you had heart. You left before I could thank you. I don't even know your name, nor you mine. However, mine is unpronounceable to you, so call me Karez."

"My name is Xi'heeh, but you will not remember that for long. I had others to bring to you. I could not leave you alone on a strange world."

Karez nodded. "And we appreciated that. This place was, and still is, perfect for us."

Steve chuckled. "Perfect? How can this be perfect?"

Karez turned toward Steve. "This is exactly like our planet. It's almost the spitting image of it."

Steve's mouth hung open.

Karez laughed. "I see you don't think this is a very good place."

"To each their own," Steve said, gazing around the dry, dusty land. "If you like this, then by all means it's fine by me. I ain't here to judge you."

"What does bring you here?" Karez grew more serious. "You can't just be visiting."

Xi'heeh stepped closer. "No, we are not. We have heard that there could be a group of people or militants or something like that in the mountains. We're here to see if we can find out more and maybe nullify them."

Karez looked around at everyone. He looked past everyone to make sure they were alone. "You didn't bring anyone else, did you?"

"No, just us," Bart assured him.

"Come inside." Karez turned and headed back through the blanket door.

Bart held out a hand to the rest. "After you."

As they entered, a short set of steps led them down about four feet to the main floor. This gave the area a roomier feel to it as it made the ceiling higher. The room was genuinely nice. It was a living room area, but it was sparsely furnished. There was a fancy brown leather couch against the far wall. A dining table with four matching wooden chairs sat off to the right of the entrance. An oval, hand-crafted, multi-colored throw rug covered about half the floor. A door beyond the table led to another room that they couldn't see, and straight from the doorway, an extra-wide set of stairs led down to an area below the main level.

"We live down there," Karez said. "There are lots of rooms cut out of the ground down below, and we have a few tunnels that go between the buildings. Once upon a time, all the people that you brought lived here. But we discovered the mountain caves so most of them moved out to live in them. It was even more like home to them there. We stayed here. My wife and children are down below somewhere. It's practically a mansion down there. Our life here is so much better. We can't thank you enough for bringing us here."

Loud thumps drifted up the stairs. A huge ten-foot-tall man appeared from below. He wasn't paying attention to what was going on upstairs and stumbled on the last step as he looked up at everyone. His gray eyes opened wide. His hair was flaming red from the top of his head to the beard on his face. He wore a tunic around his waist. Huge muscles bulged from his arms and legs. Instantly he shifted his form into that of a human of around twenty years old. He looked nothing like he had moments ago, but did keep the red hair, but not the beard. He was clothed in a white tee shirt and blue jeans. "Uh, oh man, I didn't know we had company."

"This is one of my sons. His name is also unpronounceable to you, so call him Fred."

They all stared at him.

"Is this appearance better? I didn't mean to scare anyone."

Karez made a noise of displeasure. "You should dress more as the locals do, like the rest of us. We need to blend in."

"We have seen some strange stuff," Bart said, "so we are okay. It was unexpected though. So, Xi'heeh, your people fought their people? They are huge."

Karez spoke. "Oh, Fred here is still growing. I'd say he's got another two or three feet to go before he's fully grown."

"Yes, we fought them." Xi'heeh didn't seem too keen

to talk about it.

"And you said you had defeated them?" Bart pressed on with his questions.

"Yes. We were finishing rounding them up. They are tall, but we were more powerful."

"Plus, we're not really into fighting," Karez added. "We were forced to do what we had to do to try to defend ourselves. But the K'reelian and G'mone mixture was too much for us. We tried to surrender, and they wouldn't have that. It is known in our part of the galaxy not to mess with their races. I believe we were the last to fall to them."

"That is correct," Xi'heeh said. "Now the G'mone are moving out to other places, and my people, whether they admit it or not, are being dragged along with them. I am hoping that with your help, Bart, we can put an end to that practice of conquering other worlds. That is what most K'reelian people want."

"If your people want that, why not do something about it?" Bart asked.

"Unfortunately, it is not that simple. It has to do with the joining process. It binds us into this arrangement. We are too deep into it. We would have to break that link."

"I do not know how we can help," Bart said. "We have things to do here."

"You have more to do here than even you know. I wasn't sure how to tell you before, but there is a plan to come here someday." Xi'heeh looked Bart in the eyes. "If they get here, your world would be doomed."

Karez flopped onto his couch. "My people couldn't fight again either. We gave it our all. It wasn't enough, and they took everything we had."

Bart didn't know what to say. He ran his fingers through his buzzed hair. "Well, we have a mission to find out what is in these mountains. I say we finish that up and then plan what we can do after that." Bart turned to Karez. "Have you heard anything about stuff going on up in the mountains? Have any of your people had problems?"

Karez shook his head. "Not that I heard about."

"I should let you know," Bart began, "that I have an ability to know when anyone is lying or not. Would you like to change your answer?"

Karez remained silent.

"I've heard stuff," Fred piped up. "I visit the others more than my family does. They have seen stuff going on. Some weird flying machines go in and out of the mountains. They fly low and quiet. They usually fly over land that isn't populated. They fly over us occasionally, but most of the people in the area think they belong to either Afghanistan or Pakistan. But I know they don't come from either. The machines are too well built for either of them. For that matter, they are too well built for anyone on this planet to have been involved with."

"Can you take us to where these things are?" Bart asked.

"Sure. Are you okay with that, pop?"

Karez didn't answer.

"It'll be okay, pop. They're going to need an

introduction to our people, or they'll be attacked."

Karez sighed. "As long as you return the instant that you have introduced them. I do not want you to stay there. I almost lost everyone before. We have built up a relationship with the local people. We have a life here."

"I will bring him right back as soon as we have established communication with your people," Xi'heeh promised.

Karez nodded. "I will place my son's life in your hands. But you better bring him back right away."

"Great!" Fred pumped his fist into the air and gave a small leap. "We better get moving. It'll take a couple of days to climb the mountain to get to where they are."

"We do not need to climb," said Xi'heeh. "You must not remember that I can teleport wherever we need to go. I just need to know where to set us down."

"Oh yeah, I remember that now," Fred said. "It will be a bit tricky. There is a limited amount of space there. I think the six of us may barely fit. I'll need to be in my original form as well."

"I have an internal map of this planet, but if you can show me where on a physical map, I can better internalize that."

"We don't have any kind of map of this planet." Karez stood up from the couch. "I'm afraid my hospitality is at an end with you all. I changed my mind about letting my boy help. This just won't end well." He waved his arms in a scooping fashion, ushering them toward the door.

"Oh, come on, dad."

"No, and that's final." He grew into his natural form. He was at least twelve feet tall, with fiery red hair and a beard just like his son had. Same kind of tunic, muscles, and overall look.

Bart held out his hands. "I understand, but we need the introduction from him to your people. If we don't have that, and they do happen to attack before listening to reason, many of them likely could die."

"No!" Karez shouted. "I will not allow it. Leave, now!" He stepped toward the group.

Bart motioned for the others to exit. "We will just have to make sure that Erin traps them in her force shields so that we can talk to them without hurting them."

"Wait." Karez stopped them. "Hold on a moment. Teleportation, knowledge of the truth, force shields." He shifted back into his human form. "Which of you can see paths that a being has gone." He stared at Matt, Steve, and Isaiah.

"It's me." Steve raised a hand. "How do you know I can do that?"

"The legends extend throughout our galaxy of the sword holders. Is that you? Prove to me that you can see my path from before you came."

"Uh," Steve stammered. "Wouldn't it be easier to just show you our invisible swords? You know, like not everyone has one of those."

"Magic tricks can easily hide a sword. It doesn't make them the real swords. But if you can tell me where I've been for the last little bit, I will believe that."

Steve shrugged. "Okay. Suit yourself. I can only see where you've been in this room. We'd have to tour your entire house if you want to know everywhere."

"You will guide me around, just you. Fred will stay up here with the rest of your friends."

Karez and Steve disappeared downstairs since that would be the place where Karez had begun the day.

"So..." Bart whistled a little tune. "I guess we just stand here with nothing to do for a while."

While they waited, a scream rang through the air.

"Sorry," yelled a muffled Steve. "We didn't know you were in there. I only have my ability set to see Karez right now, so my humble apologies. Oh man, I will never be able to unsee that."

Silence thickened in the air until Karez shattered it by yelling, "Aha! That's where I put that thing."

Steve led them back up the stairs. They went through the living room, and through the door to the other room that they hadn't been to.

"Oh wow, now that's cool," Steve said.

They returned and proceeded outside. After a while, they returned.

"You have some very nice chickens, Karez."

"Thank you."

They went back down the stairs. After about fifteen minutes they returned upstairs.

"That is a nice tunnel system you have down there. It's a good thing you know your way around those because even with my tracking ability, I think I'd get lost down there."

"It does take some practice, but it's not that complicated once you get used to it."

They headed back outside, and within moments returned.

"And then here we are. All back together with you talking to us. So, did I find all the places you went today?"

"Yes, you passed. I will believe in you all now and know that my son will be safe. But I thought there were only five swords. Who is this sixth person?"

Steve looked at Isaiah. "Oh, he's an acquaintance of ours that is helping us. He doesn't have a sword, but he has other beneficial abilities. He has super speed, and he can give anyone a heart attack just by touching them."

"I see." Karez sat back on the couch. "I will keep him here until you return my son."

"Wait a minute," Isaiah said. "I'm not insurance."

"It will be brief," Bart said. "It is your contribution. We need to get there faster. Have a seat on the couch."

Isaiah didn't look pleased, but he sat down.

"It was getting pretty dark out there," Steve said. "I'm not sure we can go this evening. We should wait for daylight."

"But we're not tired," Matt said. "It's only the middle of the afternoon back home."

"None of you are ever tired," Erin quipped. "You've told me that we don't need sleep anymore just like we don't need to eat. But we do them anyway."

Bart looked out the window. "Steve is right though. We will not be able to see much once we get up on that mountain. There does not seem to be a moon out either. I would bet we will need to see our footing."

Matt sighed. He nodded and sat on the couch. "So, now what?"

A tall woman with long dark hair ascended the stairs. She wore a long black gown with arm-length sleeves. A bowtie patterned band with red embroidered loops on the sides adorned the middle of the dress from her neck to her feet. The same patterned strip lined the cuff of each arm. Her aura enveloped the room.

"This is my companion," Karez motioned toward her. "She is my life, and I am grateful every time I am near her. To think we were spared together, I just..." Tears began to form in his eyes.

She smiled. The atmosphere of the room warmed. "I am called Sarah here. You are welcome in our home. In the morning, you can continue your quest. I will bring you refreshments. Please settle here for the time being."

She started toward the exit into the room they hadn't been in yet. When she passed Xi'heeh, she stopped. She turned to face him.

Xi'heeh straightened. His eyes widened a bit.

"May the prophets of my people bless you for all you have done to help my people. Without your compassion for us, we would be extinct." She disappeared through the doorway.

CHAPTER XIII

Erin grabbed Bart's hand. "Come outside with me for a bit."

"Uh, okay." Bart slowly followed her out the blanket-covered doorway.

Erin leaned on a railing attached to the front porch just to the left of the door. The light breeze moved a few strands of her hair.

Bart stood back toward the house. They stood in silence for a few minutes.

"There isn't a moon out, is there?" Erin finally said.

"No, we would not have been able to see very well. It is a good thing we are waiting. That is not why you asked me to come out here though."

Erin looked down. "No, it isn't. I-I don't know how to start."

Bart's muscles tensed.

"I care about you very much. I don't want to hurt

you, but I'm not sure what I feel right now about us."

Bart breathed. "I would say you know how to start. Wow."

Erin turned to face him. "Please, don't think bad of me."

Bart didn't say anything.

"It's just... A lot has happened to me in a short time. I remember everything I ever went through now. The sword brought all that back. I also know everything you and I went through together. That means a lot to me, but I'm not sure about things right now. I'm not the same person I was yesterday or even this morning. But I really, really don't want you to give up on me either."

Bart moved to the railing and leaned on it.

"Please say something." Erin slowly turned toward him.

"I am still processing. This is a lot to think about coming out of the blue like this. I love you very much. I understand at least the sword part of what is going on inside you. That is difficult enough to process. Having everything else on top of that must be tough. I do not understand that part of what you are going through, but I am here for you and that does not mean that I care any less about it or you."

Erin leaned on the railing beside him. "It is rough. But I don't want to hurt you or jerk you around. I just don't know what I feel right now. I want to make sure that everything we have gone through comes from real feelings and not just something I somehow fell into because you rescued me when I apparently didn't know what was happening to me. I'm seventy-five years old or something like that. That's just hard to deal with right now."

Bart looked into her eyes. "I know you are technically that old. I had that discussion with your mom just before she gave you the sword. She is rooting for us. She told me, not in these words, that it does not matter what our age may be. Besides, you must be the best-looking seventy-five-year-old ever."

Erin laughed. "You do make me happy. I'm serious when I say I don't want you to give up on me. I want us to be us. I just need some time."

"Yes, you do. I will be there for you always, one way or another."

"This is just so hard. It was easy this morning."

"Uh, actually, I am not sure you were you this morning even. If it helps though, your mom said that you were eighteen when you went into the chamber and that you are basically around twenty-one. That could be part of why you are unsure about life right now."

Erin stared over the railing at the ground.

"Take your time. I am not going anywhere."

Erin grabbed Bart's hand and squeezed. "Thanks. You have a lot in your favor, you know. Maybe I already know what I need to know."

"Hey, it is okay. Take some me-time for yourself."

She nodded and turned toward the door. Matt was just opening the blanket.

"Sarah has some food on the coffee table in the main room inside." He gestured for them to come in. "Come try it. She made some pretty good things for us."

Bart extended his hand toward the door. "After you."

***

At the first light of day, everyone was already stirring. Sarah once again produced a modest buffet for them.

"This was perfect." Erin tossed a bite-sized donut in her mouth. "Thank you for all this."

"It isn't much," Sarah said, removing an empty tray.

"It doesn't need to be for us. I just received my sword yesterday, but I'm already realizing what the guys have told me about not needing to eat or sleep. I did get a little sleep, but mostly it was too much time to think."

Bart stood up from the couch where he had been sitting. "We should get going. We'll leave Isaiah with you as we promised."

"I still do not see why I need to be the one to stay behind." Isaiah sat on the ground by the far wall still pouting.

Matt rose from the couch. "Let's just go with my parent's favorite saying, because we said so." He turned, grabbed another piece of roht, and headed for the door. "This is some very good sweetbread."

"Erin, do your thing." Bart nodded toward Isaiah.

"With pleasure." Erin concentrated. "There. I placed a force field around you, and you can't leave that spot until Fred returns."

"Oh, come on, don't you trust me?"

Erin strode over to him. She stared down at him. "You did horrible things to me. I remember it all now.

You don't have any say in how we treat you. If you're trying to amend for your wrongs, I'll gladly let you do that, but it's on our terms, not yours."

"It was your dad." He was barely audible. "I only helped."

Erin's face reddened. She took a couple of deep breaths. She started to speak, but nothing came out. She turned away for a moment, but then, calmer, turned back. "Justify it how you must. It's all the same. Keep this in mind." She leaned closer, placing her hands on her knees, staring into his eyes. "I know the whole truth, just like mom."

Isaiah looked at the floor. He didn't say anything for a moment. "Fine," he said meekly, folding his arms.

Erin straightened up.

No one else said a word. After a few awkward moments, Xi'heeh changed the subject. "We still have the issue of me not technically knowing where to set us all down. I do have the ability to see where I am landing before I do so, but if this ledge is as small as you say, it would not matter. I could know where I am going and still lose a couple of you down the side."

"I can show you from here." Fred led everyone outside. "If you look up the mountain that way." He pointed to a large mountain top. "Can you see that small ledge?"

"You mean right there?" Xi'heeh indicated the area directly in front of them.

"No, that way." Fred redirected him to a mountain range to the right of the closer one.

"Ah, okay, that one."

"No, the one even further that's between those two."

Xi'heeh strained to see the mountains far in the background. "Ah, yes," he acknowledged. "You expect me to see that far?"

"Sure, why not? I can. The space to set us is another fifty to one hundred yards from there."

"So," Xi'heeh began, "I was hoping you could pinpoint it a little more exacting?"

"Well, not really."

"I will be back in a moment then." Xi'heeh disappeared. After a few moments, he returned to this exact spot. "Okay, I have an idea of how to do this. I have seen a cave entrance just beyond that point you showed me. It is bigger than you said."

"Well," Fred looked thoughtful, "I suppose whenever I go there, I'm in my natural form. To us, that is a small area."

Xi'heeh waved everyone closer. "If we all get into a small circle here, we can land in the right place. Fred, I will need you to stay in human form until we reach there. After that, you should probably appear like the rest of your people. They are more likely to trust us if you look like them."

Bart, Erin, Steve, Matt, Xi'heeh, and Fred all gathered close together. In a moment, they disappeared.

***

Xi'heeh and crew reappeared on a tight ledge area near the opening of a vast cavern. Rocks lay all around. Many likely fell from above. No vegetation grew near the cave entrance. Down below you could see the countryside dotted with valleys and smaller peaks, slanting toward some more mountains and valleys beyond. It went on and on. Karez Kalay was no longer visible. The river just beyond it lay hidden in the terrain. The red sand field just beyond that was slightly visible along the horizon.

They moved closer to the entrance where Fred shifted into his normal form. He stood tall among the rocks. His hair was not so fiery red in the shadows of the mountains.

Inside the cave, it was pitch black. You couldn't see particularly far inside. Bart entered the opening.

"I wouldn't go inside," Fred warned. "You are being watched. My presence is likely the only reason you haven't been attacked yet."

Bart stepped back. He had no desire to start something with Fred's people. "So, what is our next move?"

Fred maneuvered himself near the entrance. He picked up one of the bigger rocks nearby and hurled it against the side of the mountain just off the edge of the cave entrance. It landed with a cracking noise, splitting in two.

A voice in an unfamiliar language called out.

"Speak their language," Fred replied. "Let them hear you for themselves."

"They can speak whatever they need to," Bart said. "In a little bit, our swords will translate anything they say."

"Mine already has encountered the language, so I

know what they are saying." Xi'heeh turned to leave. "I shall be at the base of this mountain when you have the information you need."

"Hold on." Bart motioned for Xi'heeh to remain where he was. "What are they saying?"

"Understandably they are not pleased to see me. I represent all they lost."

"That's true," Fred agreed. "They will not come out nor let you in as long as he is here. Believe me, they are very stubborn."

"I believe you," Bart said. He nodded to Xi'heeh. "We are going to need you when the time comes to move out of here. We will signal you somehow when we are done."

Xi'heeh nodded then disappeared.

"Okay," Bart began. "We have done what they want. What is next?"

Fred stepped into the opening of the cave and began to speak loudly in the same language as the inhabitants of the cave. A back-and-forth conversation riled Fred up. He began to speak louder with more animation. After about five minutes of the banter, Bart and the others started to pick up bits and pieces, mostly about concerns among the Kutarians about helping them and the safety of their people. The consensus was that if they helped, then what assurances would they have that their people would remain safe.

"All my new friends want to know," Fred pleaded with the unseen voices of the cave, "is where they can find this other cave where some strange things are happening."

"We don't want to get involved," came the reply. "About fifty years ago, one of our people was discovered outside the cave system and he was shot multiple times until he finally died. Is this how they treat people?"

"No, it is not how everyone on this planet treats people." Bart jumped into the conversation.

Silence fell. Gradually a murmur and mumble or two floated out of the cave. Then, one voice yelled, "How can we understand each other?"

"My friends and I hold the mystic swords that I know are part of your fables. These swords are real. Given time, they translate any language. We proved to Karez that we have them, and he sent us to you for more help. Although, I am not sure how much more convincing you would need other than our translating your language or our presence this high on the mountain."

There was more silence followed by a higher volume of murmuring. Eventually, three Kutarians emerged from the cave. They were all at least twelve feet tall, with the same red hair and beards. Huge muscles bulged on their bare chests, arms, and legs. There didn't seem to be one place where a muscle didn't exist. They each wore a huge loincloth wrapped around their waist and upper legs. Each held a spear that had to be twelve feet long and the circumference of the large end of a baseball bat. It was tipped with a roughly hewn stone shaped into a point with jagged edges.

"If you are the holders of the swords, one of you can defeat three of us."

Bart looked at Fred. "I thought you said Kutarians were not a warrior race. All I see is you guys wanting to fight."

Fred shrugged. "What can I say? After all these years, maybe we're finally ready to stand up for ourselves."

"Fine," Bart said. "I will fight you, but I am not going to hurt you very badly. Just enough to make you believe."

"No, the female of your species is the one who will battle us."

"You have got to be kidding, right?" Bart shook his head and wrinkled his forehead.

"Wait a minute." Erin walked over to Bart. "Are you saying that I can't take these guys?"

Bart blushed. "No, I did not say that."

"But you're thinking it. Ha, these puny guys don't stand a chance." Erin turned to face the three giants. "If you're lucky, I might take it easy on you. Bart would have been nicer to you. Bring it on." She beckoned them to come at her.

The three giants took up a position with the main one directly in front of Erin and the other two flanking him. The two on the flanks grabbed the nearest rocks which were a little larger than a basketball. They heaved them at her. About halfway there, they stopped and dropped straight down.

"Oops, you missed. And you didn't have that far to throw them either. So, how do you like my witty banter?"

The giants didn't seem to care for it. The two that threw the rocks charged, but after two steps hit an invisible shield and couldn't progress. They pressed against the air in front of them, then to the sides and back. They began to beat on the side of the shielding with their oversized fists. They could have been overgrown mimes in a street show for all the good that did them.

"Okay grumpy." Erin stared at the giant in the middle. "It's just you and me, now."

That triggered him. He rushed at her with the full force of a raging bull.

Erin ran at him. Just before she reached him, she slid to the ground and undercut him with her legs. His legs flailed out behind him from underneath his upper body, slamming him face-first into the solid rock ledge. Before he could move, Erin had her dagger out and jumped on his back straddling his neck. She pressed the dagger into his cheek.

"Don't even try to move."

The giant twitched an arm but must have decided against trying to do anything, as the arm relaxed back to the ground.

"Good boy. Now, get up." She slid off.

The giant rolled onto his knees and rested there for a moment.

"I'm not sure why your people seem to want some kind of proof other than our swords," Erin said. "I'd think they would be better than any ability we may have."

"It's because we were fooled before," said the giant still on his knees. "That is how the G'mone and K'reelian people started the invasion of our world. The legend of the coming of the swords is well known to us. They used fake swords before to make us think the fabled stories had come to pass. If you are the real sword holders, you would easily be able to beat us. And so, you have. Even using the power of one of them to do so."

Erin held out her hand to the giant. He grasped it, and she pulled him to his feet.

"We are the real holders of the swords. We need your help." Erin returned the dagger to its invisible sheath. She walked over to Bart, grabbed him by the collar, and kissed him. "How'd I do?" Bart raised an eyebrow. "Excellent, as I knew you would."

"Oh, I shouldn't have done that," Erin said with apprehension. "I'm sorry."

"Glad she's not my girlfriend," Steve quipped.

"Me too." Bart smiled at him, then walked over to the Kutarian giant. "So, can we talk now?"

The giant grinned. "Yes, we can. We don't trust people. We need to know their intent first. But we trust the holders of the enchanted swords. We know they are good. They are responsible. What do you need?"

Bart explained the reason they had come to this area, about the cave somewhere around here that appeared to have some sort of strange activity going on. He mentioned that Fred knew of something, but that they would have more details.

"I see." The giant paused. He looked at the other two. His face showed concern. After a while, he added, "We have heard things. One of our kind has been exploring the possibility that we could move some of our people to another cave system. We are running low on space here. We sent a scout to another mountain range. She returned with stories of a mighty cavern system. But she said it was already occupied. She was too frightened to describe the inhabitants, but we think we know who it is."

"Can you tell us who it is?" Bart asked.

"No, we will not presume anything. It is harmful to speculate about things you are unsure of. It is not proven."

"Will she lead us to the place?"

"She is too scared. She will not go."

"Can we at least meet her and talk to her. Maybe she can point us in the direction we need to go?"

The giant sighed. He turned to one of the other Kutarians. "Go fetch –," He made a noise that the swords apparently couldn't translate. "See if she will meet with the sword holders."

He turned to leave but ran smack into the invisible wall.

"Oh sorry," Erin said. "I forgot to take those away. Okay, you can move now."

The Kutarian held up a hand and felt for a wall. Finding nothing, he disappeared into the cave. Fifteen minutes later, he returned with another Kutarian. She slowly peeked out from the cave entrance but hesitated to come outside. She had similar red hair, longer than the men's, and no beard. She wasn't as tall, closer to ten feet, and she wasn't quite as muscular. Her one-piece outfit was made from animal fur and had a single strap over her left shoulder. It covered her torso and ended in a skirt at her knees.

Steve sat outside on a rock resting off to the side but in front of the entrance. He leaned against the mountainside. When she timidly stuck her head out, he said, "It's okay. We're not going to hurt you. We need your help."

The female giant looked at him and then the others. She saw Xi'heeh, who had returned from below. Her face froze. She stepped beside Steve and picked him up, using him as a shield.

"Hey now, it's okay. You can put me down. Please."

She didn't listen. "You are the only one I like. I don't like the others. You will stay and be my mate."

Steve's eyes widened, and his jaw dropped. "What? I just got here. I don't even know what you're talking about."

She dropped Steve and shifted into the form of a human woman about the same height as Steve. Gorgeous long black hair flowed down to the back of her knees. Her face and body were that of a model. She now wore a charcoal gray tee shirt and a nice pair of blue jeans. Dark brown hiking boots covered her feet. "Maybe you like this better?" Her voice was sweet and tender, not rough like the Kutarians.

Steve's mouth popped open. He stared a little too long. "You're stunning. Wait, did you get that from my mind?"

"Kutarian women know what their men like. I know that you like this. I can stay in this form forever if it pleases you."

"Now -," again the lead Kutarian uttered a word the swords couldn't translate. "You know that you can't be with him. I was afraid something like this might happen."

"I wish to be happy as well." She tilted her head slightly in the direction of the giant without looking directly at him while responding. "Do you deny me that?"

He remained silent.

She returned her full attention to Steve. "I was told that you want to know where the cave I witnessed the army at is. Is that true?"

Steve nodded.

"I will take you all there if I can stay with you and never return here. That's my only offer." She turned and walked into the cave entrance, standing a few feet inside the mouth.

"Okay, that was weird." Steve turned to look at Bart and the others. He threw his hands out. "What am I supposed to say now?"

"Hi, honey?" Matt struggled to keep the smile from forming on his face. "Where have you been all my life?"

Steve glared at him. "Really? Is that the best you've got?"

Matt could no longer contain himself. He burst out laughing.

Steve ignored him and faced the giant. "What is her name?"

The giant again made the same noise he had earlier.

"Yeah, I don't think I can call her that."

Fred spoke up. "Remember my dad telling you that our names are unpronounceable by you? Well, that's why you can't understand it. When we are in human form, we speak your language well, but our names do not translate."

Steve entered the cave. "Hey, I hear that I can't pronounce your name. What can I call you?"

She was still in human form and had her back to the entrance of the cave. She didn't turn around to face him. "What is your favorite name?"

"Whew, boy."

"Well, then, you can call me 'Whewboy.'" She turned to face him.

"No, no, no, sorry, that's not a name. That's just an expression that we sometimes use when we're a little overwhelmed. You need a better name than that. I just never really gave a thought to a favorite name." Steve fumbled around for the right words. "I, uh, I don't know what your customs are like, but we don't go around announcing that someone you just met is going to be your mate."

"You don't like me, do you?"

"I have no idea whether I like you. I just met you. I might like you, but given the fact that you can shapeshift, it's just, well, different. I mean, how do I know you're not something else, you know?"

"I am one hundred percent human in this form. I function just like a human. Would you like to see?" Her tee-shirt began to dissipate from her shoulders.

"No! No, you don't need to do that. You aren't familiar with our ways. We don't go around doing that. Let's just use a little trust here and say that I believe you."

Bart appeared at the entrance. "Is everything okay in here? We heard some yelling."

Steve turned toward him. "No, I mean, yes, everything's fine in here. Just give us a moment."

Bart backed away, disappearing outside.

Steve faced the Kutarian female again. "How about we just go find this other cave you found and take things as they come? I don't know you, but I do think it's amazing that you can change your form. You don't know me. Maybe you'll think I'm a total jerk after this."

"I know about you already. I did tell you that Kutarian women know all about their men. It is our way. When we see the right one for us, we know. That's all we need. I will never find another."

"Oh boy, nothing like pressure. So, do you know I have a magical sword? That I'm super strong? That I can't die? Do you know that I can do this?" Steve disappeared.

"I know all I need to know."

"I wish it were that easy for us humans." Steve reappeared. "That sure would make everything a lot simpler. So, for me, can you give me time? After all, my first meeting with you was seeing you in a different form."

The Kutarian looked him in the eye. "Would it make a difference to you if you had met this shape first?"

Steve thought for a moment. "Don't take this the wrong way, but yeah, probably. First impressions are always the biggest. But I think that I'm glad to have seen you in your original form first."

She gave him a quizzical look.

"If I had seen you like this first and then as you really are, I'm afraid that would have been a bigger surprise. Maybe I would even think you had been hiding that side of yourself from me. I know what you are, and you being you is important. You need to be yourself and not be afraid to be around others as yourself."

"Actually, I like this form a lot. I may keep it anyway. I feel good."

"There you go. That's what's important." He reached out and touched her extra-long hair. "This is beautiful long hair. Maybe you should think of shortening it though. It might end up getting in your way. Maybe there would be a better length." He pointed to the middle of her back.

"Like this?" Her hair shrank.

"Perfect."

She nodded and smiled, then moved toward the cave entrance.

"Callie," Steve said.

She looked at him.

"That's a nice name," he said. "What do you think?"

"Perfect."

"So, how do you shape-shift?"

"It's very easy. We just think of something we want to be, and it happens."

"Okay, one other question, can you... uh... well-"

"Yes, I can," she said with a sly smile.

"Okay then, uh, shall we go get the others and find

this other cave?"

Steve and Callie walked side by side out the entrance. Everyone shifted their attention to them as they exited.

"Well?" asked Bart.

"Callie will take us to the cave," Steve said.

"Callie, is it?" Bart nodded. "I like that."

"Yes, Steve says it is better than Whewboy, so I like it too."

Bart, Matt, and Erin looked at Steve, who just shrugged.

"Long story," he said.

"Can't be that long," Matt said. "You weren't in there long enough to have a long story."

"So, are we ready?" Steve changed the subject.

"-," The male Kutarian uttered the same indistinguishable sound again. "You decided to help them then?"

"My name is Callie now, please use that. And, yes, I will help them."

"So be it." The Kutarian looked at his brethren. "This woman has made her choice. She is no longer welcome here. Let's go."

The Kutarian men headed for the cave entrance and disappeared inside.

Steve stared after them. Bart, Matt, and Erin looked bewildered.

"What do they mean?" Steve asked.

Callie didn't say anything. She caught sight of Xi'heeh. She glared at him. "Why are you here? You hurt my people."

Xi'heeh bowed. "I regret the harm to your people. That is why I relocated as many of you as I could here."

"That was you?" Callie's expression seemed to soften.

Xi'heeh nodded. "I can guarantee you that the K'reelian people were not in favor of the things that happened to your people. We are pawns of the G'mone ourselves. However, that is not an excuse. We are too deep into the culture that the G'mone have established to change as an entire species."

"Can't someone do something about the bond you have with the G'mone people?" Matt asked.

"But that's impossible, right?" Erin asked.

"There are stories about the creation of the Star of B'naugh and the holy man that was responsible for that," Xi'heeh began.

"You have a lot of ancient prophecies," Matt said. "Like the one about the swords."

"This is part of the same prophecy."

"Why didn't you tell me that when I was on your planet? I could have helped you all figure it out."

"This holy man was an ancestor of my family. It is said that he may have foreseen what would happen to my people and created another talisman to release us from our bonds. However, that was never passed down from generation to generation as the Star of B'naugh was."

"What is this Star of B'naugh?" Erin asked.

"It's what was used to create these swords," Matt explained. "I don't know if I told you the name of it when

I told you all that happened to me when I disappeared. Each arm of the star was a color that matches our swords, and it gave them their powers and strength."

"When we finish this job, we will go to your planet to seek this talisman," Bart promised. "Only then can you attempt to free your people from the G'mone."

Xi'heeh shook his head. "It may not be your job. According to the prophecy, it is unclear which sword must make the pilgrimage to find the answer."

Bart changed the subject. "We need to get Fred home and retrieve Isaiah."

"No, wait." Fred held out his hands to stop them. "I want to go too. I can help."

"Sorry." Bart shook his head. "We promised your father to bring you right back, and that is what we are going to do." He nodded at Xi'heeh, who returned the nod.

Before Fred could make any further arguments, he and Xi'heeh disappeared.

Ten minutes passed before Xi'heeh returned with Isaiah.

"What took you so long?" Bart asked.

"I had trouble with this one." Xi'heeh pointed to Isaiah. "He would not come quietly."

"And why should I?" Isaiah zipped toward Callie at incredible speed and stood behind her. "I am being treated like a criminal."

"Well, basically, you are." Bart stood up from the rock he had been sitting on while they waited.

"Maybe Reginald was correct about you guys." Isaiah

took the glove off his right hand.

"Don't you even think about it." Erin pointed at Isaiah and walked straight at him, never taking her eyes off him. "I have warned you not to go against us. If you want to help repair the things you did to my mother and me, you will put that glove back on. Plus, you also likely realize that I've already put a protective shield on Callie."

Isaiah said nothing. He glowered at Erin but did as she requested.

Erin continued to pierce his eyes with hers.

He looked away and down at the ground.

"You and I will talk when the time comes." Erin was calm, almost peaceful. "At this time, I'm in the mood to forgive you, so don't mess up."

Isaiah glanced up at her, a look of hope on his face. He nodded.

"Thank you." Erin's line of sight shifted to Callie. "Where is the cavern?"

Callie shifted her feet. She pointed in the direction left of the entrance of her cave. "It's that way, but it's a long journey by foot. We couldn't possibly get there for weeks."

"Don't worry," Xi'heeh said. "I transported many of your people thousands of light-years. I can transport all of us in seconds."

"Have you heard of a town called Jalalabad?" Callie asked.

"I do not know of it, but I have studied a map of this world, and I can find it."

"Oh, in that case, you may be able to get us closer on

the first jump. I don't want to bring us right to the mountain this cave is in as it would be difficult to land us all in one place much like it is here. But, if you know where Deh Bala is, that would be a better start."

Xi'heeh concentrated. "Yeah, I have that."

"There's a field on the south side that you can set us in, and no one will bother us."

An instant later, they all disappeared.

CHAPTER XIV

They landed exactly where Callie had pointed them. They faced more mountains to the south and some to the west. Behind them, nestled in the valley of the ridges to the west was a small town with houses built from mud. It wasn't much to see, but it was home to someone. Currently, it was deserted.

"Quickly, before someone comes outside and we're seen, can you put us on that highest peak there?" Callie pointed to the south.

Xi'heeh shielded his eyes. "Level one, two, or three of the ridges?"

"Three."

They disappeared again, landing on a ridge with just enough room for everyone.

"Brrr." Isaiah shivered. "It's cold up here. Why aren't the rest of you shivering too?"

"Our swords protect us from the elements," Bart

said.

"For me, this is nothing. Now, quiet please. Let me get my bearings." Callie looked to the southwest and after a moment said, "There, can you see that opening right there? It's been made by people, it's not natural."

Xi'heeh squinted. He again placed a hand over his eyes to shield out any sunlight. "Yes, I see it. Do you want us right there?"

"No." Callie shook her head. "That would put us right in plain sight. We'd be spotted in seconds. If you look just a little higher, you'll see a ledge. There's a smaller entrance on that ledge. There are some females there that are used for pleasure and then sacrificed."

"That's horrible," Erin said.

"Their ways are not your ways." Callie continued to point to the second entrance.

"Ah yes, now I see it." Xi'heeh narrowed his eyes. "I can make out a clearing in between some trees that I can set us down in."

They disappeared again. This time it was a tighter squeeze, but they managed to land between a scant few evergreen trees and boulders without anyone in or on any.

Callie raced to the entrance, crouching right at the base of the mountain entrance. This entrance was a hole in the ground, not a hole in the mountainside. She peered over the edge, motioning for the others to carefully join her.

They stared down into a vast room where maybe twenty to thirty beds lay scattered across the room. Some of the beds had young women laying on them. Others sat at desks that had mirrors and what looked like makeup containers. All the women in the room were scantily dressed. Their clothes were comprised mainly of sheer curtain-like veils wrapped around many times to try to hide their bodies.

"I don't believe it." Matt clenched his jaw.

"I also do not believe it." A tear welled in Xi'heeh's eye. "La'prell. What is she doing here?"

"Those are K'reelian women." Matt was ready to jump into the room.

Callie held him back. "No, not like this. Some alarms go off if anyone but a K'reelian female sets foot in there."

Bart looked at her. "How do you know this?"

"I turned into a K'reelian and have visited these women. For a moment, I set off the alarm, but once the system recognized me, it sounded the 'all clear'. It was so brief no one came to check on it. I've spoken with the women. They're all afraid. They want to leave."

"I can't blame them." Erin stared down. "What are we going to do?"

Xi'heeh began to count.

"My question," Bart started, "is why you did not tell us there were K'reelians in this cave?"

Callie didn't say anything right away. "I didn't know if you would help them. They need to get out of there. This is how I best decided to help them."

Xi'heeh reported his count before Bart could reply to Callie. "I see twenty-five of them. Hang on a moment, and I will be right back. Don't do anything until I return."

He disappeared.

Everyone sat back from the hole so that they wouldn't accidentally be seen. It wasn't long before Xi'heeh returned with about thirty purple jumpsuits.

"Here, let's get them clothed at least." He started to jump in.

Callie tugged on his arm. "No, you can't go in."

"Why not?"

"You are a K'reelian man, the alarm will sound unless you come through the doorway. I need to be the one in there."

"Wait." Steve grabbed her hand. "We don't want any kind of an alarm, even a small blip that might bring attention to us. What about me going in invisible? Would the sensors know I was there?"

"I don't know. They sense motion and are tied to the K'reelian female. It's possible if the sensors can't see you that you'd be invisible to them as well. That's kind of how I got out. I turned into an insect and flew out. None of the women knew how I left."

"Let me try then." Steve grabbed the garments and turned invisible. A pile of garments now floated in the air. "So, how's this?"

"We can see the clothes, but not you," Bart said. "Callie, are you sure they will not scream or anything? And are there other K'reelians and G'mone people here?"

"I don't think they'll scream, and yes, there are lots of the others here."

Bart didn't look pleased. "It would have been helpful to know what we were getting into."

"We can't worry about that now," Steve said. "I'm going in."

"Tell them K'inta sent you. That was my name to them."

A bundle of purple jumpsuits plummeted into the room, stopping what looked like just off the ground. The women closest to the pile screamed. The others whipped around to see what the commotion was about.

"Quiet, please," said the pile of jumpsuits. "K'inta sent me to help you. Put these on." Steve flung the jumpsuits on the nearest bed.

"I am La'prell, who are you?" One of the women strode over to the pile of clothes.

"I'm... uh, isn't the fact K'inta sent me good enough?"

"I'd like to know who to thank."

"Okay, uh, I'm... uh, S'mores. Call me S'mores."

"I have never heard a name like that before." La'prell removed her sheer veil wrapping, took a jumpsuit, and put it on.

"Uh... I'm closing my eyes now."

"Why do you need to close your eyes? If they were just open, you have already seen me. It does not matter one way or the other to us if you see us undressed. We don't obsess over our bodies. Would you like to see again?" La'prell started to unzip the jumpsuit.

"No! You don't need to do that."

She stopped, then zipped back to the top.

The rest of the women followed La'prell's lead and disrobed and grabbed a jumpsuit to put on.

Within minutes they had all donned a jumpsuit. "Okay, S'mores, if that's really your name, and you really closed your eyes, you can open them again. Why are you here?"

"My friends and I are here to rescue you."

"Friends? I don't see you, much less your friends. Who says we want to be rescued?"

"K'inta told us that you wanted to escape this place. Isn't that what you'd like to do."

La'prell walked around the bed and dresser next to it. She grabbed a stick leaning against the dresser and swung wildly in the direction of Steve's voice.

"Ah, come on. I try to help you, and that's how you repay me?" His voice moved around the room. "K'inta doesn't seem to be working as a name drop here."

La'prell continued to swing for any empty spot near where Steve's voice roamed. "K'inta left us long ago. We're quite sure she was sacrificed to appease the mountain gods here."

"No, she's above through the hole in your ceiling. So is Xi'heeh."

La'prell stopped mid-swing. "Xi'heeh? How do you know him? Now I know you lie. He died on the Kutarian homeworld."

"No, my dear, La'prell." Xi'heeh stood above next to the hole. Another K'reelian woman stood beside him. "I am here. And so is K'inta. I'm coming down."

La'prell quickly came to her senses. "No, if you do, the alarms will blare. You will be discovered."

Xi'heeh teetered on the rim of the hole. Callie, or

K'inta now, grabbed his arm and kept him on the outside.

La'prell gazed up at him, the bewilderment on her face etched everywhere. "How? They said you and V'ante died."

"He did. I didn't."

"You have the sword, don't you?" La'prell stared at him, then quickly looked at the other K'reelian women. She was bouncing and smiling so hard that the others began to murmur excitedly.

Xi'heeh nodded. "I can take all of you home. You will be in our village in just a few minutes. Gather everyone in one spot."

The women huddled together. A chime sounded from the doorway. A red light over the doorway turned green.

"Oh no, someone's coming." La'prell pushed some of the women to the side and maneuvered to the front nearest the door. "Xi'heeh, back up so they don't see you. These jumpsuits will be bad enough."

The door swished open. Two elderly, fat G'mone wearing only something like boxer shorts entered the room.

"It's time for our medicine," said the first one through the door. He slicked his white hair back with his fingers. "I want La'prell this time, and I'm not taking no for an answer."

He stopped. He hadn't noticed the women dressed in the jumpsuits. "What is this? How dare you be dressed. And who is that up there."

He pointed outside the hole, where Bart and Matt

attempted to hold Xi'heeh back. It wasn't easy because their super strength was non-existent against the other sword holders. Add Xi'heeh's K'reelian genes to that, and you had a much superior fighter than the two of them combined.

"Don't do anything," Matt grunted. "Let Steve take care of it."

"I have a force field over the hole," Erin said.

"That will not stop him." Bart had Xi'heeh around the neck. "Please, do not do anything. We cannot afford to have alarms sounding all over the place."

Below, the second G'mone male moved toward a panel on the wall. He tried to press a button but couldn't touch anything but the air around the panel. Then he crumbled face-first to the ground. He didn't move.

The first G'mone grabbed La'prell. The other K'reelian women rushed to her defense. They swarmed the man and tackled him to the ground. They beat him until he didn't move.

From above, Bart yelled. "How long until they're missed?"

La'prell straightened out her jumpsuit. "We can set our occupied lights on for all afternoon if you'd like. No one else will come in while the busy light is on. Here, I'll set that up."

She walked over to the panel but also couldn't touch any of the controls inside. "What is wrong with this thing."

"Sorry," Erin yelled down. "I put a barrier over it. Let me remove that. There, now you can get to it."

La'prell ran her fingers over the switches. A purple light flashed on the wall above the door. "There, that should take all the afternoon slots up. Now, how do we get out of here?"

Bart and Matt released Xi'heeh.

"I will take you all home now." Xi'heeh breathed easier. He raised his sword and disappeared along with all the women in the room below.

"Steve," Bart yelled down into the hole. "Are you there? S'mores?"

No one answered.

After a few minutes, Xi'heeh returned with Steve. La'prell was also with them.

Bart sighed and rolled his eyes about halfway.

"She would not stay behind," said Xi'heeh. "That's why it took longer to return than it should have."

"Wow, that was a cool little village," Steve blurted, effectively ending any more discussion about La'prell returning with them. "Matt, was that where you were? That was such a cool fountain with that little cloud raining down on that field." He stopped. "Whoa, K'inta, looking good."

She transformed back into Callie. "Don't try to fool me. You like this better, and I know it. Although…"

"We need to hide." Bart pointed to two helicopters flying toward the mountain from a distance. "But where?"

"I got us covered, literally." Erin waved her hand. "There. We're all hidden in plain sight behind a reflective shield. Just hang tight and watch them pass by."

"What are they doing here?" Bart watched them approach the mountain.

"Maybe they're going to blast the place to a little molehill or something," Steve suggested.

The helicopters slowed as they approached. The lead craft descended toward the main cave entrance and disappeared inside while the other hovered behind. The second helicopter hesitated. It rotated toward Bart's group, climbing along the side of the mountain.

"You are certain you have us cloaked." Bart shifted his feet uneasily.

"Yes, I am." Erin didn't sound as sure as the scowl on her face implied. "The sword's powers are fairly intuitive. I saw what Jane did, or I should say what my mom did on occasion."

As the helicopter ascended toward them, three mountain sheep darted out from behind a rock formation, scattering higher up the side. The helicopter turned away, circling back to the entrance.

"That was interesting." Bart edged closer to the side of the mountain so he could see the helicopter as it disappeared inside the cave entrance. "At least we know where the helicopters are coming from, and who owns them. We need to get in there."

"I wouldn't go so far yet as to say they belong here, or the owners are here," said Isaiah.

Bart nodded. "I can see that. But the way the one flew up here after some slight movement by the sheep and the fact that we have not heard any loud explosions yet, likely means they belong here."

"We can see inside from the front entrance." Callie moved beside Bart. She peered over the edge and then quickly moved away from the edge. "Maybe then we can tell if they belong here."

Matt slipped passed Steve, giving him a little bump in the arm with his shoulder as we went by. "S'mores? Really? You ain't living that one down, man."

Steve rolled his eyes.

CHAPTER XV

Xi'heeh landed them on the side of the front entrance which was almost a sheer cliff face. There was enough room for them to stand without falling off. A rock tumbled down from above the cliff, barely missing Isaiah as he zipped out of the way into the opening of the cavern.

"Wait." Erin held her hands out. "I should hide us before we get too close to the opening."

A K'reelian and a G'mone guard exited the cave.

"Too late." The K'reelian raised his laser rifle.

Isaiah was too close and too fast for the guards. He sped forward, removing a glove at the same time. He touched the K'reelian guard in the face. The guard's eyes popped wide open. He dropped to the ground.

The G'mone took one step forward and collapsed face down on the ground.

"You know," Isaiah said. "You really should have

fixed that little quirk in your joining process. That's a real liability."

"It can be, but it has worked for us with every other race we have met." Xi'heeh kicked the G'mone so that he rolled over on his back.

"I just made us all invisible to anyone else here. Each of you has your own little aura now. Isaiah, Callie, and La'prell have extra protection so that they can't be harmed. These will last about an hour, so we should probably see what we can find out about this place."

"Wait a second." Bart picked up the boulder and dropped it on the K'reelian guard. "I do not know how long before these guys are missed, but maybe this will buy us some time. I hope they think he was crushed by the rock."

"So, question." Isaiah looked at Erin. "With this aura of yours around me, am I able to touch others if I need to protect myself, or am I just going to have to run away?"

"Unfortunately, I don't know. I have a feeling what keeps stuff out also keeps you from touching things. You can move freely and still grab things, but will your power to give people heart attacks work? I don't know."

"The answer is, no," Matt added. "I do know all about the swords, and that is correct. What keeps things away from you keeps you away from them. You can shoot projectiles or throw things out the shield, but if you touch something, you won't feel it, and it won't touch you."

"Great, then La'prell, Callie, and I are of little good in a fight."

"You can still hit people at super speed," Matt said.

"And Callie could technically change shapes and the force field would change to match whatever shape she chooses."

"I can help you out." Xi'heeh motioned for the three of them to come closer to him. "I have three weapons that will benefit you if you need them." He reached his right hand in midair in front of him. He produced a laser pistol and handed it to Callie. He reached into the air again and another laser pistol appeared. He handed it to Isaiah. He repeated the motion a third time and pulled out a three-foot-long laser rifle. He gave that to La'prell. "There, that should help. I caution you to only use them if something happens in there. Do not start anything, just finish it."

"That was an impressive trick." Bart nodded his approval.

"I call it my junk bag. It is the only extra ability I have used so far. I store whatever I want in there, it has no limit. I only need to think about what I want and reach in front of me. I have lots of stuff in there. Oh, I just remembered. I stuck an enemy in there once. I wonder how he is getting along in there. I suppose I should get him out someday. And, Erin, I have a bag your mother was carrying when I went to get her. Remind me to give it to you someday."

"Say I have some things I'd like to hide from prying eyes," Steve said. "Would you let me put them there?"

Xi'heeh didn't answer with words. The stare he gave Steve did all the talking.

"Right," Steve shifted uneasily. "Well, let's get

moving."

They all moved toward the cave entrance. It was dark at the entrance.

Callie moved to the front of the group. "I still have cave eyes and can see best in there. From what I can see there are three different paths. There's the big one straight down the middle where the flying machines went. Then much smaller ones to each side."

"Hold on." Steve stepped to the front. "Let me see if I can see anyone walking in there." He concentrated. "It's too dark. I see these two guards came from the tunnel to our left, but not much more. It looks like they've been here a while." He stopped talking. "Hold it, someone's coming for real. Everybody please be quiet and split to the sides of the cave walls. We'll see how well Erin's filters work."

Another set of guards, one K'reelian and one G'mone moved toward the light at the front of the cave.

"A'roc," the G'mone called out. "Where are you? H'ee? Are you there?"

They walked outside the cave. They caught sight of the G'mone lying on the ground, rushed to his side, and knelt. The K'reelian spotted his fellow K'reelian under the rock. He jumped up and went to his side. "This rock did not fall on him."

"How can you tell?"

"It is not setting naturally. I am not sure how he got under there, but he died before that happened."

"We need to report this." The G'mone grabbed a radio on his belt.

A laser beam shot out of the cave. The radio fell to the rocky ground, smashing into pieces. The G'mone guard landed on top of the pieces. Seconds later, the K'reelian fell beside the rock he was trying to push off his compatriot.

"So much for that looking natural to them," Bart said, exiting the cave.

Xi'heeh followed out the entrance. He picked up both G'mone soldiers and tossed them over the cliff. He rolled the stone off the first K'reelian and picked both up, tossing them after their bonded companions. "Hopefully if these first two have been here a while as Steve says, we will be able to move around before the next pair come looking for them. Let's get moving."

Back inside, Bart said, "We need to split up and follow all three tunnels."

"I will go only with Steve," Callie spoke swiftly.

"Man," Bart said, "What is it with you two and these alien women?"

"Hey," Steve replied, "we have some hot alien women tastes, and I find that I don't mind it."

"Yeah, what the heck I say." Matt put his arm around Steve. "When on Earth, do as the Earthlings do?"

"What does that even mean?" Bart scowled. "Steve, take Matt and Callie and go left." He pointed to the left, though he didn't need to. "Xi'heeh, I assume that La'prell will want to be with you, so you guys go right. Erin, Isaiah, and I shall go down the middle. Meet back here if you are able in less than an hour."

"One last thing," Matt said before moving. "How are

we going to communicate with each other?"

Bart shook his head. "I guess we do not."

"I was thinking," Matt started. "If Xi'heeh used another of his abilities on a communication process such as Anoriya had, then he could keep in contact with all of us."

"Why should I use an ability like that?"

"Because you're the one with the ability to transport anyone. We could contact you anytime and you could come to get us and take us wherever. This is something we could use after this mission. I was thinking maybe we should end our alliance with the President and help people on our own."

Xi'heeh thought for a moment. "It does seem having a way to communicate with each other would be good. I shall do it. I now set an open line of communication through our thoughts with each of the sword holders. We will keep each other's privacy by only opening a channel with each other by thinking of the word 'calling' followed by one or more of our names. This way we will not accidentally call each other when we are just thinking about one of us. Any one of us can reach out to any of the rest of us. I do not need to be a facilitator to start a conversation. Whoever is part of a conversation will be able to hear any of the other's words until a session is terminated by saying 'end communication.' The sword holders will always have this rapport, but I can also grant special access to this to anyone I feel needs it until I remove that access. Such as right now, I grant La'prell, Callie, and Isaiah the ability to also chat with us and each other as needed."

The others nodded.

"Hey," Bart said, "be careful in there. Matt told us about his experience with saving B'ajj. They may be desperate to nullify our powers, who knows what they are capable of?"

"Those flying machines worry me more than anyone nullifying our powers," said Xi'heeh. "I do not recognize the design. They could do almost anything."

"We have seen some of the damage they make," Bart replied. "They are dangerous. I worry more about there being G'mone and K'reelian soldiers on Earth. How and when did they arrive? Is this an advanced war party?"

"Those are very good questions," Xi'heeh agreed. "Very likely they are an advanced party indeed. I was just a ground soldier, so any plans like this would be at a higher level than what I was."

"We need to get moving." Erin started down the middle much larger path.

Bart and Isaiah followed quickly behind before she got too far in front of them.

"Let's see, Bart gave us the left tunnel, right?" Steve stared down the tunnel. "It's dark down there. How can we tell where we're going?"

"Don't worry, babe, I can see." Callie started down the path.

"Babe?" Steve watched her fade into the darkness.

"Yeah, come on, babe. Or is that S'mores? Maybe it's Whewboy. You sure have a way with names." Matt laughed. He lit up his pointer finger and held it aloft.

"Come on, S'mores, I'll take care of the light."

Steve looked at Xi'heeh and La'prell. "I suppose it's a good thing that I like both of them, isn't it?" He vanished after them.

Xi'heeh shifted back and forth. It was quiet. After a moment, he headed down the right tunnel.

"Xi'heeh," La'prell's voice was gentle. It made him pause. "I want you to know that even though I thought you were dead; I was true to you. I did not dishonor us."

Xi'heeh put his head down. He didn't say anything.

La'prell walked to where Xi'heeh stood. She placed a hand on his shoulder. He shrugged it off.

"I know you are angry that you found me in that place, I never once defiled what we had."

Xi'heeh started down the path.

"You must believe me."

He stopped again. He didn't turn to face her. "If Bart says you are telling the truth, I will believe you."

She marched over to where he stood. She stopped right in front of his face and looked him in the eyes but didn't say anything. Then she turned and strode down the path.

Xi'heeh sighed. "La'prell, wait."

She didn't stop.

Xi'heeh dashed to catch up with her. She was setting a brisk pace, but fortunately, a glimmer of light kept her in their sight. It took him a few minutes to catch up to her. When he finally did, he grabbed her arm to stop her. She twisted away.

"Hey," he said, "We need to talk this out before we

go any farther."

She stopped in her tracks. She turned to face him, her lavender eyes raging with contempt. "I just gave you a chance to talk about it, but there is apparently nothing to talk about. I have told you the truth, and you should not need Bart or anyone else to help you figure that out. You need to figure out on your own if you believe me or not. I cannot make that decision for you. That is how we shall fix the trust between us. If you cannot believe me, then there is nothing left. I thought you were dead, but I kept every filthy creature away from me. They made me sick calling it their 'medicine'. I watched all those other girls who could not fight them off. They all wanted to die. You do not know how many I kept from doing just that. They looked to me as their leader, but really, I was just saving myself. I just hope that they will fight their demons and find peace at home. I hope they never tell anyone what happened to them."

She fell to her knees, tears filling her eyes. She put her face in her hands.

Xi'heeh knelt beside her. "So, I am a big jerk, aren't I?"

She didn't look at him. "You can believe that one." She continued to sob but mingled in a laugh.

"So, will you give me one more chance to believe you?"

"I should not."

"I am sorry. I did not expect to find you there. It made me angry. Things have been strange since I received the sword as well. It was not that long ago that this happened. It was unnerving to see V'ante die and have nothing happen to me. That is nothing compared to what you have been through. You and I are joined in a better way. I will never doubt you again; ever."

She looked at him. "They told me you had died. They said there was nothing left between us. I did not want to believe them and continued to keep them away. I am yours, and yours only."

They embraced.

Clapping erupted from the corridor. A dim light twinkled.

They jumped. Xi'heeh spun around. Ten pairs of K'reelian and G'mone guards stood in front of them. They stopped clapping and raised their laser weapons.

"Oh, that was a lovely performance." The lead G'mone guard stepped forward. "I don't know how you can believe her. Each of us has been with her at least twice."

The others all laughed and nodded their heads. A couple made kissy faces. One started smooching his hand.

La'prell looked at Xi'heeh. Fear now shown in those lavender eyes. She shook her head. "Do not believe them."

"Do not believe them," mocked the guard. "I do not know how you escaped your room without the alarms going off, but not that it's going to matter. You will both soon be dead."

Xi'heeh sneered. He stared straight at the guards. He unsheathed his sword and locked it to his grip using the sword's ability to become an extension of his hand. In the dim light of the cavern, the sword radiated a purple hue. "Care to rethink who will soon be dead?"

The guards backed off slightly.

"Bah," said the lead guard. He opened fire. The others followed suit. Laser beams shot toward Xi'heeh only to disappear as they neared him. "Shoot her instead."

The guards changed direction, shooting La'prell.

She grimaced, then realized that the beams weren't hitting her.

"All five swords are here today," Xi'heeh told no one in particular. "Whatever you have going on here is done." He and the ten G'mone guards disappeared.

The K'reelian guards glanced around looking for their companions. They only saw a very frightened La'prell.

"Shoot her again," one of the K'reelian guards yelled. Then he faceplanted on the ground.

A few other K'reelians collapsed. The others watched them; terror growing on their faces.

Xi'heeh returned to the exact spot he had left from. "It should not be too long for the rest of you before your companions hit the ground from about ten thousand feet above the mountain."

Only a couple of K'reelians were still alive by the time Xi'heeh finished talking. Those two didn't live much longer.

La'prell looked at the bodies. "What are we going to do with them? We cannot leave them there. Someone will find them. They will likely be missed soon too."

Xi'heeh knelt next to La'prell who hadn't had time to get off the ground. "I do not care. The first thing I want you to know is that I do not believe what they first said. I choose to believe you as I should have from the beginning."

She gave him a big smile and a quick hug. "Thank you."

"Now, about these guys." Xi'heeh stood up. He disappeared again, this time with the ten K'reelian bodies. In a moment he returned. "Someday maybe someone will climb this mountain and think that ten men turned purple after being frozen in the snow for so long."

La'prell laughed, then stopped. Her forehead wrinkled. "Wait, Erin said she put a shield on us that made us invisible to others. Why could they see us? Can they see the others?"

Xi'heeh's face turned serious. *Calling Bart and Erin, can you hear me?*

Yes, Bart replied. *Hey, this thought communication thing works great.*

I think something went wrong with Erin's invisibility shield. We encountered a group of guards, and they could see us.

I thought I did it right. It seemed to work earlier when that first pair of guards came to replace the others.

Could it be possible that they are canceling our powers again? Bart asked.

No, Xi'heeh surmised. *I have been able to transport, and the other shield protected La'prell as expected. This may be a special unit of my people. They might have special abilities. They would not have told us grunts about stuff like this.*

I think we better be careful and assume they can see us whether I put the shield on right or not.

Agreed, said Xi'heeh. *I'll let Matt and Steve know to beware. End communication.* He turned to La'prell.

"Well, what did they say?" La'prell asked.

"You could not hear them?"

"No, you did not include me in your conversation. I could tell you were in thought, so I did not bother you."

Xi'heeh sighed. "I should have thought of that. We need to assume that they can see us. Hang on." Xi'heeh turned to the wall. *Calling Matt, Steve, and Callie. Come in.*

We're here, man, Steve said. *Hey, this is cool. Over. Roger. Ten-four.*

Quiet, Xi'heeh admonished. *I just talked with Erin and Bart. We think that the invisible shields that Erin put on us have either worn off or that the G'mone and K'reelians can see us. La'prell and I just had an encounter with a group of guards. The protective shield worked for La'prell, but they could see us. Assume that the invisibility shield did not work and that you are visible to them.*

Right, Matt said. *Thanks for the heads up. Oh, right, yeah, that ability of her sword only works if she's in the vicinity of where the invisibility shield is.*

Xi'heeh nodded at the empty air as if they could see him agree with them. *End communication.*

Xi'heeh grabbed La'prell's hand. "Come on. We better get moving." He led her down the passageway.

CHAPTER XVI

"Dowse the light if what Xi'heeh told us is true." Callie held a hand up. "Stop. I hear something."

Matt shook his hand to extinguish the flame on his finger. The cavern went completely dark. "I can't see."

"Over here and be quiet." Callie tried to lead them toward her with her voice.

"Hey, watch it." Matt tried to be as quiet as possible.

"Well," Callie said, "if you don't come over, I have to pull you over, so I did."

Calling Matt and Steve. Callie opened a line of communication. *Can you hear me?* She continued in thought.

Yeah, we can, Steve thought back.

Good, we're safer if we can still communicate but not be heard by anyone passing by. Now stay out of sight, and do not communicate any other way until it's safe.

I can't see anything.

It's okay, Steve, I can see fine. I've been in my old cave for a while now. I've developed a sharper eye. Everyone be quiet.

They stood with their backs against the wall. Nothing happened for about five minutes.

Are you sure someone is coming? Matt thought to the others.

Laughter echoed down the passageway followed by footsteps. They couldn't tell how many were coming along the tunnel, but there had to be several of them.

The footsteps edged closer. Then they stopped.

"Here we are gentlemen," said a voice.

I still can't see anything, Steve thought to Matt and Callie.

I can. Callie stared down the hallway. *They're close to us.*

"What's the matter?" said another voice.

Sniffing noises came from the direction of the newcomers. "I smell something or someone."

A light flashed on. One of the men inched away from the group. "Get inside."

Get as close to the wall as you can, Callie commanded.

If I got any closer, Steve said, *I'd be in the wall.*

A door opened. A light showed out. Five men ducked inside, closing the door behind them. From the silhouette of the doorway, two men turned in the direction of Matt, Steve, and Callie. A light swept down the passage.

I'm going invisible, Steve said.

The light swept closer to the walls. This time it caught a shadow. The beam focused on the wall and Matt and Callie stood illuminated.

The man without the light raised and fired a laser rifle in the same movement. His muscles tensed as he started to rush them. Then he made a muffled grunt and fell to the floor.

The light fell to the floor and the other man lay on the ground next to the one with the rifle. With a crunch, the light went out.

"I don't get it." Steve turned visible and rubbed his head. "They just die when the other one does. What good does that do them?"

"It's because you are catching them off guard at the moment," Callie said. "If they knew you were here, you'd have had a tougher time with them. The longer we can keep hidden, the better. We need to see what's in that room, but we need to keep the surprise factor too. We shouldn't speak out loud like this either for now."

"Sorry," Steve whispered. "It's a little hard to remember we don't have to speak."

Matt bopped him in the head, ruffling his hair.

"Hey, what was that for?"

Shh. Matt thought. *Don't keep talking out loud once someone points out to you that you're talking out loud.*

"Oh, right, oops. Sorry."

Matt sighed.

Callie led them toward the door. She leaned against the wall on the right. She raised her laser pistol. *Steve, I can't see you.*

I turned invisible again, but I'm right in front of the door.

Matt lit a finger. *Sorry, I need a little light to get my bearings.* He was on the left side of the door. *There's no door handle, how do we get in?*

There's a small panel on your side, Callie thought. *It uses handprint recognition.*

You know a lot about this place, Steve said.

I was here for a while, remember. I didn't spend all my time with the K'reelian women. I've scouted around here some. They never knew I was here.

Hey, Matt interrupted. *What about one of those dead guys?*

I got it, Steve said.

In a moment, a body floated through the air. Its hand rose and pressed the panel.

Extinguish your light, now! Callie was almost yelling the thought.

Matt complied as the door slid open. A light appeared from within. The room had been fashioned from the side of the mountain wall, so it wasn't excessively big. A row of computer terminals lined a table against a wall just inside the entrance. A few empty chairs sat in front of the table. A view screen stretched across the wall above the terminals. An armada of spaceships floated in pitch black emptiness on the screen. In the middle of the room sat a small conference table. Eight chairs sat around the table. Only five of those were filled. There were three K'reelians, all clad in their signature purple jumpsuits, and two G'mone, dressed in a baggy white shirt with a brown vest and brown cargo pants, sitting at the table.

"I don't believe it," Matt's jaw was slightly open and his eyes a bit wide as he entered the room. "J'ard. How are you here?"

One of the men at the table looked over. "Do I know you? And more importantly, how did you get in here?"

Before anyone could do anything, the screen flickered, and an image appeared. "Come in Earth Base One, are you ready?"

Matt stared at the screen. His mouth dropped further, and his eyes widened. "Reginald, it can't be."

"We were ready," J'ard said, "but this person just interrupted our meeting."

Callie stepped in beside Matt. She aimed her laser pistol at the men.

"Correction," said J'ard, "these people just interrupted us. Again, who are you, and how did you get here."

The others at the table stood up and raised their laser pistols, pointing them at Matt and Callie.

Matt closed his mouth. He turned back to J'ard. "You don't know me?"

"I've already made that pretty clear; I think."

"Interesting. I know that a companion of mine shot you dead."

J'ard raised an eyebrow. "Hm? I appear to be fine, thank you."

Maybe it's because of Erin's ability to not remember you, Steve thought.

Matt drew Timeline. The four men standing gasped slightly. "Now do you remember?"

"I have never met you, but I can see that you are one of the sword holders."

"Uh, J'ard," Reginald began, "I should explain why he thinks you're dead. Your clones were not successful in their attempt to eliminate the swords."

"You should have told me that sooner." J'ard glared at the screen.

"For some reason, I did not remember him until I saw his sword," Reginald replied. "Now I remember working with him, but I can't think of his name. This will only complicate our plans slightly."

Matt looked at Reginald. "I don't think there's anything that you can do to stop us from stopping you."

"You didn't just say that, did you? That is so cliché."

"Yeah, well, snappy comebacks aren't my thing."

"Indeed. We shall see who stops who."

"Whom," Matt said.

"What?" Reginald looked bewildered.

"Whom. We shall see who stops whom. Get it right."

"Whatever." Reginald made an annoying click with his tongue. "We shall see who stops whom. I certainly won't be losing any sleep over it. We have some tricks up our sleeves. Our forces will be more than a match for the measly planetary defenses of Earth. The sword holders can do little to stop us, except for small pockets of us at a time. And if you do that, we'll destroy massive amounts of other people in the places you can't be."

"If they get that far, Reginald." J'ard waved a hand.

"Shoot them."

One G'mone fired and then fell to the ground. His K'reelian companion flopped onto the table. J'ard and the other two looked around. The other K'reelian flew through the room and smashed against the rock wall at the back of the room. The other G'mone turned around looking for whatever made his symbiont crash into the wall.

Matt pulled a strand of rope out of his pocket and flung it at the G'mone soldier. It wrapped around his hands and legs, binding him tightly.

J'ard pushed his chair back. He ran straight at Matt but tripped as he cleared the table.

"Oops." Steve reappeared. "Did you fall?"

Matt tossed a rope at J'ard, and it began to tie him up.

The K'reelian soldier groaned.

"I better tie him up too." Matt threw a rope at the soldier. It wrapped around his arms and legs.

Steve walked over to the K'reelian and dragged him over to the table. He sat him in a chair. He picked up J'ard and the G'mone soldier, placing them in chairs next to their companion. "What do we do with these guys now?"

"Let me kill them." Callie moved toward the table.

Steve stepped between her and J'ard. He grabbed her arm. "Hey, don't. I know what they did to your people, but that's not a good answer."

"What do you mean, her people?" J'ard tried to stand up. "We haven't done anything to anyone on Earth yet."

"Show him." Steve stepped aside.

"Wait!" Matt yelled. "He doesn't know. Let's not give him any reason to find out either. It might be an advantage for us at some point."

"If you're hoping that my people will help you," Callie said, "I wouldn't bet on it."

Matt nodded. "I understand, and I'll give you that argument, but who knows? Let's leave them for now and get out of here. We have bigger things to do here."

"Hey, how about we contact Xi'heeh and have him put these guys in that 'bag' of his? I bet he could do that."

First, Matt scowled at Steve, then he raised an eyebrow. "That could be funny. I wonder where they would go?"

"Excuse me, gentlemen," Reginald spoke from the screen. "I think you've forgotten that I'm here, and I can see and hear everything you've done so far. You may have J'ard tied up and think that no one will know you're here, but you are mistaken."

Alarms blared outside the room.

"Your veil is now gone. Our forces will deal with you soon enough."

Calling Bart and Xi'heeh, Matt said.

I am here, Bart answered.

I am here as well, Xi'heeh chimed in.

As you can tell, Matt began, *we've been discovered. We ran into two people we know here. I told you about one of them I met when I got taken back to save B'ajj. J'ard is alive. The other is an old friend of ours,*

Reginald. J'ard had a clone. Apparently, the real J'ard is with us in this facility. It appears to be an advanced force. It sounds like there could be more of these posts all over Earth too.

We need to find that out," said Xi'heeh.

We're in a control room of some kind. I wish Xi'heeh could come in and go through the equipment to see if there is some information about other locations. We need to slow them down.

Callie can do it, Xi'heeh offered. *Her people know our technology.*

Excellent, I'll get her on that. Watch yourselves. End communication.

"Callie, Xi'heeh says you can try to find out if there are other outposts across the world. He thinks you can use their computers to track that."

Callie nodded. "I'll try." She ran to the console and started punching keys. "I need someone's hand over here for access. It works like the door."

Steve picked up J'ard. "That'd be you, I'd guess." He started to bring him over to the panel, but J'ard struggled more than Steve was prepared for, causing him to momentarily lose his grip. J'ard tried to stand but being tied up he was unable to and fell over. Steve picked him up, holding him tighter. J'ard continued to struggle, this time to no avail. When they reached the console, Steve grabbed J'ard's right hand. J'ard made another attempt to break free.

Matt came over to help. "You K'reelians are strong. Not strong enough though."

With Matt helping to hold J'ard, Steve was able to place J'ard's hand on the reader.

Callie tried the panel again. "There we go. Give me a few minutes to see what I can find."

Steve dragged J'ard back to the table. J'ard went limp as they passed the G'mone soldier.

"Thanks," Steve said, "that makes it easier to pull you over here."

J'ard's arms lay at his sides. The G'mone soldier picked up his feet and touched a button on J'ard's jumpsuit. J'ard disappeared.

Without J'ard's weight, Steve lost his balance, tumbling onto the chair he was going to put J'ard in. "Hey, where did he go?"

The soldiers stared straight ahead.

"You aren't getting an answer from them," Matt said. "Callie, hurry. Steve and I will keep an eye open for any trouble."

"You stay inside." Steve disappeared. The door crumpled. "I'll stand outside and stop anyone that might attempt to get in."

***

The room was dimly lit. A bed sat against a stone wall of the inside of a cavern chamber. A chair rested next to the bed. A purple jumpsuit lay jumbled on top. A small wooden chest adorned the foot of the bed. Another jumpsuit was draped across it. A dresser lay beyond the chest with a pathway between them. In the bed, from under the covers, came a giggle. Then an alarm boomed. The cover flew off the bed.

"What was that?" said a man.

"Oh no." A K'reelian woman shot out of the bed. "Get dressed, now!" She flung the jumpsuit on the chair at the man and then reached for the jumpsuit on the chest.

The man, also a K'reelian, scurried out into the living area. It was another small cavern room with a sofa and a reclining chair. He grabbed his laser pistol from the sofa as the K'reelian woman came into the room. "I'll see you another time." He kissed her, then reached for the panel to open the door.

"Wait!" The woman reached for the panel. "Your print shouldn't be in the logs, remember?"

Before either of them could touch the panel, J'ard popped into the room. He lay on the floor with his hands and legs tied up.

The woman shrieked.

J'ard rolled over. "P'thos, thank goodness you are here. Untie me."

P'thos knelt beside J'ard, setting the gun beside them, and attempted to untie him. The bands wouldn't budge. "Gri'nel, run to the other room and find a knife."

The woman ran into another room. In a few moments, she returned with a huge knife. She handed it to P'thos.

He cut the strands. It wasn't easy, but he managed to finally loosen the rope enough that J'ard was freed.

"Thanks," J'ard stood up. "Wait, why are you here, P'thos?"

"I was in the area and came to check on Gri'nel when the alarms sounded."

"Ah yes, thank you for doing that. You are a loyal friend. We are under attack. I need you to go to the central command center where the flying machines are. Get them in the air."

P'thos nodded. "Yes, sir." He turned to leave.

"Oh, P'thos." J'ard reached down for the gun P'thos set down.

P'thos turned back toward J'ard.

"You might need this." He extended his hand with the firearm.

"Yes, thank you." P'thos stepped toward J'ard to accept it.

"By the way, you forgot to zip your jumpsuit all the way." J'ard quickly shifted the weapon in his hand, aimed at P'thos, and fired.

P'thos dropped to the floor, eyes frozen with the fear that last displayed upon them.

J'ard turned to Gri'nel. His eyes blazed. "Don't ever do that again. If we were not under attack, I would deal with you now. Maybe this will give me some time to cool down." He put his hand on the panel and rushed out the door.

Gri'nel knelt on the floor and cradled P'thos' head in her lap.

CHAPTER XVII

Callie's fingers flew across the keyboard. Search results flickered on the screen. She paused for a moment. Her head moved closer to the screen then pulled back. "I have the information on the number of bases. There are five others around the world. I don't know how to save the information anywhere. I'll just have to remember the names of the places. It also says that there is a self-destruct system for this cave in case their mission becomes compromised."

Matt looked at the data. "I have an online storage system. Do they have access to the Earth's systems? If we can get that information there, you won't have to remember it."

Callie clicked a few more keys. "I think so. Here, you're in, save this text to it."

Matt took over the keyboard. He accessed his storage and copied the text file to it. "There, that's done. Okay, how do we set the destruct system now?"

"There're two options. There's an immediate option and one with a twenty-minute countdown. There's a red button and a blue button on this panel. Each one will initiate one of the options. It doesn't say which is which, so I don't know which button it is."

Laser blasts resonated in the corridor.

Matt turned to listen. "Sounds like we don't have time to figure it out. We need the extra time so we can get you, Isaiah, and La'prell out of here. If you all weren't here, I'd just push them both." Matt reached for the blue button and pushed it.

Callie's face flushed. A countdown began on the screen. "How did you know which button to push?"

Matt smiled. "You never press the red button. Everyone knows that. Let's go." He pulled out his sword and sealed it to his hand.

They reached the door. Blasts from two invisible sources directed toward the corridor continuously emanated from just outside the doorway. Occasionally a blast would come toward the door but fade away when it reached it. Bodies lay scattered across the floor.

"That must be Steve stationed in the doorway." Matt edged closer. "That you, S'mores?"

Yeah, although, I probably shouldn't answer you for that one. Steve's thought came into both Matt's and Callie's minds. *We haven't closed our conversation yet, so I'm communicating this way. I have them pinned down. They don't know where I'm shooting from.*

We started a self-destruct, Matt thought back. *We*

have twenty minutes. We need to get out.

Well, okay then, Steve thought. *Matt, come on out and let's finish these guys in the hall. Callie can shoot them from behind us.*

Right. Matt moved into the doorway. *Let's end this conversation and start one with everyone. End communication.*

Matt exited into the cave hall. With a visible target, the soldiers began to fire more intently. But the beams just dissipated as they reached their targets.

"Hand-to-hand combat," yelled a G'mone soldier as he charged forward.

The others followed him. Laser blasts burst around them as they attacked. Many fell before they made any progress.

"Wow, Callie," Steve said from somewhere beside them, "for a species that claims to not defend themselves, you sure are a good shot."

"My parents always felt we should have defended ourselves. No one listened to them, and this is what our lives have become. We live on another planet far from home, hiding in some mountains. I choose to do something about it and for that, I am ostracized. But I am better for trying. That's the real reason my people kicked me out when I chose to help you. It was just an excuse to do what they always wanted to do. You and your friends are all I have now." A couple of blasts hit Callie. She flinched. "Remind me to thank Erin for the shield."

More G'mone and K'reelian soldiers piled into the hallway from both directions.

"They just keep coming," said Matt. "We came from that way, so we know what's there. We want to go the other way." Matt raised his arm not holding his sword and pointed his fist in the direction they came from. He laid down a line of fire along the ground, up the side of the cave, across the roof, and down the other side. He repeated the motion, doubling the force of the flames. "That should burn for a while and keep anyone from crossing through there. Let's clear a path the other way."

Using his arm like a flame thrower, he blasted his way down the corridor. Steve and Callie followed shooting at anyone that dared not move.

"Again, I'm thankful for Erin's shielding." Callie stopped firing. "Looks like they're retreating. Nice to see they do that occasionally. I'm not sure many people have been able to make them do that."

"It looks like we cleared the hall of soldiers," Matt said. "Time to check on the others." *Calling Bart, Erin, Isaiah, Steve, Callie, Xi'heeh, and La'prell. Everyone there?*

What do you need? Bart's thought came through. *We are a little busy.*

We wanted to let you know there's a self-destruct system initiated. There are probably about fifteen minutes left before this place blows.

Thank you for the warning. We noticed the alarms. We wondered what had happened. So much for stealth.

Yeah, sorry about that. We had a little trouble getting some intel, but we have some news for later. Erin how much longer will your shields last?

I'd say about fifteen minutes. I can't refresh them unless I'm with you. I will reinforce Isaiah's, but that's it for now. It'll be close for Callie and La'prell unless they can get to us.

I was going to thank you for the shielding, Callie interjected. *You've saved my life a few times over already with that. I hope you get a chance to add to that.*

Can we get closer together so that I can transport everyone out? Xi'heeh asked.

We can see the main hall from where we are, Bart thought. *It is huge. It appears to be the main hanger for their helicopters. There are six in here, but there is room for many more. There may be an assembly line clear to the back of the cavern where they could make new ones, but that is not running right now.*

We just entered the cavern you are in. La'prell and I are to your right.

I see you. La'prell, your shield is extended.

Thank you.

Callie, you need to get to the main chamber quickly so I can add to yours.

That's the plan. Callie thought. *We don't know how far away we are though. We have encountered many soldiers on the way. They are slowing us down.*

We will not be able to get to you either, Bart informed them. *We are pretty much pinned down here. There are too many soldiers for us to get through fast enough.*

I can tell where you are, Matt thought. *We're on our*

way to your location. I'd say we're about one hundred yards from you, but we have a bunch of soldiers between us. Keep this line open. We'll see you in a bit.

"I guess I don't need to be invisible anymore." Steve appeared beside them sword in hand. "Callie, if it comes to it, grab my hand before the place explodes. I can extend my invulnerability to others if we are touching."

***

J'ard ran down the corridor. The stony walls glistened with wetness as he rushed past. A voice resonated through the hallway.

"Self-destruct initiated. Begin evacuation."

J'ard halted. He cursed in K'reelian. He pressed the button on his jumpsuit and disappeared.

He reappeared back inside his room. Gri'nel still sat next to P'thos' body. Her head was buried in his chest, and she was crying.

"Get up." J'ard tried to pry her away from P'thos. She resisted. "If I did not love you so much, you would be with him right now."

She raised her head. Tears turned to anger. "If you loved me, you would have spent more time with me. He made time for me."

"How long has this been going on?"

"What do you really care?"

J'ard scoffed. "Come on, let's go." He started to drag her to the door. "The self-destruct has been initiated. We need to leave."

"I want to stay with P'thos and die so I can be with him again."

J'ard froze. He stared down at her. She returned his gaze defiantly. Then he shook his head. "No, you are coming with me."

He picked her up, carrying her to the door.

She grabbed the weapon at his side and fired.

J'ard's eyes opened wide with shock. He looked down in his arms, then dropped her to the ground. She lay lifeless on the ground. Embers from her jumpsuit smoldered and faded until they were extinguished. A thin line of smoke rose off the fabric, dissipating into the air.

He bellowed a primal scream as he raced back out the door. He ran down the corridor faster than before. He didn't stop running until he reached the grand chamber where the helicopters sat waiting. "You." He pointed to the nearest K'reelian soldier. "Take your symbiont and ready the closest flying machine. We are leaving."

The soldier nodded and ran off followed by his companion.

J'ard surveyed the grand chamber. Soldiers were amassing themselves around the edges and all around the other helicopters.

"Time for evacuation protocol," he roared. Then he caught sight of Bart and Erin near the middle of the cavern. They swung their swords ferociously. J'ard reached for his laser and then realized where it was.

A soldier rushed by.

"Give me your weapon." J'ard held out his hand.

The soldier looked reluctant, so J'ard snatched it from his hands. He ran toward Bart and began firing. Nothing happened. The beams disappeared as they neared Bart.

J'ard stopped, realizing there was no way to harm one of the sword holders in this fashion. He turned to the helicopter he'd asked the soldiers to warm up. As he reached the aircraft, he barked out some instructions and ducked inside.

Some soldiers moved away from the machine and went over to some computer consoles. They flicked a few switches and began to type across some form of keyboard. The remaining helicopters whirred into motion, with the blades beginning their rotation. In moments, the helicopters lifted slightly off the ground.

J'ard's helicopter hovered down the main passageway. In moments, it was outside.

***

Steve, Matt, and Callie moved down their passage and came to a cross path much larger than the one they had just come through.

"Which way do we go?" asked Steve.

Matt and Callie shook their heads.

"So," Steve said, "none of us know which way to go."

A wind began to pick up from the passage to their left.

"That must be the way to the outside," said Matt. "I bet we need to go the other way."

"That doesn't seem right," said Callie. "It feels like the other direction is out."

"Can't argue with the wind though," Steve agreed.

Callie tilted her head, listening to something. "Quick, back into our side tunnel."

They all jumped back as quickly as they could. A helicopter, almost imperceptible to the ear, flew from the direction the wind was coming.

"Looks like Callie was right," said Steve. "The helicopter was producing that wind, not outside. Let's go the way it came from."

They ran to the left. Not far ahead they saw the entrance to the grand chamber. As they entered, the other helicopters opened fire in the grand chamber. They fired at Bart and Erin. A couple caught sight of Xi'heeh and La'prell at another entrance to the chamber and began to fire at them. After a massive display of firepower, the helicopters stopped their bombardment. When the dust cleared, Bart and Erin, and Xi'heeh and La'prell stood their ground.

"That is not going to work," Bart yelled.

The helicopter nearest to him turned toward him, bearing down on him. It knocked into him, but Bart didn't budge.

Erin sliced at the landing gear. Her sword bounced off. "That shouldn't happen, should it?"

"I would not have expected it," Bart said. "I have cut many metal things with mine. I have not found anything that could stop it yet."

"I guess we'd better find another way to stop these then." Erin sheathed her sword. "I'm going to put a barrier over the main entrance so that they can't get out." Even though she didn't need to, she waved a hand at the entrance. Then she grabbed for the side door panel and yanked. Nothing happened. "Okay, that's not fair. You have super strength; I don't appear to."

"Yes, you do," Bart said. "It is part of the swords. It is something we all have." He tried tugging on the other side door. It didn't budge either. "These helicopters appear to be indestructible, even to us. Since you have them sealed in here, we need to leave." *Matt, Steve, Callie, where are you currently?*

"Right behind you in the main entrance," Steve yelled.

Bart whipped around to see them standing in the opening.

At the same moment, a voice began counting down from ten seconds over some loudspeakers. Just about every face in the grand chambers had the same shocked expression.

We need to get out now, Bart thought to the others.

I see everyone except Isaiah, Xi'heeh informed them.

I've been in the back taking out people. I'll be over by you in two seconds. When I get there, go.

Good, because we only have five left. No one move, I have everyone else.

"Five... four... three..."

"Go," yelled Isaiah.

An explosion rocked the mountainside. Debris flew in all directions. The top of the mountain collapsed. The tunnel system disappeared, crushing all that remained inside.

***

Xi'heeh reappeared at Karez Kalay. Everyone was

with him.

"Why here?" Bart asked.

"It was the first place I thought of. I had to go fast."

Callie collapsed.

"Callie!" Erin screamed.

Matt dropped to her side. He and Steve had been standing next to her in the cavern and were still beside her after they were transported. Matt put his hands on her cheeks. "Come on, come on. Be human like you said."

She didn't move.

Matt moved one hand to her forehead. "Amazing. I know you're in there. I can feel you. Wake up."

Erin covered her mouth. "I forgot to reinforce her shielding. I killed her!"

Callie lay still, almost like she was in stasis. Without opening her eyes, she responded. "No, you didn't kill me. I'm just lying here taking in the moment." After a few seconds, she coughed and rolled to her side.

Steve fell to his knees beside her.

Matt stood up. "She'll be fine now. It's incredible. She is totally human as she's said. I don't sense any alien in her, but she can still shape-shift." Erin ran to sit beside Steve. "Oh Callie, I'm so sorry. I forgot to reinforce your shield in the confusion."

Callie sat up. "It's all right. I'm fine. I don't think I've ever felt better. What did you do, Matt?"

"One of my abilities is to heal people," Matt explained. "I didn't know if you'd be human like you said, so I may have tried to heal more than necessary. You are completely human in this form."

"Yes, I know I am. I told you I was." She shifted into her K'reelian form. "And in this form, I am completely K'reelian."

Karez came running out. "Why did you bring these K'reelian women here. Get them out of here, now!"

Everyone laughed. Callie switched back to her Kutarian form. "Maybe I'm welcome in this form?" She switched back into Callie. "But this is my form now. I am no one as a Kutarian, but I am someone as Callie."

Karez didn't say anything else.

"We need to get back to Isaiah's lab," Bart said. "We need to figure out our next move."

"What about that helicopter that escaped?" Steve asked. "I could see three life essences leaving within it. I've never sensed anyone in one before. I'd almost say that one of them was that J'ard guy that Matt met before. I could follow them with Casey, but he's not here."

Bart nodded. "I agree. You should follow them."

"I will be right back." Xi'heeh disappeared. In a moment, he returned with Casey. "Here is your vehicle."

"Excellent, thanks." Steve patted Casey. "How are you, old man?"

"Really?" Casey said. "Old man?"

"Okay." Bart raised a hand. "Attention here please. Steve, take Callie and Matt. Find out where the helicopter went. We will end communication on our old conversation. Start a new one if you need us."

"Got it." Steve jumped into Casey's driver's seat.

"Callie found that there are five more advanced K'reelian, G'mone locations across the planet." Matt opened the back door on the driver's side. "I have a file with those locations on my online storage system. I'll access that in Casey and send you a copy or let you know where other places are or something. I have a feeling that J'ard is heading to one of these other places. We'll let you know where we end up too."

Bart nodded. "We will take a look at what you send us."

Matt sat down in the back and closed the door.

Callie looked at Casey. "What am I supposed to do with this thing?"

"I am a car, not a thing." Casey opened his front passenger door. "You sit in me, and I'll take you places."

Callie slowly walked around to the other side.

"It's perfectly fine," said Casey. "Steve and I have already communicated about you. He told me about you and that you haven't seen many things from Earth. You are in for a big learning curve."

"I like you." Callie rubbed along the top of the door frame. "Are all cars like you?"

"Oh my, no." Casey chuckled as Callie sat down. "I'm one of Steve's abilities from the sword." Casey shut his door and powered up. He lifted off, banked to his right, and flew back toward the mountain to start their tracking.

Xi'heeh and the others disappeared, leaving Karez standing alone.

CHAPTER XVIII

Casey maneuvered into position near the mountain Steve directed him to. The top of the mountain had collapsed. Debris cluttered the ground. Dust particles lingered in the air. Evidence of an avalanche lay along the sides down to the bottom of the mountain. Splintered trees infested the ravaged landscape.

"Wow," said Casey. "You guys made a mess."

"Not by choice," Steve answered. "We couldn't let them keep that post open. Plus, there are five more we need to shut down. I'm picking up the life essence of the three that escaped. They're heading southeast."

"This is a very nice machine." Callie rubbed a finger across Casey's dashboard.

"Careful," Steve cautioned. "You wouldn't want to press anything accidentally."

"She is fine," Casey said. "She cannot do any damage

to me."

"We had machines on Kutara, but nothing like this."

Steve patted the steering wheel. "There isn't any other machine like this one. Casey and I have a bond too. He knows what I know and vice versa, so we share a lot. While I'm tracking the life force of these three beings, he can sense them as well. So, I don't have to lead him to them."

"Based on the speed their life forces are moving, I cannot quite match them. My top speed is one hundred fifty miles per hour. They appear to be going about one hundred seventy-five. Wherever they are traveling to, it'll take us a little longer to get there."

"That's too bad," Matt chimed in. "They could have time to prepare for us."

"I doubt they think we can follow them." Steve looked over his shoulder to reply directly to Matt. "I'm detecting an attempt to mask their trail, but it's not working. They seem to know about our sword's powers, but this attempt to stop my ability doesn't do what they meant it to do."

"We have no idea where they're going either, do we?" Matt added.

"Only the general direction that we're currently moving in," said Steve. "And that doesn't include any course change."

"Since we have some extra time," Casey said, "I have been analyzing what I've discovered about the helicopters from all our past encounters. I believe that they could damage me if they were to hit my exterior. I have been running calculations that will allow me to enhance myself with a defensive shield. I am implementing those upgrades as we fly."

"Sounds good," Steve said.

Callie yawned.

"Hey, Callie, you should try to get some sleep," Steve suggested. "You too, Matt. We don't know how long this is going to take to track them to where they're going."

Callie looked at him. "What about you? Can Casey fly without you?"

"Yes, he can, but he can't follow the trail unless I'm awake. That's the sword's power, and not his."

"Working..." Casey started. "There, done. Now it is. I have made an upgrade to that as well."

"How were you able to do that?" Steve seemed genuinely surprised.

"You gave me the ability to adapt to any situation when you created me. By that, I am an extension of your sword. That ended up being an easier update than the shielding is proving to be."

"But why didn't you do this before then? When we went looking for my sister, Michele, you said it was the sword's power."

"We are both more adept with our abilities now," Casey said. "I was still figuring things out myself. I have grown since then and evaluated what needed to be done. It was easy when I applied the right calculations. But you and the sword must be with me. I cannot randomly follow people on my own."

"Well, then." Steve looked over at Callie. She was

curled up and already asleep. She was incredibly beautiful in her human form. She knew how to appeal to him that was certain. And she must have trusted him to fall asleep so quickly. Without a certain comfort level, one does not simply fall asleep around others. He wanted to be able to have the same comfort level, but he also had mixed feelings. Talk about people coming from two different worlds. This gave new meaning to that phrase for him. It was literally two different worlds.

"So," he turned to talk to Matt. Matt was out too. "Well, so much for asking him what he thought of Callie."

"She is a fine person," Casey answered.

"I think I know that. But we don't know everything there is to know about her."

"We share thoughts, remember. I know exactly who she is, what she is, where she comes from, and what she's already done for all of us."

Steve grasped the steering wheel as if that helped Casey fly better.

"I have scanned her. I scan everyone that enters my interior. She is genuine. She is human right now. Matt said so when she collapsed earlier. I think you know that. Maybe you should get some sleep. We don't know how long this will take. Sleep might give your subconscious some time to process your thoughts."

"Are you absolutely certain you can still follow their trail?"

"Yes, but would you like to test?"

Steve nodded.

"Good thing I can sense you nodding."

"Fine, I can see their trail for about the equivalent of two city blocks. I'll close my eyes for twenty seconds and see if we're still on track. That should be sufficient."

Steve closed his eyes and counted silently. After the twenty seconds were up, he opened his eyes. Sure enough, the trail still blazed before him. "That worked. Thanks, Casey. It's always nice to get some rest." He closed his eyes again, and this time they didn't reopen.

***

Ian sat on the floor inside the chamber leaning against the door in front of the chair. He looked exhausted.

"If you hadn't spent all your energy on trying to force the door open all night long, then maybe you wouldn't be so tired. The sun is just coming up, and you haven't slept much." Sha'rell stood up. She stretched her arms over her head. "You made me tired just watching you, and I bet your shoulder hurts."

She walked over to the table where the toy bird was still bobbing up and down. She watched it. "It's amazing what some people think is interesting." She looked down the row between the tables and saw a door at the end. "I might as well look around. Nothing better to do."

The door was an ordinary solid panel of wood painted white and smooth with no ornate designs. She reached for the knob and turned it. The latch clicked, and the door opened with a faint squeak. She peeked inside. It was dark, but she thought she could make out more of the chambers that Erin had been in and now held Ian. She wasn't sure, but she thought there were four of them, and that someone might be in them.

"Get out of there," Isaiah yelled.

The unexpected arrival of Isaiah made Sha'rell jump. She leaped from the doorway back into the main room.

Isaiah sped across the room, slamming the door with force.

"I saw other chambers in there. I think there's someone in them."

"Nonsense." Isaiah leaned against the door. No one was getting past him. "There are chambers, but no one is in them. They're empty like the other three in this room. Those were all failed attempts at making a chamber like the one that eventually worked for Erin."

Sha'rell didn't look like she believed him, but she turned away from the door and back toward the chamber that Ian was in.

Bart, Erin, and Xi'heeh stood next to the chamber.

"How is our friend?" Bart asked.

Sha'rell didn't answer right away. She was still thinking about those other containers. "He is fine," she finally said. She looked around. "Where is Matt?"

Erin traced a finger across the receptacle holding Ian. "He and Steve are following one of the helicopters. We haven't heard from them yet. You could chat with him through your mind and check in on them if you'd like."

Sha'rell stared blankly at her.

"It is one of my new abilities," Xi'heeh said. He explained it to her.

Sha'rell brightened up.

"And I have just given you the ability to communicate with any of us as well." Xi'heeh then gave her a short tutorial on how to use the new ability.

Calling Matt, Sha'rell thought. There was silence. "It's not working. He isn't responding."

Xi'heeh tried. "Ah, I believe he is asleep. There is no way for him to reply while asleep."

Erin knelt next to the place that had been her home for so long. She looked at Ian. "Sad, isn't it? He doesn't even know he's a clone."

"Are you sure he's a clone?" Bart asked.

She looked up at Bart. "Quite sure. From the looks of things, he's probably about to expire too." She turned to Sha'rell. "Did he overexert himself during the night?"

She nodded.

"I thought so. He won't be of any use to us anymore. I'm going to let him out so he can die outside the glass. That's no place for anyone to die." She opened the latch.

Ian looked up at her. "Thank you," he breathed. "Promise me that you'll not let this President ruin our entire world." He tried to stand but couldn't get his footing.

Erin held out her hand. "I'll help you."

He grasped her hand. "I've always loved you my little pumpkin." She helped him to his feet. He took one step outside the container and collapsed to the ground.

Erin turned away. She looked at Bart, tears in her eyes. "My daddy always called me that. It was better than princess. I'm glad he never called me that. He wasn't my daddy, but he knew things my daddy knew."

"It will be okay," was all Bart could say. He wanted to hold her but wasn't sure it was a good idea.

"Yeah, it's okay." Erin wasn't psychic, but she knew the look Bart was giving her. She walked over to him. "I know I shouldn't, but I need someone right now to just hold me. God, my life is messed up, isn't it?" She leaned into Bart's arms.

He held her gingerly. "No, your life is just beginning. You have another chance to make it what you want."

"I hate to break this up," Xi'heeh said, "but we need to get working on where those other alien hideouts are."

Erin broke away from Bart. "Sorry," she said. "I keep doing that to you, don't I?"

"I am first and foremost your friend. Always and forever. If you need me, I will be there for you. If you do not, I will give you space."

She nodded. "I know, but I wish you weren't so nice all the time."

He smiled and shook his head. "Okay everyone, what shall we do next?"

Xi'heeh spoke up. "I think we need to check on Madam President and see what she is up to."

"We need to find those other alien installations." Isaiah had been very quiet up until now.

Bart turned to Erin. "So, what is your vote on what we do next?"

"The Ian clone said to not let Madam President ruin our world. This is about more than just one country. He specifically said the entire world. I think we check on her."

"Sha'rell?" Bart looked at her. "What do you think?"

Sha'rell looked up. She hadn't been paying much attention to what they were saying. "Me? I don't have any special abilities. I shouldn't make any decisions."

Erin walked over to her and grabbed both of her hands. She squeezed them. "You are a part of us now. You may not have abilities, but we value you."

Sha'rell smiled. Her face beamed. "I think it is important to find these other K'reelian and G'mone stations, but I trust my nephew's intuition. If he felt that they were more important, he would say so. I think we should check in on the President."

Isaiah sighed. "You all never listen to me." He threw his hands in the air. "Why don't you just put me in this container, and I'll wait until everything's over."

Erin released Sha'rell's hands and went over to him. The familiar fire was in her eyes, giving her an intense aura. "I need you to be with us. I need to know that you are with us. It's important that I can trust you, do you understand?"

Meekly he lowered his head and gave a brief nod.

"Thank you. We all agree that we need to find all the other places. It's a definite thing. But I think we need to check on her too. I think a brief visit will take less time than what we'll have to expend on fighting those G'mone and K'reelians."

"Xi'heeh," Bart looked at him, "take us to the Capitol building."

He nodded and they all disappeared.

***

They reappeared at the front gate of the Capitol building. A rally of some sort appeared to be taking place. People were all around. Police and other soldiers mingled among the crowd. Everything appeared to be calm. No one appeared to have noticed their sudden entrance, however.

"Looks like something's going on, doesn't it?" Erin said. "Let me put a shield around Isaiah and Sha'rell."

"Aunt Sha'rell, you might need this." Xi'heeh reached in the air in front of him and pulled a staff out of thin air. He handed it to her.

She took it and looked it over. "What good will this do?"

"It's a laser blaster, but it's disguised as a staff. The Emori used these weapons. The first time we encountered them, we didn't know what they were. They took a bunch of us down before we knew what had happened. I suppose fortunately for me, we figured it out quickly. Plus, you can use it as a staff in close combat if needed."

A voice over a loudspeaker broke the noise of the crowd. "Citizens of the Earth," it began. "We welcome you all that have joined us in person and all that are seeing this broadcast around the world. This is a historic day for the Earth. Please welcome the leaders of some main areas around the world. We have the leaders from Great Britain, France, Germany, Italy, the European Union, Russia, China, Japan, the United States, Canada, Mexico, Brazil, Argentina, Chile, Spain, Australia, New Zealand, Saudi Arabia, Iran, Iraq, Afghanistan, Pakistan,

India, Egypt, Libya, Nigeria, Sudan, the Congo, and South Africa."

The leaders from these countries filed out onto a stage on the Capitol grounds and found their seats. The crowd applauded with mild courtesy.

The voice from the loudspeaker continued, "These of course are not all the leaders of the world, but they represent key areas. They have come before you to announce a major breakthrough in world politics. Without further ado, let me introduce President Annika Bergstrom, of the United States of America."

The President stood up and walked to a podium set in front of the stage. "My fellow citizens of Earth, news of such great importance has come to the attention of all the world leaders. There have been lengthy discussions and we have done something that no other leaders at any point in history have accomplished. It is time to share with the world what has been going on for the past five years. First, let me introduce Dr. Reginald. He was the first to discover this important information and has been leading a team of researchers gathering all the details to share with the world leaders. It is time for him to share this information with the rest of the world, and the next steps that we must take to survive."

As a murmur arose in the assembled crowd, a man with bright red hair emerged from the back of the stage where the leaders had come from.

Bart, Erin, and Isaiah watched as he came forward. Their collective jaws dropped. They looked at each other.

"It cannot be," Bart said.

"It is," said Isaiah. "It's Reginald, but they're using that as his last name."

Reginald came to the podium, and the President backed away just off to his right. "Thank you, President Bergstrom. A plot to take over the world has been uncovered," he began.

The assembled crowd split among murmuring, snickers of disbelief, and whisperings of surprise.

"It may sound a bit farfetched, but there is ample proof that this plot exists. It started with the uncovering of secret bases about five years ago and continued with recent sightings of a new, powerful, indestructible helicopter that can destroy an army within minutes. These helicopters are silent and undetectable until they are on top of you. I can see that many of you are skeptical, and that is understandable. Roll the footage."

Three-dimensional images hovered above the stage showing the assault at the Grand Canyon. It switched to the demolition of the compound where Bart, Steve, and Erin saved some hostages. Finally, images of the destruction of the three separate regimes of the army in the desert flickered onto the screens. The devastation was complete.

The grumblings of the crowd increased. No one was laughing this time.

"Why haven't these helicopters taken over already you may be asking yourself," continued Reginald. "That is a good question, but one that has a simple answer. They are waiting for their entire invading army to reach Earth."

"I do not get it," said Bart. "If the G'mone and K'reelian want to take over, why would they allow this information to get out? And if Reginald is helping them, why would he do this?"

"You do not know them as I do," said Xi'heeh. "They do not care if their opponents know they are on their way. They are so confident that no one can take them that they will announce their intent, just not when it will happen."

"Once this armada gets here," Reginald continued, "we don't stand a chance against them unless we combine all our forces."

The crowd continued to raise the level of their muttering as President Bergstrom took the podium again.

"This is why we are announcing today a new worldwide governmental organization," she said. "The time has come for us to act as one world all working together."

Many "that won't work very well" type statements could be heard throughout the crowd.

She continued undaunted, "We have taken the initial ideal of the Federation of Earth and brought it to fruition among all the leadership of the world. I have been selected as the leader of this new United Federation by a vote of all world leaders. Each of the current leaders of countries will continue to govern their respective countries but will answer to the United Federation."

The crowd grumbling grew to a roar, but not a roar of approval.

"Now is not the time for dissent," yelled President Bergstrom into the microphone.

As if on cue, three helicopters, silent and swift, descended out of the sky. Before anyone knew what was happening, they opened fire on the Capitol, demolishing it in minutes. Anyone left inside stood no chance of getting out alive. One helicopter turned toward the stage. It opened fire, hitting a few of the leaders on stage. As it continued to shell the stage, the blasts quickly began to collide with an invisible force mid-air, allowing other leaders to escape the bombardment.

The other two helicopters turned onto the crowd. They were able to get some shots off before their laser blasts also encountered the invisible force midflight. Their doors slid open revealing five sets of G'mone and K'reelian fighters. They jumped toward the crowd but stopped mid-jump right where the laser blasts stopped. They stood hovering above everyone. They aimed their laser rifles and tried to shoot the scattering crowd, but their shots wouldn't go any further than where they stood.

"I got the stage and the main section of the crowd protected at the moment," Erin said. "We need to stop those things."

"I will get the soldiers," Bart said. "Just give me some steps up to where they are."

"You got it." Erin pointed to just in front of Bart. "Go right there and head straight up. I've extended long steps up to the top so that you shouldn't fall off if you don't go straight."

Bart unsheathed his sword, molded it to his hand, and ran up the steps.

A few stunned people near them saw Bart head up the invisible stairs. They looked at Erin, Isaiah, Xi'heeh, and Sha'rell.

"Look," yelled one of them. "Those two are purple just like some of the people up there. Get them, they must be some of the same group."

Before anyone in the crowd could muster the courage to rush them, Erin placed shielding between them. Some of the braver people gained some nerve and rushed them, slamming into the invisible shield. They fell to the ground as others stopped to look at them and help them up.

"We do not need you to make things worse right now," Erin said.

"I shall return." Xi'heeh disappeared. He reappeared above the helicopter trying to blitz the stage. Before he could fall to the ground, he and the helicopter disappeared. Moments later, he reappeared alone next to Erin and Sha'rell.

"That takes care of one. They will never return."

"Let me try something," Erin said. She turned and found the nearest helicopter. Suddenly the rotor for the main blades ground to a halt. The helicopter plunged straight down toward the cement pavement.

"There are people down there," yelled Sha'rell.

"I got them." Xi'heeh disappeared with the entire crowd that was directly beneath the helicopter plus a fair radius of people beyond as well.

The helicopter slammed to the ground but did not break apart or explode into a ball of flames. It remained intact.

Xi'heeh returned. "I moved all those people to a park well out of the way. They are safe. What happened to the helicopter?"

"I extended invisible blocks from the ground to well past the blades. When the blades hit the blocks, they couldn't spin anymore, and the helicopter dropped to the ground. I hoped that the blades would have broken in pieces, but they look to be unharmed."

Sha'rell pointed to the helicopter, "And there are some soldiers unharmed inside as well. They are coming out."

Five sets of G'mone and K'reelian soldiers disembarked the craft. They began to shoot at random throughout the crowd. They struck down a few people before their shots began to terminate at invisible walls.

"Mine," yelled Erin. "You guys get the last one." She removed her sword and remembering Bart cementing it to his hand did likewise and ran toward the soldiers.

"Any suggestions on what we do with the last helicopter?" Isaiah asked.

"Not at the moment," Xi'heeh replied.

"I vote you make it disappear like the other one," Isaiah said.

Before Xi'heeh could respond to Isaiah or even just do as he suggested, the helicopter flew low over the ground, depositing five sets of G'mone and K'reelian soldiers as they jumped from an open door. The craft then veered up and flew away.

"I guess those are ours." Isaiah removed both his gloves and put them in a pocket. He zoomed as fast as he could toward the soldiers.

Fast as he was, it wasn't fast enough. One of the K'reelian saw him take off. He calculated when Isaiah might reach him. At that precise moment, the soldier raised his hand and swatted the location Isaiah would arrive.

Isaiah hit the ground. He rolled over. The soldier stood over him. Isaiah saw the pant legs of the jumper the soldier wore. He saw bare skin just above a shoe of some sort. He moved a hand quickly landing it on the exposed portion of skin. The soldier froze and grabbed at his chest. He collapsed. A G'mone collapsed.

Before any of the others could move, another G'mone was hit with a laser blast. A K'reelian quickly spun around. Sha'rell stood with her staff laser aimed at his fallen companion. It was the last thing he saw as he slammed to the ground.

Xi'heeh appeared next to the remaining soldiers. "Where to, boys?" They all disappeared, but only Xi'heeh returned.

***

Bart reached the top of the invisible staircase. The soldiers had already discontinued firing their laser rifles into the shielding. They formed a circle, and each of them gingerly stepped forward looking for an end to the invisible platform. Below them, soldiers who had been working crowd control were attending to the injured on the stand. Many of the world leaders weren't moving. Reginald escorted President Bergstrom away from the area along with a handful of other leaders.

Bart turned his attention back to the G'mone and K'reelian soldiers. Those facing him raised their weapons and fired. Bart rolled his eyes. The beams dissipated as they reached him.

"You know, maybe someday those beams will reach me. I would not want you to stop trying something so futile."

That did not deter the soldiers. They continued to fire.

"Fine." Bart concentrated. The beams turned midflight and reversed course, striking one of the G'mone soldiers. A K'reelian fell face first onto the invisible platform.

"You all realize that I only have to hit four more of you, right?"

The soldiers all stopped what they were doing. Those already not facing Bart, turned toward him. They rushed him, growling like animals. Seven of them suddenly lost their footing and slammed to the deck. The one in front continued.

"Are you sure you want to do this?" Bart asked.

The soldier kept running.

"As you wish, but I am not pulling any punches or giving you any leeway. Oh, and your friends seem to have fallen. You are alone."

The soldier quickly looked over each shoulder and realized he was alone. That didn't seem to faze him.

When he reached Bart, he swung his rifle. Bart reached up and grabbed it, crushing it in the middle and splintering the shaft in pieces. The soldier moved with great speed and punched Bart in the face.

Bart didn't flinch. The soldier grasped his hand in pain.

"Nice try." Bart struck back.

The soldier crumbled to the surface. Another soldier trying to regain his footing collapsed.

"Three," Bart counted.

The others stood their ground. They seemed to be analyzing their next move. One of them raised their weapon and pointed it at the soldier next to him.

"What are you doing?" asked the soldier with the gun aimed at him.

"I am not doing this," the other answered as he pulled the trigger.

Both soldiers fell to the surface.

"Oh great," Bart said. "The first one I pick shoots his own companion. Eh, two left. Which of you want to be the ones to go next?"

Before Bart or the soldiers could do anything, they, and all those lying dead, fell two hundred feet to the stage, slamming hard into the wood flooring.

Bart stood up. "That was quite the fall there. Good thing I cannot be hurt." He poked one of those that had been alive above before the fall, and he didn't move. "Zero. Erin's shield must have dissipated."

"Don't move." One of the security officials pointed a rifle at Bart.

"Sir," Bart said, "Have you been watching the last few minutes? I just helped you stop these aliens. You are welcome. By the way, I do not think you can stop me." He turned and walked away.

The guard tried to follow but couldn't.

"Do not worry," Bart yelled back. "You will be free in a little while."

***

Erin moved between some of the walls she had formed. She didn't have the time, but she paused to admire her work. She could see all the walls that she had made. They were transparent to everyone but her. The degree of opaqueness was minimal, but she knew exactly where the walls were.

The soldiers hammered their fists on the wall they discovered in front of them. People cowered on the other side of the wall.

"Well, move people," Erin yelled. "Don't just stand there letting these guys scare you."

That appeared to do the trick as a few people began to move away slowly and then spun off as quickly as they could. Soon the area was free of most of the crowd. Some security guards stood within sight of the aliens, but they were unable to do anything. A couple of guards started checking on those that had fallen before Erin set up the shielding.

"Release this barrier and we'll deal with you," said one of the G'mone soldiers.

"You couldn't deal with a cold even if I let you out." Erin approached the wall. She walked along the side, staring at each one of them. "You are all pathetic. Weak. Nothing." She turned, walking back along the line of soldiers encroaching the blockade.

They slammed their shoulders into the wall to no avail.

Erin shook her head. "I'm going to free you in a moment. When I do, you're all finished." She swished her sword in the air. "Just between you and me, I'm not sure who I am anymore. I'm not sure if I'm the good little girl my mom always hoped I'd be, the one that found a home with some cool friends, or if I'm the nasty daughter of a man that once desired to rule the world in his twisted little way with me at his side. I don't think you guys want to find out. I'm free of the pains my father bound me with." She stopped at the last soldier on the east side of the wall.

They stopped trying to break through, instead, they watched as she walked past them all.

Erin drew her dagger and planted it in the neck of the K'reelian she had stopped at. He grabbed for it, but she pulled it out and spun around, throwing it at the K'reelian soldier on the other end of the line. It found its mark. Both K'reelians fell to the ground along with their companions.

The closest G'mone soldier tried to hit her with the end of his laser rifle, but Erin was quick enough to dodge and retaliate, sending her sword through his abdomen.

The next K'reelian soldier pushed the body of the companion of the G'mone soldier onto Erin and then grabbed her arms, pinning her back. Or so he hoped.

With her strength, she easily broke free of his grip and struck him in his face. He fell to the ground along with his companion, leaving one K'reelian and one G'mone soldier left standing.

They quickly turned and ran in the direction of the stage. Three security guards saw them and opened fire on them with their handguns.

"Good to know that human weapons can take care of those guys," Erin muttered to herself. She walked over to the soldier on the end and retrieved her dagger. She looked over to the stage and saw Bart walking off. She ran over to where he was coming down the steps.

"Hey," she said.

He nodded at her. "We should find Xi'heeh, Sha'rell, and Isaiah."

They appeared right in front of them.

"We are here," said Xi'heeh.

Sha'rell handed Xi'heeh the laser staff and he returned it to the abyss that served as his repository.

"Where to?" asked Xi'heeh.

"I am not sure at the moment," Bart replied. "We should see if the President, or whatever her title is now, is okay. Someone whisked her away, but I do not know where. I am certain she was unharmed."

"Just a moment." Erin turned toward the demolished Capitol building. She waved a hand, and the pieces of the building began to reform and reshape. In a few moments, the building was intact again.

"That was a nice choice of abilities," Bart said, staring at the recreated structure.

"Thanks," Erin said. "I knew this ability would come in handy. I can at least set objects back the way they were. If anyone happened to survive in there, I can make it easier for them to get out. If they didn't survive, I can't bring anyone back to life, but I can make it easier to find their remains."

"We should head back to my lab for now," said Isaiah.

They disappeared.

CHAPTER XIX

"Everyone, wake up." Casey blared a couple of buzzer sounds from his speakers.

"What? Whoozit?" Steve hit his head on Casey's roof. "Stop that, dang it."

Callie laughed. "You're funny."

"Don't get him started." Matt yawned from the back seat.

"Where are we?" Steve settled back into the driver's seat.

"I think we must be about there," Casey said. "Their velocity has decreased over the last half an hour."

"That doesn't answer where we are," Steve said.

"Tianzi Mountains," Casey answered. "It covers about twenty-six square miles and lies within the

Wulingyuan Forest Park in Zhangjiajie in the Hunan Province of China."

"These are some of the most breathtaking mountains I have ever seen," said Callie while looking out the window.

"Those are enormous quartz sandstone pillars for the most part," Casey added.

"Wow, I can't believe how dense the forest is down there with all that green growing all over those pillars. And the clouds and mist that cover the lower half of many of these peaks make it look like they go on forever."

"Careful of the bus on that road over there." Matt pointed out his window. "We don't want anyone spotting us. I can't believe buses travel up and down that winding road."

"Noted." Casey careened off away from the road. "I have also noted that the helicopter has gone down toward the base of these pillars. There is an extensive system of caves down there, and with the limestone floor, the pillars are also prone to collapse. So, it is free from public access and would be a pretty good place for another alien base."

"Let's head down there," Steve suggested.

Casey twisted around and between several pillars, changing course as another pillar would enter his view, always heading in a downward trajectory. He passed a wondrous landscape, dipped into patches of mist and fog, and emerged at the base of some pillars near a small stream.

"This is the bottom," he said. "Fortunately for me, I

can hover and do not need a road since there isn't one."

"Stop here," Steve said. "I see trails of beings that have come this way. Looks like it could be a patrol of some kind. I can see several paths at the same place at different points in time, and they seem to occur about once an hour."

Everyone exited Casey. They scoured the terrain. They saw nothing more than the beauty of the pillars as they rose into the hazy sky.

"Wait." Callie held up a hand. "I hear something in some of the trees and bushes at the base of those pillars just ahead. I think a greeting party is coming to meet us."

Steve and Matt removed their swords and used the ability to meld them to their hands. They readied themselves as best they could.

Casey lifted away from the ground. "Let me get up into the air and fog. I should be able to nail a few from above."

"I am vulnerable like this," said Callie. "There is an animal on our planet that the K'reelians and G'mone were afraid of. I need to turn myself into one. Don't worry about me though, they never defeated one of these when they were on our world. I won't be hurt."

In a split second, she turned into the most amazing creature that Matt and Steve had ever encountered, and Matt had seen some doozies on the K'reelian homeworld. A gigantic ice dragon stood before them. She was solid ice and as hard as a diamond. Not much sunlight reached the floor of the pillars, but still, diamond-shaped scales of ice sparkled as she moved. Icicle-like spikes lined her spine down to the tip of her tail. Matching spikes protruded from behind her knees. She was as big as a seven hundred square foot, single-story house with wings that matched her body size. She nudged Steve with her head and started eating the limestone rocks at the sides of the stream. When she had apparently eaten enough, she beat her wings a couple of times and began to lift into the air, flapping with ease and ascending into the mist near Casey.

After a few moments, Steve yelled, "That is spitting awesome."

Matt looked at him. "Did you just say spitting?"

"Yeah." Steve continued to watch in admiration as she soared majestically through the fog. "That means it's the pinnacle of awesome. More awesome than any kind of awesome there is."

She ripped a chunk of rock off the nearest pillar and started chewing it.

Matt shook his head. "Whatever."

A helicopter quietly passed overhead on a course targeting Callie in her dragon form.

"Look out!" yelled Steve, running toward where she was as if he could do something.

She didn't need the warning though. She had spotted the aircraft and breathed a blast of ice toward it.

Matt raised his hand that spewed water and ice and shot a huge stream of water right at the rotor blades. It mixed at the perfect time with the ice from Callie and froze the assembly to such a degree that it snapped off and the helicopter plummeted to the ground.

"Man," said Matt. "That's disappointing. It didn't explode."

"I see a little fuel leak, or at least I think it's a leak." Steve pointed to an area behind the cockpit where a trickle of liquid oozed. "Maybe a little bit of fire would be nice right now."

Matt raised his other hand and shot a stream of fire at the place Steve was pointing to. It ignited and exploded in a flash. "There, that's better."

Lasers began to rain down from Casey's position. Matt and Steve turned around to see a couple of platoons of soldiers heading at them on either side of the stream. Casey noticed their entrance and began to lay down a torrent of laser bursts. He hit five soldiers before they adjusted and dodged any remaining shots.

"I guess we better pay attention to what's happening, shouldn't we?" said Steve. "Which side do you want?"

"This one, I'm not crossing that water."

"Really?" Steve shook his head and crossed the small stream.

"Come on, boys." Matt crouched slightly as he set himself for the coming troops. "Shall we get this over with?"

The troops continued their forward progress, continuing to dodge Casey's volley. With each weave, they shot their laser rifles in the direction of Steve and Matt only to watch the blasts disappear as they neared them. A couple of soldiers hesitated, unsure what to do. That provided Casey the chance to hit them, knocking two opponents with every shot.

Two more helicopters appeared down the valley corridor. They headed straight for Casey. When they locked onto Casey, they fired their powerful laser cannons at him.

Casey took two hard hits. He screamed and flipped around out of the way, heading up into the mist.

Callie swooped down as Casey flashed by. She breathed a powerful blast of cold air at the closest helicopter, causing it to falter. It spiraled down toward the ground as the first had done, but before it hit the ground, it pulled back up into the air.

The second helicopter moved in, firing at Callie. The first few shots bounced off and ricocheted into one of the mountain pillars. A rumbling echoed through the valley. Bits of rock fell to the ground. Soon chunks followed, and then the entire column collapsed sending tons upon tons of earth into the valley right at the spot where Callie hovered. Before she could move, huge rocks cascaded down around her.

"No!" Steve yelled. "No, no, no, no, no!" He ran toward the rubble. Limestone dust billowed into the air, climbing higher and higher and covering any light from above.

Casey swooped down, firing his lasers as fast as he could at the first helicopter that Callie slowed down. He hit an optimal location, and the aircraft burst into a fireball that cut through the dust and slammed into the stream, spraying water into the air to mix with the dust.

Casey turned toward the second helicopter and flew circles around it so quickly that it couldn't target him. He again fired his lasers at the same spot as he had on the other one. It exploded and crashed away from everyone.

"Looks like Casey found a sweet spot on those things, right, Steve?"

Steve didn't answer. Matt looked around. Through the settling dust, he spotted Steve at the base of the debris. He was tossing huge blocks of stone from the pile.

The soldiers stopped when the column collapsed, but with the air clearing, they began to move forward again.

Matt rushed up to where Steve was still tossing huge portions of dirt all over. "Hey." He put a hand on Steve's shoulder trying to calm him.

Steve shrugged Matt's hand away. "Either help me move these rocks or leave me alone."

"I'm sure she got away somehow. She probably shifted into some form that can slip between the rocks. She'll be back in a bit. We need to worry about the soldiers coming toward us."

Steve turned to Matt with a fire in his eyes that had never been there before. "You worry about them. I'm finding Callie." He grabbed another chunk and heaved it toward some soldiers that had, unfortunately for them, made it to the ruins.

Matt stood up as the chunk landed on the soldiers. He laid down a line of flames effectively putting a block between themselves and the soldiers. When he turned back around to talk to Steve again, he was nowhere in sight. "Steve? Steve!"

"Argh!"

Matt whipped back around at the sound of the

scream to see two soldiers falling to the ground: one with a severe sword wound, and the other with no apparent injuries. Then another pair went down, followed by two more pairs.

"Uh oh. He's not going to stop until he takes out that entire base. And if they can't see him, they'll never know what hit them." He continued in thought, *calling Steve. Come on, I know you can hear me. You might be invisible to everyone else, but I know where you are. Don't do this.*

Nothing. Steve didn't answer.

"Dang it." *End communication. Calling Bart.*

After a long pause, Bart responded. *What is it?*

Callie went down and Steve went invisible and is thrashing the K'reelian and G'mone soldiers. I can't see him, but my sword can help me know where he is. Plus, I could follow his trail of bodies if I needed to. Are you able to come help?

We just got back from a disaster at the Capitol, but we should be able to come. Where are you?

Tianzi Mountains. It's in Wulingyuan Forest Park in Zhangjiajie in the Hunan Province of China.

There was a pause.

Xi'heeh says he knows where that is, but we may not find you right away. It is a big area.

Right. There may be a dusty haze that you can find us at. I'll make sure Casey stays in the air too. That may help. I'm going to follow Steve's trail of aliens. I'll know where you land. I'll contact Xi'heeh if you need to get closer. We'll try to meet up as soon as we can. End communication.

"Casey," Matt yelled up. "Bart and the others will be coming soon. Hang in the air and keep an eye out for them."

"Will do." Casey climbed higher to be able to scan the area easier.

As Matt turned to follow Steve, another helicopter flew out from the direction of where the soldiers had come from. It either didn't see Matt or didn't care that he was there.

Casey swept in. Attempting to use his newfound knowledge, he fired at the helicopter. It dipped out of the path of the laser beams and sped off in a southeasterly direction, disappearing into the haze.

CHAPTER XX

"We need to contact the President to see if she is alright," Bart said as soon as they appeared in Isaiah's lab. "She will not recognize us at first, but we should be able to jog her memory fairly quick." Bart paused. "Hang on, Matt is contacting me. Erin, can you initiate the call to the President?"

Erin nodded and started the process. She pressed a button on the holo-screen. The Oval Office came into view. No one was in there. "Now what? They must have her somewhere else."

Isaiah came over. "Let me try something else. She'll remember me since it's just you that she doesn't remember." He pressed some other buttons on the viewer. Different rooms appeared in the projection area. The first four he tried were also empty. In the next one, people were scurrying around. Some people were lying on the floor, and some were lying on the three couches around the room. People hovered over those that were lying down, trying to make sure they were all right. Others, mostly Secret Service agents, mingled away from the action. The President was among them. Isaiah focused on her group. He spoke. "Madam President, are you alright?"

She jumped at the sound of his voice. "Isaiah, thank goodness it's you. Where's Reginald?"

"Don't you remember? He's no longer with me."

She nodded. "Yes, now I do. Who's that with you then?"

"These are the others that work with me. They are helping you as well."

"Here, let me help you remember us." Erin removed her sword and showed it to her.

The initial shock in her eyes quickly subsided. "Ah, yes, I do remember you now. Funny how that slipped my mind."

"Well, you did have a very traumatic experience today. I'm sure that had something to do with it." Erin placed her sword in its sheath.

"Yes, maybe that's it."

Bart rejoined the group. "Madam President, we found one of the alien stations and have neutralized it. We are tracking another one. Matt and Steve are currently there. They need us to join them."

"I see." The President raised an eyebrow. "I have a different mission that I need you to do for me. I would like you to meet me in my office in an hour to discuss it."

Bart nodded. "That will be fine. We will see you

then." He clicked the button turning off the viewscreen. "She finally slipped up. That was a lie. She does not need us on another mission. I wonder if she is trying to direct us away from this second base."

"Maybe she isn't lying but just doesn't know fully what's going on," said Isaiah.

"She is lying. She cannot hide that part from me."

"Could she be trying to hold information back because she doesn't trust those around her?" asked Erin.

Bart thought for a moment. "No, I do not believe that. She is trying to keep us from something, and we may find out more at the next place."

"What if we miss that meeting with her?" asked Isaiah.

"She isn't going to remember she set that up with us," Erin answered. "Anyway, an hour from now we may be free to meet with her. We'll just have two bases closed instead of one. I say let's get going."

"Yes, we need to," said Bart. "There is something else you need to know. Callie went down."

Erin and Sha'rell gasped.

"What happened?" Erin asked.

"Matt did not have time to say. He told me where they are, and while you were reaching out to the President, I asked Xi'heeh if he knew where the Tianzi Mountains are."

"I can get us in the area," Xi'heeh said. "I may not get the exact location to start, but I can get us close. Is everyone ready?"

They all nodded, then disappeared.

***

Xi'heeh placed himself, Bart, Erin, and Isaiah down in the middle of a huge crowd of people waiting in line for the next cable car at a lift ride. Those in the immediate area of their appearance screamed and scattered, as the next hover cable car descended into the valley.

"You probably should have set us down a little bit farther away from the crowd," Bart said, glancing around.

"I will try to remember that in the future," Xi'heeh said.

"I thought you said you could blend into a crowd wherever you appeared," Bart said.

"I was in a rush to get here, and I was not thinking clearly." Xi'heeh shielded his eyes from the sun and looked around. "I do not see any clouds of dirt in the sky."

"Over there." Erin pointed toward a small cloud that didn't look like a regular cloud. "That must be near where they are."

Two security men ran toward them. "Stay where you are," yelled the one in the front.

"Whatever." Erin nodded at them.

They slammed into an invisible force and fell flat on their backs. Momentarily stunned, the guards rolled slightly on the ground.

"Let's go." Xi'heeh raised his sword, and they disappeared again.

***

Calling Bart, Erin, and Xi'heeh. Matt thought. *Looks like you found us. You need to head another mile to the west. I'm standing outside the entrance to the alien base right now.*

Wait a minute, Erin thought to the group. *Let me put that column back the way it was.*

Dirt began to shudder. Rocks began to roll slightly. Dust in the sky flew down. In a moment, they all shot into the air and reformed in their original position. The pillar stood as magnificent as it ever had.

"That is some ability you decided to pick," said Bart, watching in awe as the pieces flew around. "I just cannot get over it."

"Yeah, but I didn't get what I wanted out of this." Erin kicked at the ground and knocked a loose bit of dirt that hadn't been part of the pillar into the air.

Bart looked at her. "What did you expect?"

"I really thought I'd find Callie under there. She's not there."

"Maybe that is a good thing," said Xi'heeh. "Maybe she turned into something else and escaped."

"Hopefully she did not turn into something like a bug and was squished," Bart said.

"Gross," Erin said. "You really need to be more supportive there. Think positive."

Bart looked a little sheepish. "I do not know about their ability to change. Could she have become something smaller and not been able to switch back?"

"From what I know of them," Xi'heeh began, "they maintain their intelligence no matter what they turn into.

She could even have become a rock. It is possible that she could have been hit hard enough to lose her memory."

"She could be anything then," Bart said.

"Yes," Xi'heeh agreed. "She also could have been crushed."

"You two stop it." Erin turned to look at the pillar again.

"Can we call out to her?" Isaiah asked. "Would she hear us and turn back into something more familiar?"

Xi'heeh thought for a moment. "I suppose it is possible. If she did hit her head and cannot remember who she is, Callie may not be what she would answer to though." He saw the disappointed look on Erin's face. "But it would not hurt to try."

They all called out her name. There was no answer. No one appeared in front of them. They spread out to cover a little more area. After five minutes, they joined back up at the base of the pillar.

"Nothing." Erin was disappointed.

"That does not mean she did not survive though," Bart said.

"Yeah, I know," Erin said. "Thanks for being more positive this time though. We need to catch up with Matt."

Okay, the channel Matt opened earlier is still open, thought Bart. *Matt, Erin fixed the pillar, but there was still no sign of Callie. She may have escaped, she may have been crushed, or she may have amnesia, we may never know. We will be there in a second. Let us keep this communication line open in case we need it in the cave.*

Xi'heeh, Bart, Erin, and Isaiah appeared next to Matt.

"Where are Sha'rell and La'prell?" Matt asked.

"I left them behind when we teleported here," Xi'heeh said. "We have lost enough now. We do not need to look after them while we are here."

"Fine, we need to get in and stop Steve now anyway," Matt said.

"Can you give me an exact location for him?" asked Xi'heeh. "If you can, we may be able to cut down on the search time."

"I believe so," Matt answered. "It appears that he has stopped. I also know the coordinates of where you all are. It's weird, but kind of funky all at the same time. I'll just think it to you."

"Got it." Xi'heeh raised his sword. "I will make sure we land okay before we come in. If we cannot do that, I will bring us all back out here, including Steve."

"Can you do that while he is invisible?" Bart asked.

"As long as I have the coordinates, yes, I can grab all there."

They disappeared. When they reappeared, they were inside the cave. There was plenty of room where they landed, but it was dark. Erin removed her sword and the yellow glow provided sufficient light. Steve sat huddled against a rock wall, weeping.

Erin rushed to his side. She knelt next to him. "It's okay. It'll be all right." She held him. He continued to sob into her shoulder.

After a few minutes, Steve choked out a few words. "They killed her. And then... and then, I did this." He gestured around.

For the first time, the others looked around. Hundreds of K'reelian and G'mone bodies lay around a large chamber within the cave.

Erin grabbed Steve's head and forced him to look at her. "We don't know if they killed her or not. I put the pillar back into place, and she wasn't there. We don't know if she transformed into something else and survived or not. She may even have amnesia."

Steve sobered up for a moment. Then he put his hands over his mouth and gasped. "Oh, geez, I may have done this for nothing?"

Xi'heeh stepped forward. He knelt next to Erin. "No matter what, it was not for nothing. These are soldiers. They are not here for a holiday. They are here to conquer your planet. You would have been brushed aside like a weed if they had the chance."

Xi'heeh stood up and walked around the chamber. Using the purple glow from his sword combined with the yellow glow from Erin's sword, he scanned the area. There were lots of bodies lying around. "Did you get everyone in here?"

"Not quite." Steve put one finger to the side of his nose and blew snot out of the other side.

"Eww." Erin stood up. "That was gross. I was right there you know."

"Sorry, I don't have a regular hanky, and I had to blow my nose. So, I used the farmer's hanky."

"And... he's back." Matt shook his head. He moved closer to Steve and patted him on the shoulder. "You good?"

Steve looked up into his eyes. "Yeah. Being an all-powerful being can be tough some days, but I'm good." He stood up. "We need to get going. As I was saying, I didn't take out everyone. I'm pretty sure that dude in the other cave got away again."

"That would be J'ard's style," Matt said. "Let's get out of here."

Xi'heeh lifted his sword and they reappeared outside the cave at the pillar that had collapsed on Callie.

"Why did you bring me here?" Steve stared at Xi'heeh.

"You need to face what happened. And you need to see that Callie is not here and that there is hope she is alive."

Steve turned to the pillar. He walked over to the area where Callie would have been.

Casey flew down to the ground, landing beside him. "Sorry I was unable to save her."

"Did you see anything? Did Callie transform into something else?"

"I don't know. If she did, I didn't see it."

"I hate to interrupt," Erin began, "but I think the President is waiting for us. We should go."

"You are right," Bart agreed. "Xi'heeh drop us in."

CHAPTER XXI

The President sat at her desk looking out the window. Secret Service agents surrounded her tighter than usual. She started to stand up.

"I don't think that's a good idea," said the closest agent. He gestured to her chair, inviting her to sit back down.

She sighed. "I can't stay locked up in here forever."

"You shouldn't even be in this room," said a female agent, closing the drapes behind the President's desk.

"I told Isaiah to meet me here an hour ago, and he should be here any moment."

On cue, Xi'heeh landed the group in the middle of the room. Every agent whipped out their gun, pointing them at the newly arrived bunch.

"Don't move any of you," shouted the first agent.

"Who are all of you people?" asked the President. "Isaiah, who are these people?"

"Don't worry Madame President, they are with me."

"He's got a sword," said the female agent, pointing at Xi'heeh's sword that was still in his hand after transporting them all here. She and the other Secret Service agents opened fire. Bullets flew from their weapons for about a foot and then hit an invisible wall and dropped to the floor.

"Stand down, everyone!" shouted the President. "Why didn't I remember you at first?"

"We've taken a safety measure for our identities," Erin explained. "We don't want anyone to remember who we are. So, until we show a sword, no one remembers us, and they never remember our names."

The President frowned. "That's not going to do very much good if you have to do that every time you meet with me."

"True, Madame President," Erin said, "but right now we're being very cautious with who knows our real identity. We can't take chances that someone will track us down. It probably wouldn't end well for them anyway."

The President didn't reply, but she nodded.

"So, Madame President, what is this new assignment you want us to do?" Bart asked.

"Ah, yes, that comes back to my mind as well now that I'm interacting with you again." She went to the curtain and opened it up. "Look outside."

Bart, Matt, Erin, Isaiah, and Steve all went to the window. Xi'heeh stayed in the middle of the room, keeping an eye on the Secret Service agents.

A massive group of people congregated outside the White House fence. It appeared that they weren't in a good mood as they pressed against the fence. Military personnel readied themselves, weapons aimed at the crowd. It didn't appear that the fence would hold up much longer.

"Those people aren't happy with the new arrangements of the United Earth Federation. They have come here to challenge the new order."

"Not sure I can blame them." Bart turned away from the window. "This is new to them, and it does not appear that they had a voice in this."

"There was no time for any kind of notification anywhere in the world," the President replied. "Every intelligence agency in the world has the same information, which by the way, rarely happens. We all agree that this was the road we had to take."

"Why you?" Bart asked. "There are so many leaders in the world. Why were you chosen?"

"It was not my choice. I suggested the president of France. He declined. Although, he also was one of the leaders we lost earlier."

Steve interrupted. "Those people are about to break through the fence. We should probably do something."

"We will go talk to them," Bart said. "We will not take any action against them."

"I should stay here with the President," suggested Isaiah. "You all can let me know when you return, and I can let everyone here know so they won't try to shoot you again."

Erin moved away from the window toward him, staring him down the entire time. "Remember, I don't trust you yet. You're trying to earn that trust back. Don't you dare double-cross us."

"What?" Isaiah looked shocked. "I'm just trying to keep them from shooting you again."

Erin narrowed her eyes. "I don't need Bart's sword to know if you're telling the truth."

"I know what I have to do," Isaiah said, narrowing his eyes as well. "Go, before something happens out there."

Erin stared at him a little longer then nodded.

Xi'heeh raised his sword, and all the sword holders disappeared, leaving Isaiah behind with the President and her Secret Service agents.

The President looked at Isaiah. "Oh, Isaiah, I didn't see you come in. To what do we owe this little visit?"

"I'm not going to help you anymore. I promised someone that I wouldn't double-cross them, and I'm going to keep that one last promise."

"Well, isn't that interesting." The President sat down, folded her hands, put her elbows on the desk, and rested her chin on her fingers. "You think it's that easy? You're in too deep, Isaiah."

"I don't care." He clasped his hands behind his back. Slowly he started removing a glove.

"Oh, you'll care. We both know this alien threat is real. You don't do what I want, and the entire world will find out that you are behind the entire thing. Your measly little promise will be broken."

Isaiah clenched his teeth. "I'd say something stupid like you wouldn't dare, but I know better."

"Oh, and you can put your glove back on. I've had some new technology installed that negates your power in my office."

Isaiah was genuinely shocked.

"That's right, both your speed and ability to stop anyone's heart don't work in here. Now, how about you go outside and do something about that crowd that's gathering?"

Isaiah tried to run to the door at super speed. All he managed was a slow trot. He turned back to the President. He didn't say anything.

"That's a good boy," the President gloated. "Be a dear and see yourself out." She turned around, stood up, and opened the blinds. "Oh, looks like someone else is already out there helping. Ah, yes, I remember sending them out there now. They were in here a little bit ago, but I only just remembered. I suppose that girl is the one you've promised based on the earlier conversation. Oh, that little tramp and her ability to make me forget them."

Isaiah's eyes narrowed. He started to run at the President.

"Ah, ah, ah," she said without turning around. "Don't forget, your powers don't work here. My guards will shoot you down before you take two steps."

Isaiah eased. He turned and let himself out the main doors.

"We need to do something about those powers those others have," said the President still staring out the window. "I took care of blocking Isaiah's powers but forgot about theirs. Would someone open a communication line for me? I don't want to take my eyes off them."

The female Secret Service agent walked to the desk and pressed a button on the top. "It's open, Ma'am."

"J'ard, come in."

After a few minutes, J'ard spoke. "Yes, what do you want?"

"I apparently need to have more power blocking abilities. The sword holders were here, and I was unable to block them."

"Sword holders?" J'ard sounded stunned. "But they're just a myth."

"No, once upon a time we knew about the current group, but they're using one of their powers to block our memories of them."

"Ah, that would explain why I'm now in the third installation of our facilities. I wondered why I kept moving around. Do we know what to block?"

"Not really. It might be best to just send the generic blocker that nullifies anything."

"Right, I'm on it. You should have that by tomorrow."

***

Xi'heeh appeared with Bart, Erin, Steve, and Matt inside the fence near the front gate. The crowd jumped back momentarily at the sight of their arrival. The military unit did the same on their side of the fence.

"It's them," yelled someone outside the fence. "Look at

that purple one with the sword. They're the ones that started this. Get 'em."

"I wouldn't bother," Erin said. "You aren't going to get in here right now."

"What makes you think we started this?" asked Bart.

A tall man with sandy brown hair stepped forward. He wore an unassuming orange tee-shirt and blue jeans. He held a laser rifle pointed into the air. "We saw you there when those purple beings and guys with white hair showed up. You went to meet them."

"And, what happened then?" asked Bart.

"And then the purple guys and white-haired guys attacked you. They must have been trying to protect the President."

Bart raised his eyebrows. "Really? Are you sure those purple people and white-haired guys were not attacking the podium and we were trying to stop them? And, just what makes you think purple people exist, and if they did, just what part of the world do you think they come from?"

The man didn't say anything right away. He started to say something then sputtered. "Well, that guy's purple, right?" He pointed to Xi'heeh.

Bart turned to look at Xi'heeh. "Ah, so he is. Interesting." Bart turned back to the man. "And where did you say you think he is from?"

"Probably Saskatchewan."

Erin stifled a laugh.

"Ah, okay," Bart nodded. "Either you just pulled an area in Canada out of your butt, or now you think Canadian people are purple. Must be because it is so cold up there. I would think they would be blue though."

The man started to say something, but a small elderly woman hushed him. "Don't argue with him, Travis. He doesn't know what he's saying."

"Fine," Bart said. "Yeah, we do not need to argue. Anyway, what is the trouble here? Why are you trying to get into the White House?"

Travis held the small woman back as she tried to speak and said, "We are here to help any way we can. We're not sure why our President said there was a new United States of a Federation of Earth or whatever she called that, but we don't think that's right."

Xi'heeh spoke up. "Those purple people you saw are my people. They are good people, but they are in a situation where they are being taken advantage of by another race; that being the white-haired people. A race that bears your forefathers."

Laughter arose from those close enough to hear what they were saying. Others further back in the crowd murmured mostly about not being able to hear.

"You're kidding us, right?" Travis said. "We don't come from aliens."

"Suit yourself," Xi'heeh continued. "Just keep this in mind that they are a warlike race, and they will stop only when they have beaten you into submission."

"Do you think that'll scare us?" asked Travis.

"I believe the customary response to that question is, it should," said Xi'heeh. "I will not try to stop you from attempting to defend yourselves, but you have been warned."

"Please everyone, just go home," said Bart. "The leaders of the world have made a decision that is best for all of us at this time. We are here to help you fight these aliens. Just let us handle it."

"Ha!" yelled Travis. "You got all that on tape, people? Upload those videos so the world can see."

"Oh, can I get you all to send me links?" Steve asked? "I want to see those."

"Stop it, man," Matt pulled Steve back. "I don't want any of your funny business."

"It helps me cope," Steve said.

"Enough!" yelled the small old lady. "Let 'em have it." She pulled up her laser rifle which had to be bigger than she was and started shooting.

Some of the rest of the crowd followed suit, while others without weapons retreated a safe distance away.

The military personnel raised their weapons, but before they fired back, the laser beams, bullets, and whatever else those few in the crowd were using all hit an invisible wall and stopped.

Steve looked around Matt. "I sure hope those in the back are either not firing, or they're shooting over the others."

Matt pointed at him. "I told you to stop with the funny business."

Bart moved closer to the fence. He looked at Erin. "Can I go through the barrier?"

She nodded.

Without a running start, he jumped the fence. A few in front of the crowd noted the superhuman strength that leap took and stopped for a moment. Others kept firing and the bullets and laser beams continued to bounce off the wall. Bart walked forward and through the wall. Those that were closest to him aimed at him. Now the beams and bullets seemed to just disappear.

"Halt!" Travis shouted.

A few heeded him.

"I said halt!" He shouted much louder that time, and after a few moments, everyone stopped.

"Look," Bart began. "You cannot hurt us. We are here to help this world, our world, from being invaded by aliens a lot more powerful and fierce than our world. You have demonstrated that you are willing to fight for what you have, and that is a good thing, but you need to let us handle it."

"There's only one..." Travis started counting. "Four, five. Five of you and thousands or millions of us. How do you stand a chance against all those so-called aliens?"

"We have some skills that you do not have."

"Oh, yeah? Get 'em!" Travis and those in the crowd that had been firing rushed Bart.

Most of them hit an invisible wall. Erin purposely allowed ten past the wall she had erected. They continued forward not noticing the others couldn't go any further. One raised his laser pistol and began to fire at Bart. The lasers bounced off another shield ricocheting back at the man. The beams didn't hit the man because Erin had put him inside his own shield. Though he did stop moving forward and shooting.

The other nine froze in their tracks. After a moment

they started moving toward each other. They all took one hand off their weapons and began to hit each other with their free hand. It was more of a weak slap, but it did the trick.

"My turn," Steve said. He turned invisible. In a few moments, most of the men toward the front of the crowd who had been wearing shorts had them pulled down to their knees, revealing all sorts of fun-looking underwear.

"I can't take him anywhere," Matt groaned. He turned to Erin. "Seriously, I can't."

"This is just a small bit of what we can do," said Bart. "You are better off heading back home and letting us and the militaries of the world do what we do."

"This is our country," Travis said. "We'll do what we want to do for our land."

Xi'heeh teleported out to where Bart stood. "I understand what you want. You want a land that you call your own and no one to take it from you or tell you what to do, right?"

Travis nodded his head. "That's about right."

"I know just the place." Xi'heeh raised his sword, and the entire crowd disappeared.

Bart looked around him and then at Erin and Matt. "I wonder where he just took all of them."

"I wonder if he happened to take Steve by accident," said Matt.

Erin pointed toward where the crowd had been. "Nope."

Steve sat on a cooler eating an ice cream bar and drinking a soda.

"I can't take him anywhere. He started acting more mature when Callie came around. He's always been a joker. I had hopes that she would bring some sense of responsibility to him, but now it seems he's stepped it up some on the wacky stuff."

"He's hurting," Erin said. "He won't admit it. He's a tough guy, but still barely into becoming an adult. He found someone he likes a lot, and she may not be around for him anymore." Erin took a quick peek at Bart. He was heading over to Steve. She looked at the ground. "It's tough when you think someone's going to be there for you for a long time only to have things change. He doesn't know how to react, so he turns to what he knows, brushing it off, acting like he's clueless."

"Kind of like someone else we know?"

"What're you talking about?" Erin looked up, but she knew what he meant.

"You and Bart. You have changed, or think you have."

"I'm not the same person I was a few days ago," she said quietly but with defiance.

"Are you sure? In a way, none of us ever are who we were a few days ago. And in other ways, we are always the same. Do you care for Bart?"

"With all my heart, but my head says I'm not the same. I'm like seventy-five years old."

"First of all, are you really seventy-five? I suppose on a technicality, but I'd say if your aging was stopped, then you are what you are now."

"I remember everything I went through in that first lifetime. I remember the 1980s and 1990s. I just don't want to hurt Bart. I want to know that I can be there for him as me, not what everyone expects me to be."

"So, embrace what you were and what you've become. Combine both Erin's into the one that we know now and is part of our family."

"Thanks. I'll work through it. You're a big help."

"That's what friends and family are for. We should probably catch up with Bart and Steve. I see Casey joined them from wherever Xi'heeh left him when we transported in." He jumped the fence and headed toward them.

Erin sighed, turned, and jumped over after him.

CHAPTER XXII

The crowd of people arrived at the most luxurious plot of the greenest grass that may have ever grown. Tall trees filled with the greenest leaves lined a crystal-clear blue river that flowed into the clearest lake. Clouds floated lazily above in the clearest blue sky ever imagined. The temperature was absolute perfection. The entire area was absolute perfection.

Those in the crowd began to look around. Awe and amazement etched their faces.

"Where are we?" asked Travis. "I have never seen land so beautiful, and I've been to a lot of places on Earth."

"I have brought you to the Eden planet," Xi'heeh said. "In our lore, this is the only planet in the solar system that is absolute perfection. The air is pure. The water is pure. Everything is pure. This is the only planet that we never conquered. We attempted, but this planet cannot be conquered. It can only be utilized by a species that can live harmoniously with it. And so far, there have been zero such species. In time, everyone tries to manipulate the planet. That is not how this planet works. It is a symbiotic planet. It needs to be nurtured and loved. In return, it gives you absolutely everything you need to survive. It provides for all your needs. The wants, not so much unless it does not harm anyone. If you treat this planet with love and respect, it provides for you. If you do not do that, well then, it removes the cancer. You might want to drop your weapons."

Spindly vines began to grow beside those still holding whatever weapon they had brought. Quickly, they dropped what they had. The vines wrapped around the weapons and disappeared back into the ground, dragging the items with them.

"Hey," Travis said, "why didn't it go after your sword?"

"Because it knows who the sword holders are and currently respects who they are. If my intent were evil, it would have reclaimed its resource, and I would not be talking to you anymore. This planet is also called the Impossible planet because it is impossible for anyone to survive very long. It has been called the Doomsday planet or the Planet of Reckoning. Maybe you can be different. Maybe you can do what you need to create a civilization. Good luck." He began to raise his sword.

"Wait!" Travis tugged at his jumpsuit sleeve. "How can you just leave us here."

"You want a planet that will be just for you, right?"

"We want our planet."

"Well, this is now your planet. The food here is very delicious, and the planet will bring it to you as it sees a need. Oh, it looks like it feels you are all in need."

All sorts of food items popped out of the ground. Fruits, vegetables, loaves of bread, meats, some even hot, just appeared.

"What about a place to live?" Travis asked. "Clothes to wear, things to do."

"You will get what you need. Do not expect more than what you need. Everyone that follows the planet's rules will be well taken care of. Housing as you know it is not necessary. Your shelter will be based on your needs. If you have five in your family unit, each of you will have your own space and whatever common space is needed. If another comes along, your living space will expand. This planet's temperature regulates to whatever is comfortable to the species on it. Clothing will be provided as you need. It rains for a half-hour every night, but you will never be in the rain unless maybe you want to be in it."

"That sounds boring and like captivity." The small old woman finally spoke.

"Only if you let it, I suppose. It can be bliss and perfection. The planet will provide for you. If it feels you need to fly, it will provide a way to do so."

"Take us back!" the small elderly lady yelled.

"I will not. I will be back to check on you after the conflict on Earth is over. If you survive that long and want to go back, I will take you. However, if you do survive that long, you may have settled in here as no one else ever has."

Some grumbling among the crowd began. Some awe and wonder also showed on many faces.

"I would not divide into groups if I were you. You will live longer if you cooperate with each other and the planet."

"Why are you doing this to us?" Travis asked.

"Because we do not need your help on Earth. You will be in the way. We will be distracted trying to save you. There are no questions about that. If you heed my warnings, you will survive long enough for me to return for you. You are more likely to survive here than on Earth." He held up his hands anticipating their response. "No, do not say it. You would attempt to help and get in the way." He disappeared.

"Now what," said someone.

"No idea," came a reply.

"We can't stay here," another said.

"This is really, really good fruit," said a man kneeling to try something that looked like an orange. He had peeled it just like an orange. The casing already vanishing into the ground. "And I feel amazing. It's like a real boost of vitamin C that you can feel."

A few others knelt, grabbing something close.

"Oh, my, God!" someone else yelled. "Is this lasagna?" They tried a taste. "Oh, geez, it is. This is the best thing I've ever tasted in my life. Now I just need a fork or something." A device like a fork appeared beside them. They picked it up. "Yes!"

While everyone was looking at whatever food had turned up beside them, a mature-looking man approached them. He wore a purple hooded robe. The hood was not covering his head. His hair was short, silvery, and well-groomed. His face was etched with age, but he still seemed physically fit. The robe wasn't tied, and underneath his tan-colored pullover shirt and comfort pants were visible. He held a staff in his right hand. He didn't look like he needed the support to walk, but he used it as such. Even though not everyone was eating something, no one noticed him approaching. They were all busy eating or watching someone else eating and deciding if they should join in. It didn't take too long for everyone to partake of something.

"Glad to see you're enjoying yourselves," said the newcomer.

Those nearest to him jumped. They reached for what likely would have been their weapons had they still had them.

"Those types of thoughts will be what causes your demise," said the elderly man. "Just so you know, you won't always eat like this in the open. You can have dwellings much like you're accustomed to where similar stuff will happen. In this dwelling, you'll have a food area, and whatever you feel like eating will appear. You'll have sleep and personal areas that can be just for you, or you can invite people into your personal area as well. You'll have common areas to invite others to join you should you desire."

"Is this like a prison?" asked a lady nearby.

"Oh my, no," replied the man. "You can go wherever and do whatever you want if it's not harmful to you, someone else, or this planet. It can be as boring as you want, as amazing as you want, or as deadly as you want. And, what's deadly to one may not affect someone else, unless you plan something together."

The people began to murmur.

The man held up his arms and staff to quiet everyone. "I know you have a lot of questions. We have time for all those to be asked. Some things you will figure out. For now, just be good, and we'll set up your dwellings."

"What's your name," someone asked.

He thought a moment. "I've been here so long; not sure I remember what I was called. Just call me Elder for now. I'm the only one that's ever been able to survive on this planet. I know the guy that dropped you here said no one had, but not everyone knows everything."

"So, just how long have you been here," asked someone.

"Oh fine, a question or two first. Well, near as I can count, I'd say fourteen."

"Years?"

"No, generations. That means one hundred years to you, and yes, I know about you. The planet told me, so I'll use your measurement values."

"You've been here for more than fourteen hundred years?" someone else asked.

"I believe that's what I said, yes. Don't look a day over one thousand, do I?" He chuckled. "This place will take care of you if you let it. And to answer your next question, no, I'm not lonely. The planet is amazing there too, and about every fifty years or so, someone tries to make a go of it here. But paradise can be tricky if you don't like rules. Now, let's get you all settled into a place of your own."

"I don't think so, El-dur." Travis stood up. He hadn't partaken with the rest of the crowd.

"Ah, there's always at least one in the crowd." Elder shook his head. "There are likely others. So, Travis, go over there." Elder pointed toward a rock. "If anyone else doesn't want to give this a try, you may join him. If you wish to see how things go first, stay here. I suppose we're worried about brainwashing or some other things like that. Well, I guess one could think that."

"Ah-ha!" Travis yelled, "He admits it."

"The planet takes care of itself and any living thing on it. If by being so healthy and fit you feel you're being manipulated, well, that's your prerogative. You still have choices to make. The swordman could be gone for a long time. Maybe his side loses. What then? Maybe he never comes back. You might be stuck here."

A silence hung over the crowd. These were some of the questions they hadn't formulated yet.

Then slowly one woman stood up. "What about our families? They won't know what happened to us, and if it takes years to go back, they may not be there. I have a husband and two small kids. I want to be with them."

"Here or there?" Elder asked.

She looked down at the ground and some of the food

still lying there. She put a finger to her cheek, thinking. Quietly she said, "Here. There's more food here than my family has ever seen. We don't have much now, and here, that not much would be more than we could ever dream of back on Earth."

"You, my dear, have it right. This can be the place where your wildest needs are provided for." Elder turned around looking at almost everybody. "Now, you have two camps of thought. Travis here," he pointed at Travis, "he wants to moan and pout a while to wait and see what happens to everyone." He held out a hand toward the young woman. "And Rachel here—"

"How did you know my name?"

"I talk with the planet." He lowered his hand gesturing toward the planet's surface. "The planet is trying to talk with you all." He spread his arms out acknowledging the crowd. "If you eventually listen, you will understand, and no, that's not brainwashing, that's conversing with another sentient being. That's what all the others that ever came here couldn't do. They didn't listen to the planet. Now, Rachel here," he again held his hand toward her briefly before folding his hands in front of himself, "wants to bring her family here to give them a much better life. You have your first choice to make, everyone. If you don't want to try, go to Travis. If you want to try, go to Rachel. And for both choices, I will have the planet get in touch with the swordsman to see about your families if that'll make your decision easier."

The small elderly woman who had seemed to be one of the leaders started to walk toward Travis's side.

"But the swordsman said not to take sides," said another person still kneeling by their food.

"The swordsman isn't dumb," said Elder. "But you still have choices to make. He was also right about his world trying to conquer this one. They lost badly. Suffered such casualties that it was almost amazing that they pulled through as a species. But the planet knew their hearts and that they would rise again to menace the known galaxy. The planet found just one of his kind that would listen, and it bestowed upon him a means to defeat them—"

"Yada, yada, yada," Travis interrupted. "Yeah, we all know those kinds of soliloquies. Just get on with it."

"Hold on." Rachel held out a hand to everyone. "I think I hear something."

"Oh, come on," Travis huffed. He tossed his hands in the air.

Rachel began to move. The ground under her feet lifted her into the air. She faltered a moment but extended her arms and bent her knees slightly to maintain her balance. She began to surf around the area, moving at an incredible speed. After circling the group, the ground returned her to the same spot.

"I heard something. It told me how to do that."

"Just like it would do for the rest of your extremely long life here," Elder said. "Same goes for everyone here if you listen. Your needs here are different than where you came from. So, now it's up to you to decide."

Slowly everyone looked at each other. A few moved toward Rachel. Then more followed. Soon everyone but

Travis and the small elderly woman were with her.

"Looks like most want to see how things go," said Rachel. "What about those two?"

"Right now, I wouldn't worry about them," said Elder. "The planet will know their heart. The planet has been in touch with the swordsman. He has the location of all your immediate families. They will be arriving over the next few hours. Ah, and he started with yours, Rachel."

Xi'heeh returned with Rachel's husband and kids. She ran to them, or rather she surfed the land to them. Her husband's puzzled expression greeted her. "I'll explain later when everyone is here. For now, trust me." She turned to Xi'heeh. "Can you and your friends really save the Earth from those aliens?"

"May I ask a question first?" He walked up to her and stared into her face. "How did you remember that I brought you here before I returned? One of my companions' abilities is to block your memories of us. Once I left your presence, you should not remember how you got here. You should not have known that I can bring others here."

She stared right back. "We never forgot. Must have been the planet that kept the memory alive. It remembers you."

Xi'heeh turned slightly, wrinkling his brow. "As it should, I guess. Excuse me a moment." With that, the planet enveloped him in dirt. Rachel and her husband tried to dig him out, but the ground they were standing on quickly but gently pushed them away from the pillar of dirt now covering Xi'heeh.

After approximately half an hour, the dirt crumbled back into the ground. Xi'heeh stood still momentarily, then opened his eyes and took a deep breath. "Agreed. Dispatch them now, and they may make it in time."

Twelve seven-foot-tall pods of dirt from the planet emerged from the ground. They hovered for a moment then shot off twelve different directions into the atmosphere.

"What were you doing?" asked Rachel.

"Communing with the planet," Xi'heeh answered. "We came to an agreement on something."

"We don't have to do that, do we?" she asked. Her eyes were wide open.

"Not if you don't want to." Xi'heeh disappeared.

CHAPTER XXIII

Bart, Erin, Steve, Matt, Casey, and Isaiah sat waiting for Xi'heeh to return from wherever he had taken the crowd. People milled about, not noticing them or acknowledging that there had recently been a huge crowd of people here. The military personnel dispersed soon after the rowdy crowd disappeared, leaving Bart and the others to sit around with the mingling tourists.

Bart stood up. "Okay, we should get into Casey and head back to the lab. Xi'heeh just informed me that he has some extra work to do for those that were in the crowd."

"Oh?" asked Erin.

"He did not say what, and I did not ask. He seems to have his own way of doing things. Not sure I agree with all of them, but he does have a different culture, so we owe him some space within reason."

Steve and Matt sat down in Casey's front seats.

"So are the three of us going to fit back there?" asked Isaiah.

"If you are worried about it," Casey replied, "I can expand my exterior and create more room inside."

"I think we'll be fine," said Erin. "It's not that far from D.C. to Upper Stamford, so we should be fine. I'll take the middle." She crawled in one side and sat in the middle.

Matt turned to look at her, and she gave him a quick smile that said, 'yeah I'm going to put myself in situations to evaluate my relationship' and 'thank you' at the same time. He smiled and nodded then turned back around.

Bart followed her in, and Isaiah went around to the other side.

***

Sha'rell paced back and forth.

"You should sit down for a while." La'prell was sitting in a chair, leaning back with her feet on a table. "You are making my head spin."

Sha'rell stopped. "Sorry. I am just a little bit worried."

"Didn't your dad and brother both have the fifth sword? Nothing ever happened to them until they chose to end their service, right?"

Sha'rell didn't speak right away. When she did, all she could say was, "yeah." She fiddled with a glass bowl on the table closest to her. "This is a little different because here I do not have anything else to do."

"Yeah, it is not much fun around here. We already

found something in the data Callie got us. We just need to tell the others. Too bad there is not something interesting to investigate around here."

"Well," Sha'rell began. "Last time I was left behind, I saw this room in the back. There were more chambers like that one over there. I will swear that three of them were occupied."

La'prell's feet came off the table. She set the chair back on all four legs and glanced around. "Where?"

Sha'rell pointed toward a door on the other side of the room.

La'prell headed straight for it. She grabbed the handle and tried to turn it, but it wouldn't budge. She shook the door. That didn't help. She gave up, walked back to her chair, sat down, and resumed leaning back with her feet on the table. "Well, that went nowhere. What now?"

Sha'rell looked a little nervous. "Did you really end up in a... you know, a place of pleasure?"

La'prell removed her feet from the table. She set the legs of the chair down with a thud and sat up. "I swear on your family's honor that I never ever did anything in that place." She stood up. "I did not dishonor myself or Xi'heeh. May I hang from the local fountain arm if I did."

Sha'rell grabbed La'prell's hands. She squeezed gently. "I accept your word as your bond. This will never be mentioned in our family again. You will always be part of it."

"Thank you, I know that you had to ask. Honor has been kept."

Matt walked in followed by the others. "Hi ladies, how's it going?"

Sha'rell dropped La'prell's hands and turned around. "You are back!" She ran to Matt and gave him a big hug and a kiss.

"We were just discussing family business stuff," said La'prell.

Steve walked past everyone and didn't look at anyone.

La'prell put a hand on his shoulder to stop him. "I am really sorry about Callie."

Steve looked at the floor. "She's not gone. Please don't act like she is."

"Hey," Bart said. "La'prell is just trying to help you."

Steve shook her hand off his shoulder. "What? By acknowledging she's gone. I'm not going to do that. I'm never giving up hope that she shifted into something else."

"Good for you," said La'prell. "Never give up. I gave up on Xi'heeh because I had no understanding of what happened to him. I knew his father had the fifth sword. T'hi was a legend. But I did not know that T'hi had given the sword to Xi'heeh by that point. I was told Xi'heeh died. I did not know better. You have something more tangible to hold on to. Callie's ability to shape-shift. You may hurt very deeply right now but hang on to what you have. If I had known, I would have played my hand very differently. You will hurt for a while, but you will also become stronger."

"Sorry that I snapped," Steve said. "And thank you

for those words of encouragement."

"We need to find those other bases," Bart changed the subject to work. "It is getting a little late, but maybe we need to get a plan ready."

"Sha'rell and I have been going over the info that Callie provided." La'prell glanced at Steve to make sure she hadn't said something wrong. He didn't show any emotion. "She found a lot of stuff. She, in fact, might be the reason we can win." She woke the holo-screen and started to find the information when Xi'heeh popped in.

"Where have you been?" asked Bart.

"Tying up some loose ends and playing a wild card that will hopefully bear fruit for us," Xi'heeh replied. "It might be the reason we win this thing."

Bart, Matt, and Erin looked at La'prell.

"Interesting, lover," La'prell said. "We found something else that might do that as well."

"I am not planning on telling what I have done," Xi'heeh said. "So please tell us what you have found."

La'prell smirked and nodded. "Sure. As I said, Sha'rell and I were scanning the data Callie helped find. We came across an obscure reference to the G'mone and K'reelian joining process. We almost skipped it because we knew all about the process. Sha'rell thought that it might be fun to look at it anyway, so we opened the file."

"And what we found," Sha'rell jumped in, "was not a joining process, but an unjoining process."

Xi'heeh gasped.

Steve looked at him. "Wow, I didn't think I'd ever see him surprised by anything."

"Are you sure?" Matt ignored Steve as usual and spoke to Sha'rell. "From what you've told me, there's no way to remove the connection from someone."

"That is what we thought and have always been taught." Sha'rell was visibly shaking with excitement. "It has been a tradition for so many generations that no one even remembers when it started. Anyway, there was a reference to the sword holders and how they would be involved in removing the connection."

"If it ever happens," La'prell emphasized. "It is not guaranteed."

"Can you show this file to us?" asked Bart.

La'prell turned to the holo-screen keyboard and began to bring it up. When it came on the screen, everyone gathered in closer. They all read silently to themselves.

"Interesting," said Erin. "So, my take is there's some kind of sword holder heaven or something like that? And the ultimate and penultimate must seek out some mystic spiritualist there that will give them something or another? That sounds vague to me."

"Just who are the ultimate and penultimate?" asked Steve.

"Wouldn't the ultimate be the first sword holder?" asked Isaiah, who had stayed in the background for the most part. "I'd say the first sword holder must go on this journey."

"Penultimate means next to last," said Matt. "I'd venture a guess that the first and fourth sword holders would have to go."

"How do we get there?" asked Bart. "We do not even know where this place might be."

"Wait," said Erin. "If penultimate is next to last, then wouldn't ultimate be the last? Nothing can be more ultimate than the last thing. That would make Xi'heeh and me the ones to go. We still don't know where to go."

Xi'heeh hadn't been participating in the conversation other than with a listening ear. He was intently staring at a diagram that went with the documentation. "I believe I do know where to go. And if those other symbols mean what I think it does, only one of us might return."

"No way," Steve said. "They wouldn't do that. Why are we even paying attention to this thing? What do these people know about the swords anyway?"

"A lot actually," said Matt. "That's how the third sword holders all got pulled back to save B'ajj. It was a safety measure for the swords. Bn'ja, Ha'ka, and J'ard were trying very hard to stop the swords from being created. I find the actual timeline of the swords intriguing."

"No pun intended there, right, Mr. Timeline holder." Steve smiled.

Matt continued, maintaining his penchant to ignore Steve, "Why were the swords made when they were, and by whom they were? It's like the middle of when you'd think they would be needed. Why are we the ones for this moment?"

"I am more concerned about either of Erin or Xi'heeh not returning," said Bart. He couldn't hide his fear.

"I second that," said La'prell. "I thought I lost Xi'heeh once. I could not bear that again."

Erin looked uneasily at Bart. She couldn't bear the look on his face and turned away. She brushed away a tear before hopefully anyone noticed.

"I agree with Bart," said Isaiah. "Erin can't go."

"It's not your choice," said an unnaturally subdued Erin. "It's in the prophecy. I can tell. Besides, there's only a possibility both of us don't return."

"Hello," Steve said. "We're at this 'believing people trying to kill us and doing a pretty good job of finding ways to do so' thing again. I still say they aren't credible."

"Yes, they are," said Bart quietly. "I can tell it is true. Mostly from Isaiah saying Erin cannot go. She must. Xi'heeh too. They are the only ones with a chance. Go quickly."

Without a word, Xi'heeh raised his sword and he and Erin disappeared.

There was silence. No one could speak for the longest time. They tried to look at each other, but every time their eyes met, they quickly turned away.

"Hey," Matt finally broke the silence. "We're not doing them any favors by sitting around. We need to take out those last four alien fortresses before the armada arrives. If we can do that, it'll take away the recon from the ground, and the aliens won't have help from this side."

"How are we going to get there?" La'prell gazed at the map. "These places seem to be far away from here."

"Who said you are going?" Bart asked. "Erin is not here to put a shield around you, and Xi'heeh cannot give you a weapon from his bag of tricks or transport us out."

La'prell walked up to Bart and stood almost nose to nose. "Sha'rell and I are going. You cannot stop us. If there is a chance Xi'heeh does not return, I do not care what happens to me anymore. I know that he will do everything he can to make sure that Erin is the one to return. That is how he is."

Bart hesitated, then said, "Fine. Your life belongs to you, and you can do with it as you desire. We will do our best to protect you."

"I would be fine staying here," said Sha'rell. "I am not a fighter like La'prell is. I will maintain the base here."

Bart nodded and turned to the holo-screen. "We still need to figure out how to get to these places."

"I have Casey working on a way," Steve said. "He's the only transportation we have now. It took him a while to get from Afghanistan to China though."

Matt turned to the holo-screen containing the information on the locations. "Looks like there's a place called Bungle Bungles in Purnululu Western Australia, another near Garni Gorge in Armenia, a spot in the Andes Mountains in Bolivia, and a final one in the Rocky Mountains in northwestern Wyoming."

"Wait a minute." La'prell stared intently at the holo-screen. "Go to that file."

Matt swiped where La'prell pointed. A new file opened. It showed instructions of some sort of chamber with a large booth-like thing and some control panels.

"That looks like a transportation device," La'prell said. "I've seen one once when I snuck into the tavern at home. I wasn't supposed to be there, but no one was watching, so I went in. A couple of guys were just getting into the device and the bartender ran the controls and sent them to wherever they went. I bet they have these between the facilities, and this is how they move unseen. They would only take the air vehicles out when it was safe. We need to get in there to get to the next place."

"So," Bart began, "we just move from one to the next?"

"Yes," La'prell stated.

"Why did J'ard leave in the helicopter then?" Bart asked.

"Probably to save a couple of them," La'prell replied.

"Can you run the controls?" Bart asked.

La'prell gave a slight nod. "I think I can."

"If you can't," Matt said. "I can. You're right that does look like what we used to go into the city when I was on your world. Those change everything. We just need Casey to get us to the closest one in northwestern Wyoming."

"I say let's rest here tonight first. It looks like we don't need Casey to think of anything for us after all," Isaiah said. "There are some beds in the lab next to this one. It was kind of a research facility for us where we conducted some overnight studies on some subjects. I'd say we all get some rest now."

EPILOGUE

The lock clicked. The door slowly opened, squeaked, and stopped. It moved again, squeaked some more, and then swiftly opened far enough for her to enter. She quickly shut it, ignoring the squeak this time. The others were all either asleep or resting. They wouldn't hear the squeaking.

"I knew it," she said to no one. "I knew I had to find a way in here. I should have thought about picking that lock sooner when no one was here."

The room was lit only by some dim lights surrounding three chambers like the one Erin had been in. She moved toward those chambers. The glow was enough to tell there was someone inside each of them but not enough to tell who they were. In fact, their bodies were hidden behind a thin curtain surrounding them.

She tried to maneuver around to look under the veil, but it was no good. There was no way to see who they were. She tried to open the door on the closest one. The lock held firm. There was a panel near the handle on the door. A green light glowed solid. Another red bulb beside the green one was dormant. "I suppose the green light means the lock is working," she said to herself.

"That would be correct."

She jumped. She wasn't expecting an answer to her question. She turned to face the voice. "Oh, it's you."

"Yes, it's me." Isaiah stepped closer to the glow of the chambers.

"How did you know I was here?"

"I have an alarm that goes off on this little thing." Isaiah pulled out a small cube-shaped device. A tiny light was flashing red.

"Are you mad at me?"

"You know, for once in my life, I'm relieved that someone else knows. I think I'm getting soft in my old age."

"Maybe you're trying to do good things now?"

"Perhaps. Now that you know, I have a favor to ask of you. If something happens to me, I want you to wake them. You can't wake them until the final event occurs."

"How will I know when that is?"

Isaiah zipped so close to Sha'rell that she jumped back; her hands held up in a defensive posture. Her knees were slightly bent ready to fight if need be.

"I thought you didn't fight," Isaiah said.

"I will defend myself if needed, but I do not like to fight."

He held up his hands. They were gloved. "I'm not going to hurt you. Those days are past."

She eased her stance.

He leaned in and whispered into her ear.

"Oh my." Her reply was mild for someone learning a secret.

"And not before. You must promise me, not before."

She nodded. "So, who are they?"

"They were in a similar situation to Erin. They were experiments gone wrong. Promise not to tell anyone?"

She nodded.

"These are their names." He leaned in again, whispering.

"Oh my!" This time, her eyes widened. "And what do I do to wake them?"

"Here, let me show you."

GLOSSARY

So, for those of you that hate it when a writer makes up all kinds of fake names and stuff like that, I've provided you with a little glossary to help guide you through some pronunciation. I hope it helps!

- A'ROC (Air ock) – K'reelian guard stationed on Earth at an outpost in Afghanistan.
- B'AJJ (BAHzh) – Creator of the mystical Swords of B'ajj. Mate to Bu'an. Became the first holder of the sword, Truthseeker.
- B'NJA (Ben JAH) – G'mone. Mate to Ha'ka. Son is J'ard. Highly probable he is named after the author's youngest child. By no means is the character a reflection of the author's child! Tried to destroy the swords before B'ajj could create them.
- BU'AN (Bwonn) - Mate to B'ajj. Became the first holder of the sword, Blockade.
- DEH BALA (Deh Bala) – A town in Haska Meyna District in the south of Nangarhar Province, Afghanistan, bordering Pakistan.
- EMORI (e MOR ee) – A species that used laser

weapons disguised as staffs that almost fought off the G'mone and K'reelians.

- G'MONE (Gah MOAN) – Humanoid species bent on universal domination that currently resides on the planet K'reela. All G'mone are white with white or white-blonde hair. The male has a symbiotic connection with a male K'reelian that increases their fighting ability but has the drawback of killing the other symbiont when one dies.
- GAN (Gan) – Alien that Bart, Matt, Steve, and Erin met in The Swords of B'ajj: Truthseeker.
- G'RELL (Gah rell) – G'mone symbiont of T'den and a minion of B'nja and Ha'ka.
- GRI'NEL (Grih NELL) – J'ard's wife who was having an affair with P'thos.
- H'ona (HO nah) – T'hi's wife, Xi'heeh's mother, Sha'rell's sister-in-law, and Qu'arry's daughter-in-law.
- HA'KA (HA kuh) – K'reelian. Mate to B'nja. Son is J'ard. Highly probable she is named after what the author's oldest child called herself when she was two or three years old. By no means is the character a reflection of the author's child!
- H'EE (He) – G'mone guard stationed on Earth at an outpost in Afghanistan.
- J'ARD (JAR duh) – Son of Ha'ka and B'nja. Highly probable he is named after the author's middle child. By no means is the character a reflection of the author's child!
- JAVILYN (JA vill inn) - Holder of Truthseeker after B'ajj and prior to Bart Taylor.
- K'REELIAN (CREElian) – Humanoid species bent on universal domination that currently resides on the planet K'reela. All K'reelians are purple. The males are bald, and the females have lavender hair that usually grows long. They all wear a similar

purple jumpsuit. The male has a symbiotic connection with a male G'mone that increases their fighting ability but has the drawback of killing the other symbiont when one dies.

- KAREZ (Kuh rez) – Kutarian shapeshifter that Xi'heeh relocated from Kutara to Earth with his family.
- KAREZ KALAY (Kuh rez) – The dwelling place of Karez and his family.
- K'INTA (KIN tuh) – K'reelian name that Kutarian shapeshifter Callie called herself when she would visit a G'mone/K'reelian outpost in the Afghan mountains.
- KOOLTH (Kool th) – Alien that Bart, Matt, Steve, and Erin met in The Swords of B'ajj: Truthseeker.
- KUTARA (Koo tara) Planet of the Kutarians. Taken over by a G'mone/K'reelian force.
- KUTARIAN (Koo tar ian) Inhabitants of the planet Kutara.
- La'Prell (LA Prell) – Mate to Xi'heeh.
- P'thos (Path ohs) – Underling of J'ard who was having an affair with Gri'nel.
- QU'ARRY (Quor ee) – K'reelian friend of B'ajj and his symbiont. Protector of the Star of B'naugh. Became the first holder of the sword, Gateway. T'hi is his son, Sha'rell is his daughter, H'ona is his daughter-in-law, and Xi'heeh is his grandson.
- ROHT (WROTE) – Afghan sweet bread.
- SHA'RELL – (Shuh REL) – Qu'arry's daughter, T'hi's sister, H'ona's sister-in-law, and Xi'heeh's aunt. She and Matthew Walker are an item.
- STAR OF B'NAUGH (Star of Beh naw) – Multicolored five-point star-shaped ornament that B'ajj and Qu'arry used to create the Swords of B'ajj. Qu'arry's family passed the star down from generation to generation until the right blacksmith

could be found to create the swords.

- T'DEN (Tuh DEN) – K'reelian symbiont of G'rell and a minion of B'nja and Ha'ka.
- T'HI (Tie) – Qu'arry's son, Sha'rell's brother, H'ona's mate, and Xi'heeh's father. Became the second holder of the sword, Gateway.
- V'ANTE (VON teh) – Symbiont of Xi'heeh.
- XI'HEEH (Zeye HE uh) – T'hi and H'ona's son, Sha'rell's nephew, and Qu'arry's grandson. He is the third holder of the sword, Gateway.

ABOUT THE AUTHOR

The idea for this series of books came to James as a teen. He dreamed of having swords like this and imagined what it would be like to own such a sword. He decided that he should write down his ideas and thus the journey began. *The Swords of B'ajj* continues with the third installment, *Timeline.*

James lives in Lincoln, Nebraska with his wife. They have three children.